F

The Dan... ...... Series

"Wickedly funny . . ."—*Kirkus*

"Smart, surprising plot . . ."—*Booklist*

"Fresh, fast-paced and great fun . . ."—*Library Journal*

Also by Susan C. Shea

Murder in the Abstract
The King's Jar

MIXED UP
with MURDER

MIXED UP
with MURDER

A Dani O'Rourke ⚖ 👠 *Mystery*

SUSAN C. SHEA

REPUTATION BOOKS

MIXED UP WITH MURDER

Published by Reputation Books, LLC
Reputationbooksllc.com

Book Design: Lisa Abellera

This is a work of fiction. Names, characters, places, and incidences are either the product of the author's imagination, or are used fictitiously, and any resemblance to actual persons, living or dead, business establishments, events, or locales is entirely coincidental.

ISBN 978-0-9862031-3-8 (paperback)

ISBN 978-0-9862031-4-5 (ebook)

First Edition: February 2016

10 9 8 7 6 5 4 3 2 1

Reputation Books

To Candida, my sister and hero,
and to Tim, forever.

ONE

I was feeling lucky, sitting in the taxicab on Monday morning, having checked into a tidy inn in Bridgetown the evening before. I loved this part of Massachusetts, only an hour from Boston but loaded with small New England coziness. I hadn't been here since my divorce, and not often when I was married. Late spring was the perfect time to be visiting a pretty college town complete with a white-steepled church and carefully preserved clapboard houses dating from the early nineteenth century.

I peered out as we drove through Lynthorpe College's stone gates and onto the campus with its paved walkways, open lawns, and stands of leafy, deciduous trees, the kind I don't see in my San Francisco neighborhood of eucalyptus and Monterey cypress. The air was warm with a fragrance I didn't quite recognize, mixed with the smell of fresh cut grass.

Young women and men strolled down the paths in groups, laughing and talking, most carrying backpacks, some dressed so casually that I wondered if I was looking at pajamas and slippers. I'd be lying if I said it took me back to my college days. I went to a determinedly urban university in New York City, its only patch of lawn fenced in so students wouldn't be tempted to take their shoes off and walk on it when the sun reached down between the buildings to briefly warm it. No one would have shown up for class in flip-flops and baggy shorts. We were far too serious, destined for Wall Street or Oxfam, swathed in long sweaters and longer skirts with black tights or panty hose. I glanced instinctively at my bare legs in Jimmy Choo heels, reassuring myself I had left the 80s far, far behind.

Lynthorpe College's president, the man I was here to see, occupied the most impressive building on campus. The sign on the façade said it was built in 1809, which had given the ivy plenty of time to climb to the mansard roof. There were administrative offices on the first floor and a handsome staircase up to the suite of offices he and his staff occupied. President Rory Brennan's middle-aged assistant told me the great man would be free shortly. "Shortly" turned out to be fifteen minutes, at which time the door to his office opened abruptly and a red-faced man carrying about thirty extra pounds and a large file folder steamed out, passing the sofa where I sat without a glance.

Suddenly, the man stopped, pivoted, and came back to where I sat scanning a glossy color brochure about Lynthorpe. "Ms. O'Rourke?" he said in a gravelly voice and stuck out his hand. "Larry Saylor. You don't know how glad I am that you're here. I need your support on this business." Before I could do more than mutter a greeting, Saylor hurried out of the office, giving off waves of irritation or distress, I wasn't sure which.

The assistant pretended she hadn't been staring. She told me the president was free.

"Ms. O'Rourke? I'm Rory Brennan." The deep voice came from a tall, powerfully built, middle-aged man who stood smiling at me in the doorway. He shut the door behind us as he shook my hand. Light streamed in tall, arched windows and made a halo of his smooth-combed silver hair. He strode to his desk and pointed to the coffee pot on the credenza behind him, raising his eyebrows.

"No thanks," I said. "I'm coffeed out. The hotel where you put me up is exceptionally hospitable." There were rows of folders lined precisely along both edges of the massive, burnished mahogany desk, a lot of folders. His eyes flicked to them as he sank gracefully into his chair, then came back to meet mine.

"We do a lot of business with them," he said. His voice was hearty, upbeat in a noncommittal sort of way. *Maybe the same way you sound when you're checking out a potential donor at the Devor*, my inner voice said. Point taken.

"Congratulations on the upcoming endowment Mr. Margoletti is giving the college," I said. "That's quite a coup."

I meant it. Vincent Margoletti, Lynthorpe Class of 1970, had offered his alma mater twenty million dollars and the bulk of his contemporary art collection. I was here because Geoff Johnson, the board chairman of the Devor Museum of Art and Antiquities in San Francisco, where I was chief fundraiser, was also on Lynthorpe's board and had recommended me to Brennan. They needed some consulting help to assure a gift this size, with so much original art, was accepted without legal hiccups.

President Brennan tipped his head in acknowledgement and tented his fingers. "Yes, indeed. I've been talking with Vince about this for quite some time. You know how it is."

Interesting. The way Geoff told it, Margoletti had approached the college out of the blue four months ago, taking everyone by surprise. Geoff had told me Margoletti had never given a big gift to dear old Lynthorpe before now, even after he joined the college's board.

I smiled back at the president. "The collection will turn heads in the museum world, and the money he's giving to build a new art gallery for it will mean your campus becomes a destination for scholars and the public."

He frowned and the cleft in his chin became more pronounced. "Yes, and that's why we can't let anything cause problems, Ms. O'Rourke."

"Dani, please," I said, seeing where he was going. "I think that's why Geoff hoped I might be of some help, to make sure this goes smoothly and that all the details about the gift are transparent right up front. The last thing you want is to find, for example, that any of the artwork has any competing claims of ownership pending at the time of the transfer."

"God forbid," he said sharply, as if it had only now occurred to him. "I'm sure Vince would never put us in that position." He paused. "I'm afraid he might be insulted if we even mentioned it to him." He looked and sounded far less pleasant all of a sudden.

"This is all routine, President Brennan. My guess is his lawyers, who are doing the valuation of the artwork, are way ahead of me on this." If Vince Margoletti's lawyers were half as aggressive as he was, the gift contract they were preparing was likely to have as few moving parts as a steel trap.

"I hope so. Vince surprised me the other day. Told me he absolutely wants this wrapped up right now for tax purposes. I'm afraid you have less time than we originally planned when Geoff Johnson and I first talked about having you help us out."

Geoff had called to invite me to lunch a few weeks earlier. "I need to ask you a favor," he had said on the phone. "I've already spoken to Peter about this, and he's fine with it." Peter Lindsey is my boss and the museum's director, and I was intrigued at what Geoff might have felt needed his approval.

"Lynthorpe College has been around a long time. I'm on the board there, you know."

I did. I make it my business to know a lot about what our major donors do with their time and their disposable income. "You set up several scholarships and helped raise money to expand the business school, didn't you?"

"Seemed only fair," he said.

Fair enough, since he retired as the CEO of a Fortune 500 company a few years ago with a golden parachute, and lives pretty well. If Geoff's undergraduate education had helped him get there in any way, some payback was in order.

"Something big's about to happen to Lynthorpe," he said. "Not public yet, but, frankly, it has the potential to change the college's reputation, at least in the higher education world. So, are you free for a quick lunch?"

When the board chairman invites me to lunch, the only answer is yes. We met in the museum café. His smile was a bit strained and I heard him sigh.

"Something wrong?" I said. "You look a little down."

"Ah, nothing to do with our meeting. A guy I knew jumped under a train down on the Peninsula. You never know what makes a person so desperate they'll do something like that. I think a lot of people who knew him are sad and confused today."

"I'm sorry. Anyone I'd know?"

"No, I don't think so. Not a philanthropic guy so far as I know. Anyway, that's not why I wanted to see you. I just got back from a board meeting at Lynthorpe. Everyone's doing high fives, but I don't think they've thought through some of the nuances of this gift."

I speared a piece of lettuce from my salad. The lines on his face, part of being a veteran of the international business world, were etched a bit deeper today.

"All the way back on the plane, I was thinking about what they need right now. Dani, they need you."

My mouth opened of its own accord, fortunately after I had swallowed the lettuce, but I didn't say anything even though he seemed to be waiting for a response. In the awkward silence, I tried to decipher his meaning. He couldn't mean I should quit the Devor and go to Lynthorpe, could he? Peter wouldn't be okay with that, would he? Or, would he be glad to get rid of someone who seemed to attract trouble? It wasn't fair—

Geoff interrupted my thoughts. "I'd better explain. The donation Lynthorpe is about to receive is coming from Vince Margoletti."

"*The* Vincent Margoletti?" I said, finding my voice. "Silicon Valley attorney to the tech wizards, midwife to the hottest companies in the Valley?" And, added my always-prowling professional self, possessor of two of David Smith's beautiful metal sculptures and a shocking and scandalously expensive piece by Damien Hirst? "Wasn't he the subject of a hostile article in *Forbes or Fortune* last year?"

"The same." Geoff sighed. "A classmate of mine at Lynthorpe and a fellow board member. He's close to becoming a billionaire by now. Started collecting art recently."

"I've heard a little about his acquisitions, of course—we all have. He has a handful of pieces Peter and the curators here would love to get, even on loan. You know becoming a collector at this stage of a successful career isn't unusual," I said. "Guy makes his fortune early, gets bored with the accumulation and starts looking to spend."

Geoff put his untouched sandwich back on his plate. "We don't move in the same business circles. My guess, though, is that he collects for investment purposes, rather than as a passion."

"I get a sense he's not your favorite person."

"My friends in the tech industry imply he's more feared than liked. Was one of the first in Silicon Valley to see the huge potential in hooking up with brilliant, young innovators, and became almost a good luck charm for a few of the biggest names in the new technologies. People say it went to his head, that he now believes he can do anything, and pushes some pretty questionable deals. He doesn't scare me, but he's not a guy I'd choose to go fishing with."

"I don't see where I fit into Lynthorpe's situation, Geoff. I'm happy at the Devor, and I'm not a lawyer, much less plugged in to the tech world."

"The president of the college and the dean of the liberal arts school have stars in their eyes and no experience handling a mega gift like this. I'd say the art alone is worth somewhere between eighty and a hundred million dollars, mainly because of a few celebrity works like the Hirst animal in formaldehyde. I thought you could consult with them, make sure everything's as it should be before they accept Margoletti's generosity."

"I work in the museum world. Not the same thing as academia."

Geoff gave me the look I'm betting he hit his own managers with in his days as a successful CEO. I still wasn't sure what I could add that the college's own staff couldn't, but I was pretty sure I'd be visiting the campus. Since Geoff gives the Devor a six-figure gift and lots of social endorsements every year, I was willing to bet Peter would go along with anything short of sexual slavery or a three-month paid sabbatical.

"Is there something in particular that's worrying you?" I said.

"This stays between us," he said, pushing his plate away and tossing his napkin down.

"Of course."

Geoff toyed with his spoon for a minute before looking up at me. "I admit it's my prejudice that's driving this request, Dani. Vince cut corners even in school. If there's an angle to play on this gift, something that's to his advantage but not necessarily to Lynthorpe's, I'm sure he'll play it."

"Like what? Reneging on a pledge? Retaining partial ownership past a reasonable time?"

"I have no idea, but I think someone has to be watching the school's back."

My stomach muscles were tightening. "You don't think something criminal's going to happen, do you?"

"No, I can't imagine what that might be, but I'd feel a hell of a lot better knowing you've walked the college's staff through the process of accepting a gift this large and complex. You have the experience they lack."

He drummed his fingers on the table. "First, the board needs to be sure he has the ability to write the big checks they need up front to revamp the art building so it can house and protect a world class collection. Second, the art needs to be guaranteed as to legal ownership and value for insurance purposes. You know how to do those things, while the president and the dean are too intimidated by Vince—and too eager—to be paying attention to the details."

"We get that here too," I said. "Even Peter occasionally gets impatient with me when I want to slow things down a bit before we accept a painting or promise to name a gallery."

Geoff chuckled. "I remember one or two of those skirmishes, and that's why I want you for this assignment. Lynthorpe's financial vice president's a solid guy. Spend some time with him and help us look the gift horse in the proverbial mouth. He's agreed to my idea and the college will pay your way and a reasonable consulting fee. You'll love the campus. It's small and quiet, set in the middle of rolling hills an hour from Boston. Beautiful this time of year."

"So Peter's okay with that?" I said, thinking about what I could do with some extra cash, like a week at a spa in Napa or the mouthwatering Gucci hobo bag that was in every fashion magazine this year.

"He says he can spare you for a week or two, which ought to be plenty."

I stared at my coffee cup, thinking fast. I hadn't taken any of my accumulated vacation for over a year. I wouldn't be trekking in some remote area where my office couldn't reach me. As long as my downstairs neighbor wasn't planning a trip back to her native Quebec, she'd feed my cat every day if only in anticipation of the present I'd bring her back from Boston. A week at a quaint New England college in the full blush of an East Coast spring doing some straightforward due diligence on a transformative gift being offered by someone I probably wouldn't even meet?

"I'd love to. It'll be a nice break from the routine."

Two

*P*resident Brennan was still speaking. "Our own attorney isn't concerned. Of course if someone like Geoff wants an extra pair of eyes looking at it I have no problem." *In other words,* said my inner voice, *he is going along with this only because Geoff's pushing for it, not because he really believes it's necessary.*

Brennan and I chatted for another ten minutes, most of which was spent with him reminding me indirectly not to screw this up and me assuring him that I wouldn't. He worried that the donation—what was being given and what not—might not have been properly spelled out in Margoletti's letter of intent and hoped I'd take care of that discreetly. He looked relieved when the intercom on his desk buzzed, signaling that our meeting was over. As we exited into the reception room, a short, slender woman in her twenties with dark hair worn in a ponytail jumped up from the sofa and all but danced over to me, her hand outstretched.

"Ah, here she is. Dani, this is Gabriela Flores. She'll be at your service while you're here. Gabriela's a researcher in the development office and she's also a graduate of Lynthorpe."

We said our hellos and left the president ushering in the next visitor in the same warm tones he used with me when our meeting began.

"So, how did your meeting with Mr. Saylor go?" the young woman asked me as I retraced my steps down the stairs and to the path outside the building in her wake.

I must have looked a little confused because she said, "He was going to be there, I thought."

"He was leaving when I arrived. He introduced himself, but seemed in a hurry." I wondered why he hadn't stayed, and why Brennan hadn't mentioned him.

Gabriela didn't seem too concerned. "We're all so glad you can help with this project."

"All? I'd be surprised if everyone's glad to have a consultant horning in right when things get exciting for the staff," I said, laughing.

She laughed too. Her brown eyes sparkled. "Well, maybe some of us more than others. But, honestly, I for one am relieved to know you'll be examining this offer carefully. Frankly—"

"Hey, Gabby," someone called out. A young man in Dockers and a blue button-down shirt jogged to catch up with us.

"My husband," Gabby said by way of introduction. "Dermott Kennedy. He's teaching history here this year, part-time."

"Yeah," Dermott said, grinning at me and giving his wife a kiss on the cheek. "Nepotism."

"So not true," she said. "As if I have any pull with the dean." She turned to me. "Dermott got his doctorate last year, but tenure-track jobs are hard to find. We're lucky we both got jobs here. Where are you headed?" This last to her husband, who hitched his faded backpack higher on his shoulder as he explained he was hustling to attend a departmental meeting.

"Not that I'd be missed. They only tolerate me because I'm properly humble and have no illusions that I'll ever get tenure." The briefest of frowns darkened his face and then he changed the subject, making arrangements to pick her up after work before he took off in the opposite direction at a trot.

"Nice guy," I said. "How long have you been married, Gabriela?"

She blushed and self-consciously touched the thin gold band, still shiny with newness, on her ring finger. "Six months. I've known him for several years, though. We met here in his senior year. I was a sophomore. And, it's Gabby. So, where would you like to start?"

Protocol demanded I start with the director of development as well as the dean of the school that would be managing the collection, and Larry Saylor, whose office had to vet the gift and agree to its valuation. Gabby told me the first was easy since he was waiting for me. The dean might be harder to find right away, and Saylor would be anxious to see me even if he hadn't been able to stay for my meeting with the president.

"Mr. Saylor has been the financial vice president at Lynthorpe for thirty years. He's a great guy, you'll like him," she said. "I'm the development office's researcher, and my boss assigned me to work directly with Mr. Saylor on the Margoletti project." She stopped at the door to what looked like an old house half covered in blooming wisteria, hesitating. "He told me he isn't sure what to make of some of the information we've collected, and hopes you can clear it up."

"What kind of information?" I said.

"I'm not exactly sure. My job is to gather everything I can, but he handles Lynthorpe's financial matters and so he does most of the analysis. It's so great that Mr. Johnson proposed having you come to Lynthorpe. You know more than we do about making sure someone who promises a multi-million dollar gift doesn't back out, on top of evaluating an art collection. Whatever it is, Mr. Saylor told me the president and the dean weren't worried. Of course, no one wants to question anything, or upset Mr. Margoletti. I heard he has a temper."

She opened the carved wooden door. "Sorry, I'm gossiping. Please forget what I said. How about I take you to the art gallery after your last meeting today? The collection's small now. Come back next year. If all goes well, this place will be so exciting." She beamed, and after I said that sounded like a plan, introduced me to the development director's assistant and sped off to set up the rest of my day. Her energy revived me. This might be fun after all.

After listening to Jim McEvoy, the director of Lynthorpe's fundraising program, for twenty minutes, I understood why Geoff had asked for my help. The director began our meeting by complaining in a high-pitched whine that the board of trustees didn't understand fundraising. Then he went on about his close working relationship with the president, laced with implications that the gifts the president claimed credit for were really the result of his hard work. He had started in on the difficulty of finding good staff when I interrupted as politely as I could to ask about the Margoletti gift.

"Geoff Johnson told me it's by far the biggest the college has received."

"Well, it's big, yes, but we have gotten other big gifts," he said. "Last year we got a two-million dollar bequest. Nothing to sneeze at." The difference between two million and the roughly one-hundred-million-dollar gift we were there to talk about was a lot to sneeze about, but I didn't point that out.

"Frankly, Danielle, the sooner we nail this, the happier I'll be. No fuss, no muss, you know?" This was beginning to sound like a refrain. "Larry Saylor's a wonderful man and I would never say a word in opposition to him, but I do think he's finding problems where they don't exist. In fact, I had to be firm with him last week when he told me he wanted to talk to Mr. Margoletti directly about a simple bookkeeping matter."

"Bookkeeping? Related to the cash or the art?"

"He didn't share that with me. I said he should tell me and I'd bring it up with Vince, but he said he had called Mr. Margoletti's office himself and was working to clear it up. Between us, I'm surprised Rory asked him to get involved in this. It's clearly my office's job. Larry's in a little over his head." He sniffed.

I recognized the symptoms of bureaucratic turf wars. Luckily, I would be outside the fray. My cell phone vibrated, saving me from having to comment, and I excused myself to peek at the display. Damn it. Dickie, my ex. When I had bumped into him at a trendy Asian restaurant near the Devor a few nights before I left, I mentioned that I was going to do some consulting work for Lynthorpe. He had reminded me that his old prep school was in the next town, and told me it was holding its annual alumni reunion right about now.

"Come with me, Dani," he had said. "I hate these things and everyone asks me embarrassing questions about us. If you're there, they can't."

That's the kind of reasoning that drives me nuts about my ex-husband. I never know where to start in telling him how illogical it is. Since I had attended one of the reunions with him right after we were married, I could think of many reasons to say no. A lot of middle-aged men in navy blue sweaters emblazoned with the school's crest, standing around drinking gin and tonics and guffawing about the time they threw Jimmy in the cold shower or glued the headmaster's Bible to his desk, ha ha. If I were lucky, I'd be on a plane back to San Francisco a whole week before the rah-rah alumni parade and the annual picnic and mosquito convention. I ignored the phone's buzzing.

The development director agreed to have Gabby bring me copies of the documents related to the Margoletti gift so I could start reviewing them right away. He jumped up the moment his assistant poked her head in the door to say my guide was waiting to take me to my next meeting.

"Have you had anything to eat? We have some time," Gabby said as we exited the building.

I breathed in deeply the fragrant air. Peonies? Magnolias? Whatever they were, the perfumes were different from San Francisco's ocean breezes flavored with Chinese cooking, and I inhaled greedily. When I admitted to Gabby that I hadn't figured out where to get lunch, she detoured to the student union, where I grabbed a salad and sat with her on a shady patio, surrounded by twenty-year olds chattering and laughing, and seemingly unaware of the big, bad world beyond the college's stone gates. Lucky kids.

"I had the rest of the day worked out for you, but something's come up," Gabby said, munching on a chocolate chip cookie that I tried not to fixate on. "Mr. Saylor was set to meet with you next, but he got called away from the office, believe it or not, to play golf."

"Sounds good to me," I said. In some non-profits, golf is major donor networking time, so it could be job-related.

"He said to tell you he would love to take you to dinner tonight near your hotel, if you're available. He wants to get started on the review as soon as possible. If that's okay, I'll let his assistant know and she'll leave a message on his cell phone. The golf club doesn't allow cell phones to be used on the course."

I agreed, and she flipped open her own phone and passed the information along. "The dean of the liberal arts school is too busy today. He's in charge of the academic unit that includes the art program. He says it's important that you meet with him, but it will have to be tomorrow. I set it up for first thing, if that's okay. That means we can go to the art gallery now if you like."

I begged off for an hour or two, explaining that I had to call my office. We agreed to meet at Lynthorpe's art gallery late in the afternoon. I used part of the time to send Dickie a text message saying I would be gone by the weekend of the reunion. Then I turned the phone off.

Gabby was waiting for me at the gallery door when we reconvened shortly before five o'clock. With her ponytail and skinny pants, she looked more like a student than a member of the development staff. As promised, she handed me a plastic folder full of papers, my homework, from the development office's files.

The building was the shabbiest I'd seen since I arrived, a boxy structure newer than the imposing building where the president's office was located, and less personal than the development director's den in a converted house. A "Closed" sign hung crookedly inside the glass doors.

"You can see why a gift to completely redo the gallery is so exciting," Gabby said as she unlocked the door. "They're talking about razing this and starting again, assuming all goes as planned."

She flipped on lights. The main space was empty. Moveable walls, a few ladders, and some canvases were scattered around. "The senior show is being hung," Gabby explained. "It's the last of the academic year. Mr. Margoletti is hoping the demolition work can begin right after graduation."

"You started to tell me why you have reservations about this gift, Gabby. I'm really interested to hear your concerns."

"Mr. Saylor will explain tonight over dinner," she said quickly. "He's the right one to bring this up. I'm only a low level staffer. All I really know is it came out of his review of the material we pulled together from a lot of sources. Something he hadn't seen before. I think he's been trying to resolve it with Mr. Margoletti's staff and members of his family."

"Margoletti's divorced, isn't he?"

"He has a grown son who went to Lynthorpe for a couple of semesters, a guy about Dermott's age, although Dermott doesn't think they ever met. I heard he didn't do very well and dropped out."

She led me around a corner and into what must have been the permanent gallery, a low-ceilinged room dwarfed by several large and undistinguished ceramic pieces. Along one wall was a line of small oil paintings, country scenes with ponds or lakes.

"Charles Woodbury," she said when I walked over to look more closely. "Nineteenth century, had a studio in Boston, if I remember, and is in the collections of a number of regional museums. Occasionally, a scholar will come to study them."

"Lovely," I said. "Is this the kind of work the Lynthorpe gallery has collected to date?"

"Yes, mostly New England artists up through about 1960. No big names that I recognize."

There wasn't much more to see in the gallery except that no self-respecting collector would allow his treasure to be housed in such dilapidated, un-secured quarters. Vincent Margoletti's gift would be a game changer and I was getting excited on Lynthorpe's behalf. The college was about to break into the big time and it was a heady feeling. No wonder the leaders here were nervous.

THREE

*W*hile I waited in my hotel room for Larry Saylor to pick me up for our dinner meeting, I started reading the development office's files about the gift and the man who was making it. There wasn't anything in them about the critical magazine article that I remembered reading. The gist of that piece was that the attorney, who had become rich enough to turn around and invest as a venture capitalist, had brokered some of the biggest business deals of the last decade. Impressive, but in other cases, he engineered deals that benefited insiders but set other investors grumbling. In a handful of cases that went to litigation, his firm agreed to confidential settlements, which suggested some fault but conveniently muzzled everyone involved. I thought I recalled the gossipers saying part of his fees were paid in private stock in the new companies, on whose boards he then sat. Margoletti wielded blunt power in the Valley, like him or not. I'd have to ask Gabby if Saylor had decided to hold the article back for political reasons. The file included a list of the boards he sat on and another of the pieces he was donating, some published estimates of his wealth, and some clips from social columns and non-profit annual reports.

The correspondence with Lynthorpe in the file made it clear Vince Margoletti wanted his treasure to go somewhere where it would be the star attraction. Understandable, especially for collectors who had spent lavishly to score big name artists and wanted major bragging rights.

Half an hour later, I glanced at my watch. Saylor was running late. Maybe he got stuck at the "nineteenth hole" with a garrulous college donor. I was glad I'd had a salad earlier. I turned the phone back on in case he was trying to reach me by cell phone instead of the hotel's line. Two messages, one from Dickie, the other from Geoff. Since it was earlier in San Francisco, I could call them both back.

Geoff wasn't picking up his phone but Dickie answered on the first ring. "How's it going, cupcake?" he said, starting off on the wrong foot as usual. I am not his cupcake and have not been since the day he phoned me from the top of a snow-covered mountain in another country where he'd gone skiing by himself to tell me our marriage was over because he had met his soul mate, Miss Sexiest-Underwire-Bra-You-Ever-Saw-and-Only-$39.95 in the hot lingerie catalog.

Our divorce was way too public, in part because of the supermodel's status with the paparazzi. Dickie's two Porsches, Paris apartment, and four hundred and fifty million dollars, none of which I took with me out of the marriage, fueled the gossip columns for several months. When he periodically tells me that he will do better next time, I remind him there will be no next time. He doesn't need to know that I have argued that point with myself more than once, and that my heart still flips for a millisecond when he looks at me with that lopsided smile. When that happens, I remind myself of the miserable weeks I spent hiding out at my sister's house, convinced I could never go back to San Francisco and what I was sure would be constant snickering and whispers behind my back.

"I'm flying in next Thursday evening. How about I drive over and see the campus? If you're winding things up, we can swing by my school to see the old place and I can take you to dinner at one of my old haunts."

"I've been to your old haunts before, remember? Greasy cheeseburgers and French fries? Soda and potato chips?" One meal like that and I obsess that I'll be back in the size fourteen corner of my closet, which I fought my way out of only last year. My women friends tell me I'm lucky to be tall and that a few extra pounds don't show. My mirror disagrees. "No thanks."

"Let's leave it open, okay? I promise a good meal. I'll call you when I get in." He signed off before I could say no a few more times.

I realized I didn't know how to reach Larry Saylor or Gabby and it was getting late, so I left a message at the front desk for my absent dinner companion telling him I was in the hotel's restaurant. I worked my way through a tired Chicken Cordon Bleu that might have come out of a microwave, made more interesting by a piece of coconut pie I had no business ordering.

There were no messages for me when I got back to my room, so I spent the next hour reading about Vince Margoletti and his plan for Lynthorpe College. Rory Brennan's update about Margoletti's sense of urgency made it clear he was a man who, having made up his mind, was impatient for results.

Gabby was waiting for me when the cab dropped me off the next morning, and was surprised to hear Saylor hadn't shown up. "I'm sure he got the message," she said. "His assistant is terrific and she said she left it on his cell phone. I'll call to set something up while you're at the dean's office."

Coe Anderson was short, on the plump side, and wore a silk handkerchief in the pocket of his suit jacket that coordinated nicely with his tie. The suit was several cuts above the president's and was accessorized with a gold pinky ring.

His harried assistant kept interrupting us with papers he had to sign, announcements about upcoming meetings that had to be shifted, and calls from people who could not be put off. In between interruptions, he whipped out a stick for chapped lips and applied it. "A little too much sun at my club last weekend," he said with a smirk, waving it in my direction. Anderson favored me with fake expressions of apology every time he broke off our conversation to deal with "the million little crises that a dean's life entails," as he put it in a high tenor voice that bore traces of a southern accent. My own inner voice, which does not suffer pomposity gladly, was kept busy with the kinds of retorts one should never utter out loud as Dean Anderson sighed loudly, flipped calendar pages, peered into file folders, and otherwise demonstrated how important he was.

His main point with me was the same as the development director's and President Brennan's: Don't mess this up. "Gabriela tells me she took you to the gallery, so you don't want me telling you how badly I need the funds to create a space up to the quality of his collection."

Having heard the chorus twice already, I was impatient enough to ask if he thought there was something that could cause a delay.

"Absolutely not. I had dinner with Vince the other night and he's champing at the bit to get going. I'd say he's on the verge of being annoyed if we act like we're looking a gift horse in the mouth."

I paused to admire his ability to use matching clichés before asking, "Do you think he might renege?"

"Of course not. You know how these things are. The longer they sit around, the easier it is for other people to pick at them, that's all."

"Who do you think is objecting?" I said, thinking he was referring to the vice president for finance. I felt sorry for Saylor, who would clearly be the fall guy if Margoletti's gift didn't work out.

"No one. I shouldn't have spoken."

"Rory Brennan said almost the same thing to me, Dean Anderson, but I haven't seen anything so far that would cause a problem. I started reviewing the papers last night," I said to calm him. "Based on my work at the Devor Museum, I think the collection may grow to be worth more than his lawyers are claiming. Housing it properly and safely is going to be critically important."

The dean beamed at me, throwing his arms wide and tilting back in his chair. "What did I tell you? A sweet deal. So, can we cut this short, get your stamp of approval, and get moving? My wife wants to do a private dinner party the night before we announce this formally, and she's on me like a hen after corn to set a date." Another smirk and another application of lip gloss. He swung forward in his chair and stood up, ready to see the last of me.

"I want to do a bit more reading first. I should check media coverage of Mr. Margoletti's business dealings. These days you want to be sure your donors aren't likely to be exposed for business practices that may make it awkward to accept their money."

It was actually comical. Dean Anderson froze, one arm outstretched toward his door, the big smile still pasted on his face, for a count of five.

"Awkward," he said, lowering his arm as his face turned pink and his voice hardened. "Awkward? I'll tell you what would be awkward, Miss O'Rourke. Telling him Lynthorpe College is too pure to accept twenty million dollars in hard cash. Telling the richest, most successful member of our little board of trustees that his money isn't good enough." His southern accent was becoming more pronounced, I noticed. "Never mind me being the butt of jokes from here to Memphis . . ." He trailed off, glaring at me. So that was the source of his drawl, I thought, to distract me from the hostility in his voice and face.

"I'm not suggesting anything. I was brought in to make sure there are no surprises later. We do this kind of due diligence all the time at the Devor." This consulting business was harder than I had imagined. At the Devor, I felt comfortable stating my opinion and arguing for something. I knew everyone, they knew me, and we all had to work together a year from now. Here, I felt off-balance. Was Coe always like this? Was he about to lose his job? What was it I wasn't getting?

"Well, I'm sure the Devor Museum can afford to be choosy, but let's be realistic. Without this gift, Lynthorpe College is another small school in a crowded market. Plus, people already know that Margoletti's offered this to us. If we turn it down, do you think he's going to tell his pals that? No, he's going to put an entirely different spin on it, Miss O'Rourke."

"You mean he'll suggest he pulled the gift because Lynthorpe couldn't manage it correctly? You may be right, but let's not get ahead of ourselves."

"Then what are you saying?"

"One, we do this background check quietly," I said, holding up my fingers and congratulating myself on getting a manicure before I left so they looked authoritative. "Don't mention to outsiders that it's happening. Two, we operate on facts, and not gossip. In other words, because a magazine article questioned his business deals, that's no reason to turn the gift away."

Anderson had been calming down until I mentioned the article. He sputtered for a minute, but I sat silent. He went back to his chair.

"Three, we're ready with some spin of our own if the situation requires it. I'll propose something if I think we need it."

"How long will all this take?" he said, somewhat mollified. "I'm supposed to meet with him again in a day or two."

"Go ahead with your plans since finding a problem big enough to derail the gift is unlikely. If it falls apart later, no real harm done. In the meantime, he'll be happy. I promise I'll be as quick as it's possible to be and still be accurate."

The dean had to be satisfied with that. He looked at his watch, told me he had meetings the rest of the day, and instructed me to report to him directly as the research progressed. Since the president and the director of development had given me the same order to report directly to them, I had choices to make, or lots of copies. All three men had obvious control issues, as we say in California. I murmured something noncommittal and had stood up to go when the door opened.

This time, the dean's assistant looked more than hassled. Her face was white and her hands shook as she looked from him to me. "Gabriela's here. Something's happened. The president wants to see you in his office right away, Dean Anderson."

Gabby rocketed into the office, one hand clutching the other, and stopped abruptly in front of the dean's desk. "The police called. They found him." She gulped audibly. I was having trouble following her. "Dead."

"Who?" the dean said. "What's going on?"

"Mr. Saylor," Gabby said in a strangled voice. "He died. In a lake on the golf course. He drowned."

"Drowned? Where did you hear this?" Coe Anderson said, making it sound like an accusation.

"From his assistant. She's with President Brennan and the police right now. President Brennan wants the Cabinet members there right away. I guess the police want to ask you all some questions." Gabby couldn't stall her tears any longer and she started weeping. "He was such a nice man."

I stood up and put my arm around her, leading her to a chair. Anderson stood too and with a muttered comment that we could use his office as long as we needed, he was out the door. His assistant hovered for a minute, came back with a box of tissues, then left, doubtless to share the news with other people down the hall.

There wasn't much I could do, so I sat and thought while the woman sitting next to me snuffled softly. Was that why Larry Saylor hadn't met me for dinner? I don't golf, but I never thought of it as a lethal sport.

Gabby's tears trailed off and she blew her nose. "I'm sorry, Dani," she said in subdued tones. "This is such a shock."

"Maybe this isn't the time to continue my review of the Margoletti donation, Gabby. Everyone will be preoccupied with this tragedy and it will be a while before they want to turn their attention to fundraising. I think I should head back to California."

"Oh no," she said, "you can't do that. Mr. Saylor said he needed to have you check out what he noticed in the records. At least say you'll look at his files before you go. I know he'd want that."

"His files are different from the development office's?"

"There's material we hadn't summarized, documents he was still reviewing. I'll pick up what you need. When you've read it, you and I can meet. I'll tell you what I can about it and you can decide what to do from there."

"I hardly think this project's going to be anyone's main thought right now." I have developed an allergy to being anywhere near where people are dying. Chalk it up to having had the awful luck of stumbling into more than one ugly situation in the past. Plus, the longer I stayed here, the greater the chances Dickie would track me down and start nagging me to spend a long hour chatting with his former headmaster's wife or, worse, the prep school's bursar, who showed signs of suffering from age-related dementia when I met him years ago.

"Mr. Johnson told Mr. Saylor that if anyone could be counted on to help us, it was you." Smart girl, my inner voice said. Perhaps sensing my instinct to bolt, she was reminding me who my boss was and what he would want. Geoff's worried face swam into my mind. Damn.

We agreed to meet at the same café patio where I'd had my lunch the day before. "I'll read," I said, "and I'll talk to you tomorrow. As soon as possible, I'll give the president my report in person or from San Francisco, so it's available whenever he can turn his attention to it. But I think it's best I stay off campus. Things are going to be busy, and, from what you said, Larry Saylor was so well liked that his death will throw everyone off balance. Does he have family?"

"His wife died before I came to Lynthorpe. The college was his life, at least since I've known him. Oh, Dani, I can't believe this." She stifled a new sob, and squared her shoulders. "I think he was the smartest, most principled man I ever met. Except for Dermott, of course."

She jumped up and left and, while I walked over to the cafeteria, I thought about the abruptness of death, and what a loss like this could do to a small campus community. I regretted not having met him except in passing, given how much Gabby admired him.

A half hour later, I was finishing a chai latte when Gabby arrived, her eyes still red, and handed me a sheaf of paper. "These aren't copies, so please take care of them," she said. "I may have done something I shouldn't have."

I gave her a quizzical look as I thumbed through the thick stack.

"He kept this on a work table where we met to go over the research. No one was there, so I picked them up and left. What if the police want to see them?"

I couldn't imagine why the police would care, but liked Gabby even more for her caution. "Tell you what. I'll work in the library so I don't take them off campus, make notes and get them back to you in a couple of hours if that's okay. You can put them back today. No harm done." I made sure I had her office phone number this time. "I wanted to ask you something," I said, remembering again the negative article about Margoletti. "The development director's file didn't include a particular piece on Margoletti from a national magazine in which the writer reported some really harsh opinions of him. Does it ring a bell with you?"

She sighed. "Oh yes, it came up in any Google search and I copied it, but Mr. Saylor was reluctant to pass it along to the president, and I can understand. It's mostly gossip and innuendo. My guess is he mentioned it when they met, though."

"Didn't it say something about a deal or two that benefited his clients but supposedly squeezed others out of a share in the rewards of their own technology ideas? My memory's a bit sketchy."

Gabby said she thought so, but would make sure I had a copy before I left campus.

I could see why everyone at Lynthorpe shied away from talking about an article in which their board member and major donor was labeled something close to a crook. Who wants to be the one to carry that hot potato to the powers that be?

FOUR

*T*hree hours later Larry Saylor's reasons for wanting to get someone else's perspective made more sense to me. Stripped of the negative press, Vincent Margoletti appeared to be a great guy, posing with other attendees at charity tennis matches, symphony balls, and art gallery openings. A gushy photo spread of his house in Atherton, which is an estate-studded San Francisco suburb, focused on his taste for luxury. A large, vividly colored Anselm Kiefer painting dominated the white-on-white living room décor and the article mentioned his growing art collection. A photo of him in *Town & Country* with his son in Florida, the younger Margoletti muscular, grinning in jodhpurs and a helmet and holding a champagne flute, was captioned "Vincent and Jean Paul Margoletti celebrate polo win." None of this set off alarm bells. There are some people who, through skills, connections, luck and timing, manage to earn vast sums of money. That they spend it lavishly on themselves is none of my business unless it intersects with my fundraising for the Devor.

When I turned back to Vince's professional bio, something piqued my curiosity. Vince sat on a number of corporate boards, again, no surprise. The people who are on boards tend to look for new members from their own set, which means the same people wind up sitting on numerous boards. It's not progressive, but it's not illegal. What caught my eye were penciled asterisks on the page next to the names of several companies on whose boards Vince Margoletti sat, big names in the last decade's tech burst, still privately owned, the research said.

What did it mean? Possibly nothing, but in my consulting role I needed to make sure the companies weren't delaying their decisions to go public because they were in financial trouble. That's something Lynthorpe's vice president and treasurer would have needed to know. After all, if Margoletti owned ten million shares in a company that was about to go belly up, they would be worthless. Would he have the cash to make good on his pledge once Lynthorpe committed to spend the money on building the art gallery? More than one institution had been left with massive construction loans when a donor failed to follow through on a cash pledge, and a small college like Lynthorpe would be particularly vulnerable.

There was a draft of the gift agreement, of course, in lawyerly terms, with a list of artwork included in the transaction along with a copy from his accountant's office. On a yellow sheet of lined paper, Saylor had handwritten a list. "Call VM office," was at the top of the page, which must have been what the development director was unhappy about, wanting to be the big cheese where contact with the donor was concerned. The next said only "Call Sotheby's." Sotheby's and Christie's are the two major auction houses that handle most of the top tier secondary market for art worldwide. Their breathless promotion of big-ticket paintings gets lots of media coverage and no wonder, with prices in the multimillion-dollar range becoming more common every month. Right after that on the handwritten to-do list, a reminder to "check all against master," whatever that meant.

Farther down the page was a phone number preceded by an international code I didn't recognize, with a check in the left margin to show, undoubtedly, that he had made the call. The next two items were times of appointments with the dean and the development director on the same day two weeks ago. The last one noted the meeting with President Brennan two days ago, the day I arrived and saw him coming out of Brennan's office, too irritated to do more than mutter a greeting to me.

I recalled the discomfort of the three men I had met with, and the implicit messages to avoid stirring up trouble, and wondered if their meetings with Saylor had made them—or him—nervous. How frustrating that Larry Saylor had passed away before we had an opportunity to talk. He must have been seriously concerned to risk making his peers at Lynthorpe angry with him. Who would want to be blamed for losing a huge gift, especially one that so many others were clamoring to take credit for?

And how convenient, my inner voice chimed in, *that if he was seriously questioning Margoletti's gift while the donor and the senior college officials were pushing hard to get it accepted quickly, he should happen to die.* The thought made me shiver.

I was tapping my pencil on the pages when Gabby spoke behind me. "There you are." The girlish enthusiasm and big smiles were gone. Even her ponytail looked less perky. "The president's assistant says he'd appreciate it if you could drop by for a few minutes this afternoon."

"Of course. I'm pretty well through with this material, if you want to get it back to Saylor's office," I said. "Any chance I could make copies of this handwritten list of meetings?"

She nodded. "Everything if you'd like it."

"Thanks. Only the material that he annotated for now. You did a great job researching Margoletti's Silicon Valley ties. Did Saylor satisfy himself about the value of the shares Margoletti owns in the companies on whose boards he sits?"

She dropped into an empty chair, looked around cautiously. "I think so. It's a humungous position for someone who started out as a solo practitioner thirty years ago, don't you think?"

"Yes, but not without precedent. I'd guess Margoletti's a sharp businessman who drives a hard bargain. I thought maybe the college's chief financial officer was worried that the shares weren't worth enough to guarantee such a large cash gift."

Gabby shook her head slowly. "He didn't discuss that with me. He did ask me to see if there was anything in the California papers about Margoletti's son, his hobbies or his job, stuff like that."

"And did you find anything?"

"Sorry. He mentioned it only the day before you came and I was too busy to start looking." Her voice trailed off and she squirmed in her chair. "I got a message from the dean a little while ago. I need to bring Mr. Saylor's files over to his office. I'm sorry to rush you, but his assistant was pretty firm that he wants everything related to Mr. Margoletti transferred to him."

"Let's walk back to Saylor's office now. We can talk on the way," I said, standing as I gathered everything into the folders Gabby had left with me. "Do you have any clue about why he met several times in the last two weeks with the senior leadership here?" I didn't say that his concerns were apparently pointed enough to spark the animosity of his peers.

"I know he was worried about something he found out," Gabby said. "I don't know what it was. He told me he needed to talk directly to Mr. Margoletti."

"And did he?"

"I assume so," she said. "That's who he was playing golf with yesterday."

FIVE

W *here is your own personal policeman when you need him?* Charlie Sugerman, half of a seasoned San Francisco team of homicide inspectors, and, if not my boyfriend exactly, then as close to that position as he was willing to get, would have teased me about letting my imagination run wild. If I were looking into his startlingly green eyes, I could have let go of my jitters right away.

Gabby's news made me uneasy. My proximity to murder in the past, I reminded myself, didn't mean Larry Saylor's death was anything other than an accident. *Yeah, right,* said my inner voice. *Then why did your stomach turn a cartwheel and why is the muscle in your eye beginning to twitch?* An investigator turns up material he thinks may call for increased scrutiny of a donor. A few days later, he drowns while playing golf with the donor? Not good, definitely not good.

I took a deep breath and exhaled noisily. Gabby looked at me questioningly. "Too much caffeine," I said. "How about you make me a copy of this page of notes he wrote to himself? Then I'll head over to the president's office on my own while you round up what the dean wants."

"I'm supposed to meet Mr. Margoletti later this afternoon. He's coming in to talk with Mr. McEvoy and they want me to start working on a list of potential donors to the new art gallery."

"Does Vince Margoletti know you're doing research on him?"

"I doubt it."

"May I suggest something?"

She nodded.

"For now, don't volunteer that you've been checking into his financial background. It makes some donors feel awkward to be reminded that people are looking the proverbial gift horse in the mouth. Know what I mean?"

She smiled. "Not to worry. That's my ongoing instruction from my boss about every donor."

I was glad to hear it, especially if there was something in Margoletti's background that had seriously worried Saylor. I stood at the top of the stairs while Gabby copied the notes I wanted at the nearby machine in an alcove and then walked with her into Saylor's office. The vice president's group occupied a space that was divided by a reception area, with his executive office on the left, and a set of rooms on the right. A few staff members were clustered in the doorway, talking in low tones. They glanced at Gabby and nodded, but no one said anything to us as we headed into Saylor's office. The young researcher replaced the originals on a large table near a window.

The room was masculine and well furnished, tidy, with a large desk and a bank of file cabinets on one wall. A handful of glossy business magazines was scattered on the table.

"Stories about the companies Mr. Margoletti is involved with as their attorney or a board member," Gabby said when she saw me fingering one. "The guys who started them are so creative. Dermott and I were impressed when we read about them."

"Is Dermott interested in business theory?"

"Not really. He only wishes he made more money. The life of a Ph.D. in history is not anything like this high tech world."

"So true. I read last week about a fourteen-year old who sold his company, if you can even call it that, to one of the big online search firms for more than a million dollars."

Gabby sighed.

"Does it bother you?"

"Not me. The comparisons are hard, though, when you're looking at having to pay back big student loans. We'll be fine. We're a lot better off than that poor guy from Reomantics."

"Poor? I doubt any of them are poor," I said as we exited the office.

"He was about to make it big when someone else started a company using the same idea for software, or so he claimed. It was one of the cases Mr. Margoletti was involved in. At first he was this guy's attorney, then he dropped him and became the other man's representative. It was in the articles I collected."

"What happened to the original CEO?" I said as much to myself as to the researcher.

"After all those hassles, he was back to square one, trying to come up with another idea when, wham, he rammed into a freeway pillar and died."

That did it. I was officially creeped out.

The scene in the president's office was different from when I first visited. His assistant was standing behind her desk, talking softly but urgently on the phone and gesturing to a wide-eyed student, who was shifting from one foot to the other while he waited for instructions. Several middle-aged men and one woman were squeezed onto the couch and chairs, checking their smartphones and glancing up periodically. The door to the president's office was closed, but I could hear the president's baritone voice even though the words weren't distinct.

With no place to sit, I waited by a window, looking out at the peaceful campus and the clumps of students crisscrossing walkways and lawns. While I watched, a gray squirrel dashed across a utility wire from one treetop to another. I could see why someone could get comfortable working here for decades.

"Ms. O'Rourke? The president can see you now." The assistant interrupted my daydreaming. As I walked to the door, I was aware of the curious glances the seated people gave me.

Brennan was still in executive mode. He got up and came around his desk, gesturing to two men seated in comfortable chairs.

"You've met Dean Anderson, I believe?" Coe Anderson nodded and murmured hello. "And this is Vince Margoletti, the donor we've talked so much about."

Given what Gabby and I had been talking about, it was hard to look at him and not see trouble. He rose from his chair, played with his cufflinks for a split second, long enough to make sure he had my full attention, then extended his hand. "I understand you're good friends with my old classmate Geoff Johnson. Great guy." His voice signaled lukewarm interest, whether in me or Geoff I wasn't sure, while his eyes seemed to be measuring my response. I did my best to keep my expression neutral, pleasant.

"I work for him, indirectly," I said. "He's a real friend to the Devor Museum."

"Yes, so I understand. Although I may give him a run for his money here, right Rory?" He looked down at his perfectly buffed nails before raising his head to look at Lynthorpe's leader.

"Indeed, Vince," the president said. "Your magnificent gift would turn heads anywhere. You know how grateful I am personally. We all are, of course," he added as Dean Anderson twitched in his seat and re-crossed his legs suddenly.

Let's all fall over ourselves with gratitude. Margoletti was not very subtle cueing up the compliments. Taking the chair Brennan pointed me to, I wondered what this meeting was about and wished someone had given me a heads up. In the absence of any hard information, I looked for clues in the body language of the three men sitting there. I noticed that the development director was missing. He was probably too busy tallying up hundred dollar checks from the alumni fundraising drive. *Catty*, I chided myself.

Brennan was at turns serious and almost jocular as he threaded his way through a monologue on the situation. "Our cherished colleague and friend is gone, and the last thing we want to do is carry on business as usual," he said. "I'd like nothing better than to send everyone home to grieve and remember Larry, each in their own way." He paused, looked down at his folded hands as if in prayer.

Out of the corner of my eye, I could see Vince Margoletti's hands on the arm of his chair and I noticed one was opening and closing in a tight fist. Arthritis? Tension? At one point, he flicked his wrist and dollar chimes began ringing in my head. His Patek Phillippe watch had more complications, as they're called, than my eyes could register crammed onto the watch face. Definitely over one hundred thousand dollars, about the same price as one of Dickie's beloved Porsches. This man had money.

Brennan lifted his head and sighed audibly. "But life doesn't give us that luxury, does it? Coe and Vince and I have been talking, Danielle, and thought you might have some advice for us based on your own extensive experience."

Watching Brennan's face and listening to his unctuous comments was a distraction. What I really wanted was an excuse to stare at Vince Margoletti. I'd read so much about him by now, a lot of it hinting at his toughness, that his appearance caught me off guard. Newspaper and magazine photos didn't do him justice. Of medium height, he was slim, fit, had a full head of expertly cut, curly blonde hair set off by a slight tan. The hair might have been helped by a bottle of bleach but, if so, it was skillfully done. He was wearing what I'd bet was a bespoke suit from the best London tailor. Other than that clenched fist, his movements were relaxed and smooth, he spoke easily, and his straight-backed posture put my own to shame. I had been expecting someone different, visibly harder, more grasping.

Brennan was moving on to his real point. "We have had what I consider a wonderful idea to honor Larry. The gallery and the collection will be named for Vince, of course, but there's a way to remember Larry too. Vince, why don't you explain it to Danielle?"

Margoletti looked at me with dark, opaque eyes that then slid away to focus on the wall behind me. "Larry worked hard to make this dream of mine come true," he said. "I understood he had to push back now and then in the college's best interests. Ultimately, I knew the Vincent Margoletti Collection would become a reality."

So Saylor had brought up at least some concerns about the proposed gift with Margoletti. I wondered how much Saylor might have sugarcoated his concerns in his attempt not to trigger the temper Gabby mentioned.

"I respected him for that and I think I answered all of his questions to his satisfaction."

I decided this was my chance to ask the question that had been burning at me since Gabby told me. "Did you discuss it yesterday, while you were playing golf?"

There was a moment of silence. The three men froze. Then, Margoletti said, "No, the game was purely social. Rory, Coe, Larry, and I wanted some time together not talking business, right?" He turned to the others, whose smiles were a little tentative.

"Oh, I hadn't realized you were all together." I didn't point out that I was in the room because the pesky details of that business hadn't been worked out. Margoletti may have read my mind.

"We met to discuss the details earlier. I was trying to keep the gift as simple and straightforward as possible." He went on quickly. "After what happened, I've suggested to Rory and Coe here that I put in another million dollars so that one of the main areas in the new art building can be named for Larry, perhaps a study room, or a sculpture atrium. I don't see anything particularly complicated about that. Do you?" He turned one palm up in a question and I noticed him spreading open the fingers of his other hand, laying them deliberately along his thigh.

"Offhand, no," I said. "If you're talking about enlarging the building's footprint or needing an extra type of security or climate control system, the costs for the additional space might be proportionally higher, but you and Coe would find that out early on in the planning phase. Larry Saylor's campus colleagues will appreciate the gesture."

Coe Anderson was beginning to resemble a bobble head doll. The president was doing his avuncular beaming thing at Margoletti and me. I was puzzled as to why I was here since this didn't seem like an issue that would detract from the college's decision to accept the gift. I looked toward Margoletti and suddenly caught a glitter in his eye that made my skin prickle. It vanished almost immediately and he was once again the polished philanthropist, but in that moment I had seen something different, something much closer to the man I had been reading about. His cold eyes had been sizing me up, measuring my response again. He looked tense beneath that controlled exterior and I wondered why. The proposal he had made was reasonable and generous, and I knew by now that I had no real power in the approval process. If the president were determined to accept it, the majority of the board would go along with it.

"However," he continued, "we need to sign the papers and make the announcement without any more delays. I've got paintings just sitting in a warehouse in California because I have no place to show them. At this rate, I begin to worry we'll forget what's there." He smiled to show he was joking. "I know my friend Coe here is dying to tell the media, and I want to show my respect publicly for Larry."

President Brennan jumped in. "I couldn't agree more. In light of this tragic event, we want to be able to announce Vince's gift right away. It will help the campus deal with Larry's death." Turning to me, he lowered his eyebrows and signaled my instructions. "I'm hoping you might be able to finish your interviews and satisfy Geoff Johnson without delay."

So that was it. These three were determined to pressure me into doing a fast sign off. If I didn't respect Geoff Johnson so much, or hadn't seen the look in Margoletti's eyes, I might have folded right then. Brennan's phone rang. He spoke a few words, okayed something, then hung up and turned back to the group.

"I have a suggestion," I said. "I'm proceeding without Larry Saylor's guidance, concentrating on the key provisions of the gift. I can do most of what I still need to do on the phone. I should review the letter of intent with Lynthorpe's attorney, which I'm sure you understand since it's the core of the legal arrangement,"

I said to Margoletti. "And it makes sense, given my museum background, that I look at the valuations your lawyers have placed on the donated art, to see if it tallies at least roughly with current market prices. I have a copy of the list of included artwork that your lawyers drew up, Mr. Margoletti."

Margoletti dipped his head fractionally, seemingly relaxed, although I sensed something—impatience, concern? I couldn't figure it out but something about this conversation was making this powerful man uncomfortable.

"Frankly, I think it's possible the collection is undervalued, given the heated market and the high demand for the limited number of works that have come to market by some of these artists."

"I'm not too concerned about that," Margoletti said. "I'm ready to sign over the artwork today, if it will get the project moving."

"That's very generous," I said. "I'll collect documentation on the donated pieces—"

Margoletti cut me off. "I hardly think you need to personally review the details to that degree, Ms. O'Rourke. Hardly the best use of your consulting time. Use the list my lawyers submitted. They attached fair market values to everything, I believe." His hand made an involuntary fist again and a muscle in his jaw twitched as he stared at me. "Lynthorpe's own staff will be curating the collection and can do the fine print stuff, isn't that right, Rory?"

"Absolutely, Vince. I'll personally see that our staff does a bang-up job."

"All the same, Lynthorpe will want to make sure the collection can be insured properly," I said. "If you want to close quickly, a second valuation is something I'll recommend that the college commission right away." I didn't mention my curiosity about the shares he held in private companies. Until I had a better idea of what Saylor had been worried about, I thought it was better to do my checking under his radar. "This shouldn't take long, and I don't need to do it here on campus while you're all coping with this shock and its aftermath. My suggestion is I gather any papers he had on this project, take them back to San Francisco tomorrow, and finish my report from there. If I need to, I can come back for a few days next week, when things will be calmer here. The cataloging and final estimate of the value of the pieces can come after the gift has been made, as long as Mr. Margoletti's tax attorneys agree."

Coe Anderson had been silent, but he jumped in now. "As long as you can finish what is merely a formality quickly and let Geoff and the board know you see no problems. We're trying to keep this quiet so we can do a big splash of an announcement."

"Do you have the staff for that?" I said,

"Vince has recommended a national P.R. firm to make sure we get high level coverage, but the word is leaking out locally already. I don't want anyone stealing our thunder."

"I'm afraid it won't be possible to give you Larry's files," Brennan said with a deep frown. "I can't fathom why, but the local police have insisted on sealing his office."

Six

"Why on earth would the police do that?" Coe said, red spots appearing on his cheeks. "Can't you tell them it's not necessary, Rory? After all, this is your campus. What right do they have to be here, anyway?"

President Brennan chewed on his lip. "To tell the truth, Coe, I don't know what I can do. I'll talk to the chief when we're done here. It seems overly dramatic, but I guess there's not much excitement in small towns, and the chief's determined to look as good as the police he sees on television."

Silently, I thanked Gabby for her quick action this morning, but decided I'd keep quiet about my earlier access to the originals and the fact that I had a copy of Saylor's handwritten notes in the briefcase sitting next to my chair.

The president turned to me. "Perhaps you're right, Danielle. It would be best to do what you can from San Francisco for the moment. If you need anything from us, call my assistant or the young woman from the development office for help. We can finish this up early next week."

Margoletti spoke up. "If not sooner. Ms. O'Rourke, if I can help in any way, please don't hesitate to call. I don't think you'll need a lot of what I assume is voluminous research, but if there is anything more you need, you can come directly to me." He handed me a thick, cream-colored business card. "My office can find me on a moment's notice. I want this process to go smoothly. We all want the same thing, don't we?"

The men stood as I picked up my briefcase. This might be the only time I had to ask, and I blurted out the question that was bothering me before I had fully weighed the wisdom of asking.

"I'm a bit confused, Mr. Margoletti. I understood you were playing with him when Mr. Saylor died, and now I realize all three of you were there. Was it you who called for help when he fell into the pond? Or," turning to include Coe Anderson and Rory Brennan, "any of you?" What I really wanted to ask was how did a grown and presumably healthy man manage to drown in what Coe Anderson had assured me was shallow water, but I wasn't brave enough to go that far.

The dean jumped in, ready to be offended. "Of course not. I was shocked when that young woman burst into my office to say he was dead. I had no idea when Rory and I left the clubhouse that he'd been taken ill."

The president murmured his agreement and Margoletti's brow furrowed while the corners of his thin mouth turned down. "Unfortunately, none of us was with him." He turned to include Coe and the president. "The four of us played together and went to the bar for drinks after. But Larry had messed up at that hole and decided to go back on his own after the last scheduled foursome had played through and see if he couldn't improve his performance. He left us right as we were ordering a second round."

I glanced at the two other men, who had adopted the same serious looks. Coe hadn't mentioned having been on the course with either Saylor or Margoletti when we met earlier and I wondered why not. Surely, he would have worked the prominent man's name into the conversation. "Who did find him, then?"

"The groundskeeper went out looking when it got dark. He couldn't account for the cart Larry had signed out," Brennan said in clipped tones. "I'm not sure how this is relevant, frankly."

"We had all gone our separate ways by then, so we didn't realize there was a problem," the dean said, pronouncing 'realize' in three distinct, southern-accented syllables.

Margoletti sounded genuinely sorrowful, but his eyes darted up to the ceiling past my shoulder. "We were saying earlier that we wished we had persuaded him to join us for another glass of wine in the bar." Hadn't I read that people do that upward thing with their eyes when they're not telling the truth? Or was it downward?

The phone rang then and broke some undefined tension in the room. I said a quick goodbye and opened the office door. I could hear the president on the phone already asking his assistant to track down the police chief as I left. The dean was insisting in a shrill voice that the files should now revert to him. The people waiting on the couches looked me over again as I left, and I made sure I held in my sigh of relief at being released from the hot seat until I hit the sidewalk.

~~~

There were two police cars parked in the No Parking zone outside the president's office. Passing students eyed them curiously and I wondered how far news of the administrator's death had traveled on campus. I noticed that a few of the young women focused their stares on the dark-haired cop who leaned against the side of one patrol car, and no wonder. His short-sleeved shirt showed off muscled arms and a flat stomach. The square jaw, dark sunglasses and impassive expression on his face were right out of an action film. He clenched a toothpick in his mouth, which gave him a chance to bare his white teeth slightly. For me, the macho effect was diluted by the impression that he knew exactly how he looked.

A second uniformed policeman got out of the driver's side of the car and came around to speak to Macho Cop, who turned his head slowly away from the passing parade of students to listen. He pushed himself off the car and sauntered off with his partner toward the building where the development office was located. It seemed like a lot of police attention for a drowning accident. Maybe President Brennan was right and there wasn't much else going on in town to compete for the attention of the uniformed cops today.

I reminded myself I had a lot to do if I was going to head back to San Francisco sooner. The air was sweet and the breeze hardly more than a whisper, and I was wearing the right shoes for it, so I decided to walk the mile to my hotel. On the way, I used my cell phone to call Teeni Watson, my assistant, to tell her I planned to be in the office Thursday.

"You solved all their problems already? Damn, here I was thinking we'd have some party time before you rolled back in."

"Easy, girl. Plenty of time to party when your Funk Art exhibit opens." Teeni is a graduate student at the University of California's Berkeley campus, whose doctoral dissertation is in the form of a project she's curating for the Devor. I get heartburn thinking about what I'll do after the exhibition, when some smart museum snatches her up. "Oh, before I forget, your cute cop called. I told him where you were. I hope that's okay?"

"Sure. Did he say why he wanted to talk to me?" Like, maybe ask me out on the off chance he could actually keep a date? Charlie was sweet and desirable, but a lot of trouble as a romantic possibility. As half of a busy San Francisco Police Department homicide team, it felt as though he was on call all the time. The local TV reporters might say that murder rates were down in the city, but you couldn't convince me of that. Gang fights, drug deals gone bad, innocent victims who opened their doors to the wrong people—I know the city isn't worse than other places. However, from my angle of vision as someone who would enjoy finishing a Friday night dinner in peace, or watching a play past the first intermission without having her date glance at his pager and start making his excuses, the city was in a non-stop crime wave. It certainly hadn't done anything for our love life. After months of dancing around it, we had finally spent a couple of late nights together and they were delicious, except for the time his pager would not stop buzzing even though he was theoretically off duty. He had finally apologized and snatched it up off the bedside table, explaining that on rare occasions—hah—it was all hands on deck.

"No, but he has your cell phone number, right?" Teeni said. "I figured he called you directly."

"Not yet. Anything else I need to know before I get back?"

"You got a call from a guy named Burgess from a law firm in the Valley. Said you wouldn't know him, but he'd like to talk to you when you have time."

"Did you ask him if someone else could help him?"

"Yeah, but he said no. Said he'll explain when you call him back."

"Okay. I'll deal with it later."

"How are you enjoying being a big shot consultant among the preppy set?"

"The good old boys are making it clear my job is to rubber stamp their plan, and the guy who raised the red—well, the yellow—flag about the gift died before I could find out what was bothering him."

There was silence for a long moment. "Hold it," Teeni said, dropping her voice a half octave. "You're telling me you've been in that town for two days and someone is dead already? Oh, girl, you'd better get on home. You are bad luck."

"Not fair. I barely met the man. Anyway, it was an accident."

The silence from the other end of the phone was as pointed as a sharp stick, but that's not fair. I can't help it that a few odd things have happened around me. They didn't happen to me, or because of me, and anyone in my position who worked with rich, powerful, and sometimes eccentric people would have had the same experiences. At least, I like to think so. I have admitted to myself that once in a while I don't leave well enough alone.

Teeni's unspoken rebuke did its job and I promised myself I'd focus on Mr. Margoletti's intentions and his enviable warehouse full of art for the remainder of my consulting gig. First, I had an errand to do. I walked past sidewalk planters filled with azaleas and ducked in a couple of stores in search of a present for my cat sitter. Since she doesn't actually like cats, the scores of needlework cat pillows and framed cat sayings were out. Ditto red and green plaid stadium blankets, thick mittens (on sale at this time of year), and Grandma Moses prints, charming as they were. I left empty-handed and, without any further excuses, went back to my room to think about Vince Margoletti's proposed gift and how to get it to go quickly.

I jumped when my cell phone rang, not in surprise, but in relief at the distraction. I was having trouble concentrating on the gift, and kept drifting into consideration of how someone could drown on a golf course. Who knew? From the viewing perspective of a TV set, I had always assumed the water was all shallow puddles.

It was Charlie and I was quick to dump my random thoughts on him. He didn't think it sounded the least suspicious, which reassured me. "It could have been his heart. People have heart attacks everywhere. They'll do an autopsy and that'll answer a lot of questions. If anything at the scene hinted at violence, they'd already be talking to his golf partners and anyone else who had been around him that day."

I told him a little about Margoletti, but Charlie had never heard of the guy. "Our circles don't intersect, Dani. Wait 'til he kills someone on my turf and then I'll know."

"Not likely," I said, laughing at the idea. "He has everything anyone could want. He's not going after someone's sneakers or fancy car."

"There's always something that a person wants and doesn't have," he said, "and, sadly, some of them can't figure any way to get it other than to take it violently. I know."

"You see that side of life every day, don't you?"

"Hey, I'm not the only one. Remember—"

I cut him off. I didn't want a repeat of my conversation with Teeni. "Call me this weekend if you have some time off, okay? I'll be ready for some distraction. For now, I have to go bury myself in paper."

"Distraction? Is that all I am?"

"I didn't mean . . . actually, yes, I did mean a distraction, the very best kind, a serious sort of distraction."

He chuckled. "I guess I'll have to accept your definition for now, and think of a way to prove it to you when you get home."

Sweet. We were definitely getting somewhere in this relationship, even if it was slow going. I said a few nice things that seemed to please him, and we left it at that.

SEVEN

I was happy to be back in my office. It was one of those rare, drizzly days in May, not quite rain falling or fog misting. I'm not a workaholic, but if there's one thing I know, it's that paper multiplies like breeding rabbits when it sits in the in-box. In addition, it was almost time to submit next year's budget, my least favorite task. Teeni, dressed in dangly earrings and a red leather skirt that appeared to be poured onto her curvy frame, was distracted by details about the Funk Art project, and only put out her fist for a quick bump as we passed in the hall. "Hey," she said, "back in fifteen."

Deep into negative numbers, I jumped as a shriek from somewhere down the corridor interrupted my contemplation of the computer screen, causing me to drop the bagel I'd picked up in the downstairs café, cream cheese-side down, onto the printout on which I was trying to make revisions that would turn red ink into black.

Before I could get up to see who might have won the lottery or, more likely, scalded themselves with hot coffee, Teeni burst into my office.

"Hot damn," she said, pumping an arm in the air. "I'm a finalist. I'm one of two. I know I'm going to get this job, Dani, I know it."

To a stranger, it might seem odd that someone looking for a new job would share her excitement with her current boss, but everyone around here knows the story. Teeni is a woman of many talents, the least of which is being my super efficient aide. Her passion is art history, and museum outreach. She's a budding museum curator and her retrospective of California Funk Art opens here in two months. It will get rave reviews, so Teeni's days in the office down the hall are numbered. I'm trying to get used to the idea, but it's not easy. Like everyone else, I relish Teeni's company and count on her talents.

"Which one is this?" I said, wiping cream cheese off the page. "Dallas? They're hot for you, I know."

"They haven't called yet," she said. "This is the women's college in Maryland I told you about, the one that received a humongous collection of American 'outsider' art. They want an American art specialist who can create a series of exhibitions, plus pull in new gifts of art and, of course, money."

"They're going after the right person," I said, trying to sound enthusiastic. "You know how to keep board members and staffs happy, look someone in the eye and ask for big bucks, and talk to artists. That's what I'll tell them when they call for a reference. Now, if only you could fix this damn budget for me."

"Never fear. For that kind of recommendation, I'll get the annual fund director to shave ten percent off his projected costs, and get the old copier working like new." She winked and sailed out of the office, taking all the oxygen with her. The spreadsheets looked drearier, the computer screen more boring, and the bagel unappetizing. I tossed it into the wastebasket and stood up.

Being vice president of fundraising activities at the Devor had its high moments—parties, openings, dinner with society mucky-mucks, working with the brilliant museum director. This rainy day wasn't one of them. My hair had gotten wet on the way to the office and was threatening to sort itself into corkscrew curls. The classic Calvin Klein slacks I had been so happy to fit into again after dieting back down to a size 12 had also gotten damp and were creased in all the wrong places. I paced the confines of my office for a few minutes, trying to fire up my brain cells and tamp down my urge for chocolate.

I had forced myself back into my chair when she buzzed me a half hour later. "It's the most cheerful man in San Francisco for you," she said.

"The boss?"

"Are you kidding? With third quarter reports on his desk this week? Trust me, you don't want to run into Peter in the elevator right about now."

"Oh. Then you must mean . . . ?"

"Yes, I do," she sang out. "And brimming over with good cheer."

"Tell him I'm in a meeting, or that I don't have time to talk."

"He's way ahead of you, Dani. He said if you tried that I should tell you he'll send a basket of fruit, a very large basket with balloons attached, which he knows you would hate."

"Oh, for heaven's sake. Okay, put him through but be prepared to hear the phone in this room slam down in about thirty seconds."

"Be kind," Teeni said. For some reason, she finds my ex-husband funny. She didn't know him back in the day.

"Dickie, I just got back from Lynthorpe and I'm buried in paper. Can this wait for another time?"

"Hello to you too, Dani," he said, using the hurt little boy voice that makes me want to strangle him. "You finished so fast? Bummer. I mean for the reunion."

"Going to your reunion was a non-starter, Dickie. I have to believe you understood that."

"Hmmm," he said, and changed the subject. "I've got an idea that might be good for the Devor. Do you want to hear it?"

"Okay, okay," I said, simultaneously rude and suspicious, even to my own ears.

"There's a charity polo match in Palo Alto Sunday. I'm sure a few of the Devor's biggest donors will be there for you to chat up. Champagne by the bucket, some South American players to keep up the level of the game, maybe even an incognito member of the royal family. What do you say?"

It was tempting. The international players I had seen were pretty hot, with flashing smiles, muscled limbs, elegant manners, and all the earmarks of extreme wealth. The British royal, if it was the same one attached to a famous player who graced the society matches every year, was only one through a former marriage and was a disappointment—scrawny, unhappy-looking, and a little drunk. The champagne would be good, however, and the atmosphere quite upscale. There's not much that is more conducive to daydreaming about being an aristocrat than the tradition of strolling cross the grassy field in between chukkers, fluted glass in hand, pausing in the happy chatter to tap clots of uprooted turf back into place with the toe of one's trendy shoe. Especially if the heel is flat or at least wide enough not to sink into the turf, which happened to me the first time I pretended to know what this polo business was all about.

"Thanks, Dickie. I appreciate the thought. Can I call you back when I have some idea of what else I need to get done this weekend?"

"Absolutely. Right up to the morning of."

"Wait," I said, suddenly having a horrible thought. "You're not playing, are you?" I was remembering the last time he set out on borrowed ponies to relive his college experience, only to have a bad fall that resulted in a weeklong stay at Stanford Hospital, where his mother insisted on camping out in his room even though he and I were married at the time. Mrs. Richard Argetter II (I was Number Three) had argued that, having lost her husband a year earlier, she had no intention of losing her only child, which also might have been a reference to our marriage, an arrangement of which she did not approve and which she did all she could to undermine.

"No one's going to let me near a pony. They're happy to have me as a member of the club as long as I pay my dues and tip the grooms, but you know me. I'm much too lazy to do the practicing that would keep me in the saddle, and too old to bounce off the turf if I crash."

"Good," I said. "Not that you're lazy, but that you're staying out of the fray. Maybe Peter will want to go." I knew from experience that if I stayed on the phone longer, or was too nice to him, Dickie would sense an opening and wind up inviting me to dinner or to Paris, which is about as likely to happen as me taking up spelunking.

It had been my intention to wait until Charlie Sugerman called me, but I only lasted until lunchtime Saturday.

"Hey, are you back in town already?" he said when I reached him.

"I had my cell phone with me," I said. As in, you could have called me to check.

"Yeah, but it's nicer to talk in person. I don't suppose you're free tonight?"

I'm in my thirties, past the vague "mid-thirties" and definitely past the time when girlish pride rules my behavior. In other words, I wasn't going to play too hard to get. "Free as a bird. Are you asking me out?"

"Sure, er, well, maybe."

Nice, very nice. Sound of romantic balloon bursting.

"Your best friend Andy Weiler and I offered to trade on-call status with the guys on another team, one of whom is about to become a father. If it stays quiet tonight, let's do pizza in North Beach. Sound good?"

What could I say? It sounded somewhat good, but not like a sure thing given San Francisco's murder rate and Homicide Inspector Weiler's habit of jumping on every case that comes along. I long ago decided he had no personal life and that he was working to keep Charlie from developing the bad habit of having one. Seeing as I didn't have a lot of other offers—none, in fact—and Charlie is special, if hard to pin down for any length of time, I said, "You're on," crossing my fingers.

My luck was holding and we were on the tiramisu and espressos when Charlie said, "What do the cops say now about the guy who drowned?"

"It's not clear. The police searched his office, and I did notice a couple of officers walking around campus. My impression is everyone at Lynthorpe thinks that the checking around is only a formality."

"What does the coroner say?"

"Easy, Inspector. You're talking to a complete outsider. I'm not sure they have a coroner in this little town."

"If not, they'll call in someone, most likely from the county. He must have had a regular doctor, and the people he was playing with ought to know if he was feeling okay. People having heart attacks frequently have symptoms in the first stages, long before they go into crisis. Where were they, anyway, while he was drowning?"

"In the bar. He went back up to the course after their first round of drinks was finished. Then they left. One of the foursome was the donor whose gift I was hired to review."

Charlie nodded as he sipped his espresso. "Hardly suspicious. After all, if the gift is approved, he's happy. If it's not, he still has his mega-bucks to offer someone else, right?"

"So it would seem." Charlie had a nice way of cutting to the heart of the problem. What did Margoletti have to gain by killing his alma mater's vice president? If there were a problem, they'd deal with it privately. Part of me was shocked that I would even consider Margoletti as a violent criminal. He was a hard charging lawyer, which is not, I reminded myself, the same thing as being homicidal.

"The first few hours in an investigation are full of unanswered questions," he continued, "but these things sort themselves out pretty quickly. The cops will interview everyone on the golf course and by the time you get back, it'll be settled."

As we walked back to my car, which was parked in the multistory garage next to the North Beach police station, Charlie's arm rested on my back, sending little electric charges through me. Suddenly, I heard my name. I turned around and saw Dickie coming out of a far fancier Italian restaurant than our cozy pizza joint. The pressure on my back vanished in an instant, as did the good feelings. I felt myself stiffen. It was bad enough that my ex was interrupting my reverie. It was even more annoying that he was holding the elbow of a stunning woman while he did it.

EIGHT

I sized her up in a nanosecond and didn't like what I saw. A brunette about my own age, dressed with exquisite style but not flash, easily a size eight, a face I grudgingly admitted was lovely, wearing a serene smile and—I made time to check—no wedding ring.

"Hey, fancy meeting you here," my ex said. "Dani, I don't think you know Isabella. Izzy, this is my ex-wife. You're Charles, the cop, I mean homicide inspector, right?" All said with charm oozing out of his pores while I felt my lips tightening. I knew I looked wary, but damn it, Dickie had a way of ambushing me and this was the wrong time and place to bump into him and Ms. Perfectly Wonderful.

I wasn't sure what to make of them together. He had been pressuring me to come to his prep school party. Now, he was out with someone else. I had no business being jealous. *So why are your claws out?* Damned if I knew.

We all made polite noises, agreed North Beach was lovely tonight and wasn't the full moon pretty? My instinct was to bolt if I couldn't relax, but my curiosity was gluing my feet to the pavement. "So, Isabella, do you live in San Francisco?"

"Oh, no," she said with a throaty laugh and an exotic accent. "At least not yet, although Richard tells me I wouldn't miss Rome one bit if I'd give San Francisco a chance." She turned toward my beaming ex, showing her dimples—dimples!—and touched his arm with perfectly manicured fingers.

"It usually isn't this warm at night," I said before I could stop myself. "We get a lot of fog."

"Ah, but I love cool weather. Rome is so hot in the summer, you know?" she said, still smiling. I thought she was perhaps making too much of those dimples. "And then it gets so cold sometimes in the winter. Brrr." She lifted her shoulders in a charming gesture of vulnerability.

Dickie beamed, Charlie cleared his throat, and I decided a matching simper was the best choice at the moment. Before Dickie could suggest a nightcap or some other gruesome social gesture, I said, "Well, nice to meet you." Charlie echoed my escape line in a hearty tone and we headed off purposefully.

"She seems nice," he said as we dodged hurrying Asian pedestrians headed back toward Chinatown loaded down with plastic bags, and small groups of young people making their way in the opposite direction toward the sleazy Broadway clubs.

"If you like the type," I said, tuning out the voice in my head that pointed out she and I were close to being the same type, minus the dimples, the designer wardrobe, and the Italian accent.

"Your ex seemed more relaxed than the other times I've met him."

"Perhaps that's because there wasn't a dead body lying on the sidewalk, or your partner suggesting that I might have killed someone. It's easier to be casual when murder isn't the topic of conversation."

Charlie laughed. "Maybe that's it. I notice you didn't tell him about what's been happening at that school back East."

"No, and I'm glad you didn't. He'd be all over it, fussing and thinking he had some role in fixing it."

"Cops can live without eager beaver amateurs," Charlie said, still chuckling. I glanced up at him. "Oh, not you. You're not a busybody, you're always in the middle for some reason."

"Please don't joke," I said. "I'd quit this consulting job in a heartbeat if I could. Even an accidental death makes me want to run screaming in the other direction. But Geoff would see me as a quitter, and, anyway, I feel I owe something to the vice president who was so sure I could help."

"Okay, no jokes, but you have to admit it would take some stress off you if your ex found someone special. She's really attractive."

I had to agree on all points, but I wondered why that didn't make me happy. After all, I did want Dickie to focus on someone other than me, didn't I, so why was I feeling snippy? Residual anger maybe, a conditioned reflex of some kind? I was getting tired of thinking about it. I missed Charlie's hand steering me, and the picture of the rest of the evening that had been building before Dickie interrupted things. I was about to suggest a drink at my apartment when Charlie's cell phone rang. We kept walking while he fished it out of his leather jacket.

"Again? Man, what's up with these guys? Okay, I'm close by. Meet you in five."

No, no, no, I yelled mentally. *Don't let this happen.*

He turned to me with a rueful smile. "I was really hoping for a quiet night." He stopped on the sidewalk and pulled me close, facing him. "You know how much I love spending time with you. That evening we had, well . . ." He leaned in to kiss me, then let go of me. "But duty calls. Weiler says two guys decided to do a reenactment of an old cowboy movie in an alley in the Western Addition. One's dead, the other shooter's long gone and, of course, no one's seen or heard anything. I'll walk you to your car, but the rest of the evening's out, I'm afraid."

Oh, good. Not only do I get to see that my ex is entranced with his new girlfriend, but the guy I would like to have my own fling with is off chasing bad guys instead of cuddling with me. Why couldn't I fall for a banker or a plastic surgeon, someone who kept regular hours?

Twenty minutes later I was stomping around my apartment muttering to Fever, my overweight cat-with-attitude, who had apparently decided during my last trip out of town that my neighbor Yvette was much nicer as a lap. Yvette didn't like cats in general or, as far as I could tell, Fever in particular. Maybe that's why he now rubbed up against her jeans, threw himself down in front of her well-worn ballet shoes, and tried to slip out of my apartment door and run downstairs to her place every day.

So there we were, not exactly glaring at each other, but not offering much in the way of mutual comfort and support, when the phone rang.

"You're back," sang out my best friend Suzy Byrnstein. In my mood, I had a sharp remark on the tip of my tongue, something about stating the obvious. It wasn't her fault people were killing each other in San Francisco tonight, I reminded myself, so I curled up on the couch with a mug of mint tea for a talk. Fever, after looking longingly at the door and weighing his options, jumped up next to me, and settled in for a nap.

Suzy is an accomplished artist, a trust fund baby who didn't let that blunt her ambition and focus. She's represented by a gallery in San Francisco and another in Santa Fe, where she once had a serious automobile accident for which I still feel responsible. She's the best gossip hound I know and we hadn't talked in almost two weeks. When I asked her what was up, I knew I was inviting a long, excited monologue, which was good since I didn't want to admit I was playing second fiddle to a couple of urban cowboys, never mind Italy's Miss Congeniality.

I had time to replace my teabag and fill the little pot with hot water a second time before Suzy wound down. Then I filled her in on my consulting gig and the sad circumstances that brought me home early.

"Let me get this straight," she said. "You get sent to a strange town and the next day the person who needed your help is dead?"

"I wouldn't say it quite like that. You're implying cause and effect."

"Oh well then, pardon me. You get to town and, as so often happens when anyone comes to town, someone dies. Does that work better for you?"

"Don't joke. I didn't know him and Charlie told me it's most likely a coincidence, but you know how easily spooked I am."

Suzy heard the pain in my voice and her tone changed instantly. "Oh hon, I am sorry for making you feel worse. It is horrible, and I wonder if you should even go back there."

"Most of the work can be done here although I want to consult with several people on campus. I'll have go back to present my report verbally to the president before I can write up a final draft, but I'll wait until the funeral is over and the president's ready to think about this again. They really want to wind this up quickly and book the gift."

"Want me to come back with you?"

"Thanks, but I intend to keep my head down and stay far away from whatever investigation the local cops do."

"The police are involved even though it was an accident?"

"From what I understand, it's only a formality. Meanwhile I plan to hit the phones to a few people in Silicon Valley. After all, not many powerful people around here are openly referred to as 'snakes' in the local press, and I'm interested to know why the man who's giving all this money and art to the college has such a mixed reputation."

"Sweetheart, where there's smoke, there's always a fire smoldering," my friend said. "I might have a contact for you. Ethan's a cousin of mine who invests in tech start-ups. Why don't I call him and see if he'll talk with you?"

"That'd be great. I might pick up a less biased perspective than I'm likely to get from entrepreneurs looking for funding. Margoletti made so much money from getting inside high tech winners that he's now investing big time in the next generation of innovation in the Valley. I'm guessing those people might be afraid to criticize him for fear they'll get blackballed from early funding. Tell me more about Ethan."

Ethan Byrnstein and three others had put up a million dollars for the first phase of a new company that was betting everything on a simple idea for reaching customers on the Web. I asked if it had gone public since then.

"You'll have to check with him, but I'm guessing not. He has the uncanny ability to back the wrong horse every time, but his heart's in the right place, and he is so enthusiastic. It's a good thing Ethan's dad also did well in our family company so he has money for these experiments. It's another good thing his dad died before he could see Ethan and his sister burning through their inheritances."

"Is she an investor too?"

"No. Gail's a softie. I swear everyone with a sick or injured or abandoned animal charity has hit her up at one time or another. You should see her house. The walls and tables are covered with framed photographs and figurines of cheetahs and elephants and house cats she is credited with saving. Thank heavens she doesn't bring the live ones home."

My own animal was giving me the eye and my tea was cold, so I said goodnight to Suzy, threw some kibble into Fever's bowl and ground the coffee for tomorrow's pot. A half hour later I was in bed, polishing off the latest in my favorite alphabet series of mysteries and congratulating myself on having a reasonably enjoyable and productive Saturday night in spite of San Francisco's crime wave.

NINE

*P*eter Lindsey and I drove down to Palo Alto Sunday morning for the polo match. Peter's almost the dream boss: funny, informal, loyal to his staff, and smart. I say 'almost' only because he doesn't always give me what I want, a situation I'm particularly aware of at this time of year when we are submitting our budget proposals for the coming twelve months. Today he had an idea for scouting out a prospect and I had a desire for champagne and strawberries, so we were gossiping and laughing as I drove. Suzy had called me earlier to say her cousin would be in his office in the heart of Silicon Valley, and would be happy to see me if I wanted to drop by later in the day. I had talked briefly to him, and he seemed intrigued.

"Do you think Margoletti's someone who could still be a good contact for us?" Peter asked, looking up briefly from emails on his smart phone.

"I wouldn't bet on it, not while Geoff's the leader of the Devor's board. No love lost there, I gather. Could be a conflict of interest for me anyway, using Lynthorpe's contacts to turn a donor in our direction, although I have to say I'm kicking myself that we didn't go after him. I had no idea he was ready to give away his collection so soon after beginning it."

"How about his son, then? He's the polo player, right? If he's here today, I'd like to meet him. Presumably he'll inherit someday, which gives us lots of time to get him interested in the Devor."

"I know nothing about him except that someone mentioned he went to Lynthorpe for a little while."

"I have another idea," Peter said. "There's a high ranking amateur player from New England who went to school in the Boston area and whose late grandfather collected Matisse paintings in the 1920s. Sandy mentioned one piece in particular she wishes we could get. Says she thinks it's still owned by the family. Maybe Margoletti Junior and the grandson are polo buddies."

Sandy was the Devor's European paintings curator. "I wouldn't recognize the son."

"We can put out feelers," he said as he put away his phone and looked out at the cobalt surface of the lake formed by the San Andreas Fault that lay off to the right of the highway.

"Do me a favor, Peter," I said as we got close to our exit. "I don't want to talk about what happened at Lynthorpe last week, even to Dickie. Would you keep it between us for now?"

Peter nodded. "I understand. It's not exactly a party topic. I promise, not a word."

Palo Alto is twenty degrees warmer than San Francisco on a nice day, which this was. Dickie had reserved a table under the center tent and we found him there, looking like a character out of an F. Scott Fitzgerald novel. He wore a navy linen blazer and aviator shades, with one blonde lock of hair falling in his eyes, his movements lazy and graceful. Suzy says he's a bad boy, which is way too forgiving in my opinion, but even after everything that's poisoned our relationship, I have to admit he's one of the most attractive men I've ever met. As we walked over, he was laughing at something the guy leaning over him was saying, while several women in fluttering silk and crunchy linen gossiped nearby. A round bowl of red, white, and blue flowers on the table made the whole scene look like a Renoir painting I once saw at the Chicago Art Institute.

Dickie looked up and waved. "Perfect timing," he called out, rising and shaking hands with my boss as a bugler played the first notes of the national anthem. Dickie likes Peter and vice versa. I think it helps that Peter is a confirmed and quite public bachelor.

Isabella wasn't in the group, which was a shame. I had decided that I was cool with his dating her and had enjoyed a daydream of being super gracious to make up for the other night. She would like me, we would double date, and my ex would be impressed. *Oh well, the halo next time.*

There's a slow but lovely pace to the game of polo, at least for the casual onlooker. It's marked out with rhythmic thudding hooves of ponies charging up and down the field, occasional clusters of men and horses in a kind of scrum, the riders flailing around with long mallets in search of a ball that's rolling around under the animals' hooves, then more riding up and down the grass. Occasionally, the ball makes it into the net, at which time the ponies get to slow down. It's easy to see why the horses only play one chukker, or period—there are eight in a game—before going back to the trailer area to get rubbed down by grooms while other lucky ones have their turns on the field.

As the second group of horses took the field with the same riders, I asked my ex if he knew Vince Margoletti's son. "I hear he plays."

"Sure. He's here today," Dickie said and pointed to a player on the other side of the wide field, leaning over to pat his pony's glossy brown coat. The helmet buckled under his chin didn't hide his long dark hair laying on the collar of his white shirt, although it may have overemphasized a jutting chin that looked a little large for his nose. The chukker began and Margoletti's son immediately got the ball. Dickie explained that he was playing offense. Over the course of the next fifteen minutes, I couldn't help but notice how aggressively he played, pushing his horse for speed when chasing the ball, muscling his way into the scrums, and using his horse to intimidate other players by racing up or down the field close to other riders, even bumping into the opposite player. Twice, I winced as his mallet slammed into an opposing player's leg.

"Is that legal?" I said the second time it happened.

Dickie grimaced. "J.P. was a member of my club for a while, but he hangs out with a different crowd now. He pushes," Dickie said when I looked confused, "plays rough, offends people. He bets on matches too, so there's more at stake for him."

"Like father, like son," said a woman sitting nearby, who had been looking through binoculars. I'd met her a few times when Dickie and I were married. She was fiftyish, divorced from money like me, but had kept the houses in Marin County and Lake Tahoe. This afternoon, she was wearing a large, yellow diamond that caught the sun in a fiery gleam. "But they have the money to do it."

"I met Vince at Lynthorpe," I said, "the college in New England he graduated from. I'm guessing he's not back yet."

"He could have hitched a ride on someone's private plane."

That's the kind of response that always did, and always will, separate me from my ex and his friends. A private plane. Of course, silly me.

Dickie called out to the man he'd been chatting with when we arrived, "Alex, seen J.P.'s dad today?"

"Not yet," Alex said, ambling over. "But if he's around, we'll know it soon enough, especially if J.P.'s team wins."

The woman with the diamond smiled, although her mouth twisted in a sign that the scenario annoyed her. "If he's here, he'll make sure we're all aware of his golden boy's brilliance. Who knows? We might even see some of the lowlifes who hang around J.P. hoping to get their money back."

"Money back?" I said, thinking this didn't sound at all like the smooth Vince Margoletti I'd just met.

"Rumor has it J.P.'s in over his head with gambling debts."

"No," Dickie said, "can't be. Not with a father like Vince to cover him."

Just then, the local team scored and we paused to clap. A minute later, when the period was over, I watched Vince's son ride back to a long horse trailer, hop off his horse, and whack his mallet against the side of his boot while the groom led the horse, its sides heaving, away and a second groom walked over with a fresh mount. Someone handed him a water bottle and I did a double take. It was Vince, and he was beaming and saying something. I sidled over to Peter, who was now chatting with the diamond lady, and tugged on his sleeve. "Father and son at 11 o'clock," I murmured. Peter and I turned in time to see Vince reach out to slap his son approvingly on the back as J.P. turned away to mount up.

The champagne was still flowing as the last chukker wound down, although I was reluctantly passing on refills since I had to drive farther down the Peninsula after the match. The players dismounted near the horse trailers, and a few accepted towels from their grooms and scrubbed their faces before wandering over to meet the onlookers. Vince made his way along the sidelines to our group and the woman with the diamond ring, who seemed to shrink back in her chair as he approached. I stayed close enough to listen and watch, but not close enough to get sucked in. So far, the senior Margoletti hadn't noticed me. Vince did exactly what she had feared. He replayed J.P.'s goals, his toughness on the field, and his riding skills, move by move. All she could do was agree in monosyllables every few minutes.

Peter edged into the group, sticking out his hand to shake Margoletti's. A few minutes later, the polo-playing son walked into the tent area and Peter got his introduction. The two of them began to chat. Dickie glanced at me, then came over and took my arm. "We have to rescue Deirdre. I figure you have some kind of agenda with the big man anyway." Before I could object, Dickie was saying to Vince, "I think you know my former wife, Danielle O'Rourke?"

Vince turned, seeming genuinely surprised to see me there. "Of course. What a coincidence. I guess you decided you didn't have to stay at the college. Have you finished your review yet?"

I was rethinking my decision to pass on more bubbly as I made what I hoped were soothing comments to Lynthorpe's major donor. While I was complimenting Margoletti on the Anselm Kiefer canvas that I had seen in the magazine spread, his son broke away from Peter and stepped over to us.

"Has my father been bragging about how much money he paid for the Jeff Koons sculpture?" he said by way of introduction. "Or maybe about the auction where his agent beat out some sheik's for a set of Warhol movie star prints?" Without the helmet on and closer up, I noticed that he was good looking, with the same tan that was so sexy on the South American players. His large jaw was offset by thick hair that curled well below his ears but was perfectly cut. His voice was louder than his father's, but his laugh, which began right after his question, was jarring. It sounded like a donkey braying. He stopped laughing as abruptly as he started, and upended his champagne flute, gulping the delicate wine down like water. To be fair, he had played a hard polo match on a hot day, but the sharp look his father gave him and the agility with which the younger man snagged another full glass from the tray on the table made me wonder if he might like wine almost as much as I like chocolate and might be as susceptible to it.

Vince recovered his smooth manners and introduced us, explaining to J.P. that I was reviewing the gift at the request of the trustees, and that Lynthorpe would be making the public announcement of the deal in a day or so, a slight exaggeration meant for my ears, no doubt.

"A day or two?" J.P. said, sounding surprised and looking at his father. "So, feeling generous, Dad?" Abruptly, he raised the glass in a mock salute, then gulped down most of the wine.

"J.P. seems to think I'm giving it all away," Vince said. "I'm trying to convince him there's plenty left. Enough to go to Argentina to the players' camp and to keep a string of ponies, anyway." His smile was tight.

"Allowance, Ms. O'Rourke," J.P. said in a cheerful voice. "Unfortunately, I don't have my father's talent for business, although I'm working on it. So, I beg rides on Alejandro's private plane when he isn't carrying a bunch of girlfriends to and from camp, and stay with Dad here in the States the rest of the time. You should know you're getting the best in this deal." Again, the jarring laugh.

"It's not for me, not even the museum I work for," I said, hoping for a quick exit from this father-son argument. "It's for Vince's alma mater. Did I hear right that you went to Lynthorpe too? It's a beautiful campus."

"J.P. has put his degree on hold," Vince jumped in to say. "If you're going to be an A list player, you have to put in the time and the discipline earning your place on the team year round. You're moving up fast, J.P." He reached out an arm to pat his son's shoulder, but the younger man moved slightly beyond his father's reach while seeming only to focus on the glass in his hand. Vince's arm fell to his side before he raised it again, cocking his elbow to peer at the same fancy watch I had noticed in President Brennan's office. "We have to leave, I'm afraid. J.P. got in late yesterday and he's flying off first thing tomorrow. I hope to see you again, Ms. O'Rourke. You have my card and you'll get in touch if you have any questions?"

Vince walked quickly over to the woman with the diamond ring and kissed her on both cheeks while explaining J.P.'s tough schedule. J.P. squinted at his father, then turned to me. "So, it's a done deal, the money and the art?"

"Well, not quite yet. We're moving as quickly as we can, though, because both President Brennan and your father want to close right away. It's only paperwork and the college has assigned someone to help me gather and vet it. Should be soon." I smiled reassuringly, although I wasn't sure from his comments that this actually was going to please him.

As his father continued his rounds of the people under the canopy, shaking hands and kissing the women, J.P. said, "How well do you know him, my father, I mean?" He took off his sunglasses and I saw that his eyes were so dark they were almost absent of color, much like his father's. "You know how he made his money?" One corner of his mouth lifted in what could have been a smile.

"In general. Nothing specific," I said, wondering where this was going. "Are you an art lover too?" Was he pouting because he wanted the Warhol?

The young man held up his glass as if to toast me, then drained it. "Oh yes. You could say that. In fact, I can't live without it." And with that, he was off, striding across the turf to another tent across the field from which came a little scream as a guy in white slacks aimed a foaming bottle of bubbly at a girl in a large-brimmed hat.

TEN

*A*s planned, Peter hitched a ride back to San Francisco with a couple he knew while I headed farther south into Silicon Valley to meet with Suzy's cousin who was working, Valley style, on Sunday. Highway 280 threads its way south from Palo Alto's rural west side into what was once an agricultural paradise and is now, at its bottom end, almost completely paved over. The road itself is graceful and beautifully planned, with long curves that give drivers ample time to absorb the breathtaking landscapes shaped by the San Andreas Fault and the pastures studded with live oaks. Ghostly white fog banks frequently pour over the crests, and down the slopes of the soft hillsides. This heavenly view extends for almost forty miles, but ends rather abruptly when the road flattens and the new world order begins. Crisscrossed with multi-lane highways, low-roofed business complexes and mirror-finished shrines to some of technology's biggest icons, Silicon Valley is either a dream or a nightmare, I'm not sure which.

I was looking for an address midway between Santa Clara University's tile-roofed campus and San Jose International Airport, a red dot on my GPS in the middle of a grid of long blocks that all looked alike. Ethan Byrnstein had told me to look for a tan stucco building surrounded by palm trees, but I was beginning to think he had been joking after I swung in and out of three huge parking lots that looked like what he described. I checked my coordinates and called his cell number and learned I was only a couple of blocks away.

"I wish you hadn't said it was tan," I said, laughing as he let me in the glass door a few minutes later. "I think every building in a ten mile radius is tan. For next time, this one's cream."

He looked at me blankly. Men and decorating details? Not a close match.

"Suzy told me you're on the track of something mysterious," he said in a booming voice as we walked down a long corridor lined with empty, pale blue, chest-high cubicles. "I told her there's no place like Silicon Valley for intrigue and gossip, never mind some of the most calculating people you'll ever meet." He chortled.

I explained I was trying to finish what should have been a simple assignment for Lynthorpe. "My job is to assure them a gift contract they're ready to approve protects the college's interests. Because the donor is prominent and has a mixed reputation, I want to include a side note to the president and the board about his standing in the community, so they're ready for any criticism they might get."

"You mean, in case the money's tainted or even stolen?"

"Probably more subtle than that, but, yes, I want them to understand if questions might be raised. . . . Whoa, this is Dilbert territory," I said as we marched along. Most of the space was empty, but I heard voices coming from one area, and a young woman in cargo pants and a Stanford red tee shirt passed us at one point, saying hello to Ethan as she did.

Ethan did not live in a cubicle. He had a corner office, the sign of his stature as an active board member of the software company he had invested in. The venture capital firm he represented was one of the smaller ones along famous Sand Hill Road in Palo Alto, but its stature was growing, he explained, because a couple of their picks had performed exceptionally well recently.

"Suzy will be glad to hear it," I said, then bit my tongue. He might think she had been criticizing his prowess.

He only smiled and said, "As will my wife. But this is a high risk, high reward culture and you have to know that going in. Okay," Ethan said, as he waved me to a chair. "I can guess that the college won't turn down the money. People will overlook a lot when there's big money at stake. Who is it and how much is on the line?"

He whistled when I told him, and again when I told him about the art collection.

"Well, they're sure playing in the big boy pool, but I'm guessing you already suspect that. What can I tell you?"

I explained that I had access to plenty of information about Vince Margoletti, but that it had to be part of my job to get a picture of his capability of writing the big check to support the new art gallery construction in a timely manner. It also fell to me to privately advise the president if the donor was likely to become entangled in any unsavory legal or ethical issues.

"Any more, you mean?" Ethan said, rocking back in his chair. "You've read the publicity about the stock price scandal, I assume. He didn't come out of that one blameless."

"Yes, I skimmed it and will pass it along to Lynthorpe's chief, although I'm guessing he'd rather eat worms than read it and have to factor it into his decision."

"I ate worms once," Ethan said, looking at the ceiling thoughtfully. "In Africa. Fried in some kind of batter. Not half bad."

"Margoletti's role in negotiating the deal for the CEO and the board members was only described sketchily," I said, to bring Ethan back to the here and now, "but I saw the accusations by one entrepreneur that he was cheated out of his own original idea."

He nodded. As we talked, I silently thanked Suzy for the tip. Ethan knew quite a bit about Margoletti, in part because he and the other founding partners of the company in whose headquarters we sat had briefly used Margoletti during their incorporation work. "We changed lawyers pretty quickly," he said, frowning as he fingered a toy robot on his desk. "Margoletti had a habit of thinking he should make decisions for us. He was constantly reminding us that he was more successful than any of us. It was one Friday surprise after another for the few weeks before we pulled back."

I raised my eyebrows, not sure what he meant.

"One time he wanted his name added to a couple of our patent applications."

"Is that legal?"

He shrugged. "It's up to the person or company filing the patent whose names are on it. Anyway, the next call was to bring a new guy onto the team, an engineer of his choosing. Stuff like that."

"And the problems with the suggestions?"

"A new company stands or falls on its control of patents and licenses. If the founders of your company have patented a valuable piece of intellectual property, they stand a chance of controlling the market for their product at least for a while. Think about the drug industry and gene modification patents. You don't spread that unique competitive advantage around. Frankly, I was surprised Margoletti had been successful getting a handful of other founders to let him get that close in the past. My board and our founder said no and decided Margoletti wasn't the right attorney for us if he didn't understand that."

"How did he take it?"

"Like you'd imagine. Pissed off, told us we had little chance of succeeding without his help."

"Sounds like a threat."

"We took it as his assessment of our naiveté."

"So, what happened?"

"When our new attorney contacted him for the files, he danced around for a week. Lucky for us, our new lawyer was a junkyard dog and the matter got settled when he threatened to report Margoletti to the bar association."

"Did Margoletti do anything illegal?"

"No, but like you said, our new lawyer hinted that Margoletti had worked a couple of deals in the past that left some suckers in the lurch."

"Margoletti stole their ideas?"

"Privately, I wouldn't bet against it. Took them on as clients, then dumped them on some pretext and hooked up with a competing firm that claimed the idea and submitted patent applications pronto."

"If that's widely believed, how come he's still operating? What you're describing sounds illegal to me. I'd think his name would be poison by now."

"Good question. It's hinted at, not often spelled out in public for one thing, and while a few people have threatened to sue, not one conflict has actually gone to trial. Second, he's rich and powerful, and he can hurt you with a few well-chosen words in this town. People who don't like him stay away from him, but he can be seductive. There's always some newcomer who's so full of dreams of riches that he'll buy into Margoletti's siren song of how they'll create the next Apple together." He paused. "This is all background, right? I'm being pretty candid here."

"Completely. I'm trying to get a picture of the guy, wondering if the money he's giving his alma mater may taint the school later on."

"Look, he's already on the boards of a handful of charitable groups. If you look around, you'll find out he's giving money, doing guest teaching at Stanford and UC, stuff like that."

"So you're saying he's not about to do anything sketchy?"

"He's at the time of life when he wants to polish his reputation. He has all the money he needs. I'm guessing *Forbes* lists him as a billionaire next year. He's not evil, just not someone I'd trust with my revolutionary idea. If I had one," he chuckled. "After all, I'm a V.C. too and I have the same goal of making money from other people's genius. I hope I can do it without leaving a trail of unhappy people behind me."

"Okay, then let me throw one more question at you. And this is confidential on my end too. Any chance the stock he holds in private companies might not be worth all that much?"

"If his companies are in later stages of private funding—big partners weighing in with major investments on a product, not an idea—his stock will be valuable when it goes public. You know he can't unload it all right away? There's a waiting period to unload that type of pre-public stock, but unless it tanks right after going through its IPO, the initial public offering to all potential stock market investors, his stake should be okay."

We chatted for a few minutes about Suzy and her latest one-person exhibition in Oakland. I got up when a guy who looked like he belonged in high school, wearing shorts and a rumpled shirt, rapped on Ethan's door and poked his head in to say someone wanted him to come look at a PowerPoint report. He had the kid walk me back to the front door, which was a good thing since I'm not at all sure I would have found it on my own.

Halfway back to San Francisco, tired from the polo field sunshine and the champagne buzz, my cell phone rang. Ethan wanted to tell me something else. "I remembered something that's not so nice. A company Margoletti was involved with was in the news. The founder died suddenly. Not sure there's a connection, but...."

A chill ran through me. "You can't remember the man's name?" I said, wishing my memory for names hadn't gone on break.

"Not offhand. It was a car crash, I think. Not here, but in Boston. All I recall is some chatter at an entrepreneurs' mixer."

"Was Margoletti's name mentioned?"

"Only that he was the guy's attorney early on."

I thanked him but didn't tell him I'd already heard Vince Margoletti's name linked to a car crash. I wondered if there was some cause and effect, or if this was a coincidence. I didn't like coincidences much.

ELEVEN

*T*his consulting gig was turning out to be harder than I thought. With Devor work piling up and the pressure on to bless the Margoletti gift quickly, I felt pulled in different directions. It didn't help my mood when I heard a sharp tapping on my closed office door Monday morning. I hadn't even finished my cappuccino, I grumbled to myself as I yelled for whomever it was to come in.

"Got a minute?" It was Geoff.

I recalled with a twinge of guilt that I hadn't returned his phone call while I was at Lynthorpe, and apologized now. "I am so sorry the vice president at your alma mater died before we could meet. Did you know him well?"

"No, not really, but he met with the board regularly, and I always thought he was good. They were lucky to have him. A heart attack, Rory said in his email."

"Yes, a real shock. He'll obviously be missed. But I have access to his materials about the gift, so I think the due diligence will continue." He only nodded, seeming distracted.

"Are you okay, Geoff?"

"I know you were busy. I wanted to share something. Remember my mentioning the man I knew who was killed by a train?"

I nodded.

"Bart Corliss," Geoff said. "A decent man, developed some tracking software for medical records that became viable at the right moment in the market. Got ready to take his company public while investor money was still flowing. I didn't make the connection then, but I've since been reminded that he had a business tie to Vince."

My antennae jumped to attention. "Wait. You don't think Margoletti had something to do with this man's suicide? I know you said you don't trust Vince."

"Good Lord, no, nothing that dramatic. I don't like Vince's proximity to Corliss in light of his way of doing business."

"Sorry, I'm not tracking, Geoff. What proximity?"

"Vince was the company's attorney."

"Is Vince on the board?"

"No, but word is he was paid in shares at a very favorable option price before the public offering. Meaning," Geoff said when he saw the puzzled look on my face, "he'll be able to sell his shares for a whopping profit now that the company's listed on the stock exchange."

Geoff's face had taken on a little color as he told me the story, and he was rubbing the fingers of one hand with the other. For him, that's major emotion.

"But Corliss got rich too?"

"That's what's bothering me. The police have confirmed Bart committed suicide, and that doesn't make sense. He was at the top of his game."

"Family troubles, maybe?"

"Well, we'll never know, I guess. But I'm sensitive to anything Vince is attached to these days. How's the vetting going?"

Seeing Margoletti as somehow involved in the deaths of two company founders wasn't computing for me. Why would he? If it was true he had a ton of stock in Corliss's hot company, he could make good on his cash pledge to Lynthorpe and still have enough to keep his playboy son in riding boots and horse trailers. I was beginning to think that Larry Saylor was intimidated by the size of the gift and afraid to sign off for fear of overlooking some detail, and that Geoff was letting his dislike of the man color his thinking. I had to tread lightly.

"Well enough. I'm plowing through paper this week and hope to have a draft of the report done very soon for Rory Brennan."

Geoff was watching me, nodding, and then he said, "Have you run into any resistance from the administration?"

"You mean Rory, Coe, or the development director? Nothing serious. They all seem worried that something will slow the process down. Vince's demands for a quick resolution have made them nervous. Why? Have you heard something?"

"Well, the dean did send me an email. Nothing to worry about. I think they may not have realized the complexities involved in accepting a large art collection. It makes me doubly glad you're there. Don't let anyone push you to sign off on an agreement with holes in it."

I told him I would move as fast as possible and Geoff seemed satisfied. Looking at his watch, he said he had to get to Peter's conference room for an executive committee meeting and waved goodbye.

Peter and I had had a drink after work Monday. I wanted my boss's perspective before I flew back to Lynthorpe.

"It's tricky, I admit," he said over martinis in a trendy place that served astonishingly good sushi and every kind of martini yet invented. We were in a dark room with concrete walls, and floors livened with a forest of bamboo plants. "I might push you to present hard proof of illegal or deeply immoral activity if I were Brennan, something big likely to come out in the future. All you have now is the vice president's private concerns and the donor's reputation as a shark, balanced against major cash and an art collection I wish we'd had a crack at getting for the Devor. Any news about Teeni's job search?" he said, switching gears.

"She's excited about the college back East. Have you gotten a call for a recommendation?"

"I'm guessing it will come soon. She's a strong candidate for damn near any position at her level but, cynically, even if she wasn't a board's first choice, they would include her in the finalist pool because it would make them feel good to be able to say they had an African American candidate."

"I thought of that," I said, sipping the last of my green appletini and wondering if I should order a second, "and so has she. Teeni has a nose for this kind of thing and hasn't let the gamesters keep her in their candidate lists for show. She bows out as soon as she gets the hint."

"Maybe she'll sniff out tokenism in all of these offers and we can keep her," he said, "even though we don't have the right position for her."

"The museum world is getting more diverse. She'll land something good and we'll throw her the party to end all parties when she packs it in here."

Peter pushed me a bit about how much longer I'd be at the consulting assignment since we had a busy few months coming up at the Devor. Teeni's exhibition was the highlight of a season that included VIP tours of two local art preserves in Sonoma County, an artist-themed film festival, and an audience participation art installation that was already attracting cultural reporters wanting to do feature stories. We do all of these events because it builds support for the arts and attracts new donors, but it's always a stretch for our small staffs, and the boss was making it clear he wanted me back after next week. Brennan's assistant had called me earlier in the day to say the president hoped I'd return tomorrow or the next day to present the report so they could proceed with their announcement.

"Give me a couple more days and I'll be finished, promise. In the meantime, why don't you see if Dickie has a contact number for J.P.? We can invite him to something special and you can grill him about the owner of the Matisse."

Luckily for me, Lynthorpe had insisted on business class. I spent the five-hour flight going through every piece of paper related to the donation of art that the development director and Gabby had been able to give me. The list of paintings was straightforward, a number of lesser known artists whose work might or might not stand up to scrutiny in twenty years, some reliable standbys from the middle of the twentieth century, plus a few marquee names. Larry Saylor had the same list but I hadn't asked Gabby to copy it since I had skimmed McEvoy's packet earlier. Margoletti, or more likely his art consultants, must have bid hefty amounts at Sotheby's or Christie's auction sales to get a few of them. He had a real trophy, a moody painting of an empty street by Edward Hopper that had sold at auction only a year ago for thirty million dollars before it came into his collection.

Most of the paperwork was fine, although there were a few, like the Hopper and a Lichtenstein, for which the documents were incomplete or missing, at least from my stack of material. Maybe he wasn't giving them to Lynthorpe, and who could blame him? Most of the rest was routine, the provenances confirmed by the sales documents, and the pieces listed as being in storage, at his home or office, or in a few cases on loan for museum exhibitions. A few were also consigned for sale, and those needed to be cleared up as part or not part of the gift as of the date of the transfer. I would focus on making sure the full list was cleaned up before Lynthorpe signed the gift papers. Simple stuff really.

By the end of the flight, as I scooped up the piles of paper I had sorted through, I figured I had a handle on the art. If I could get a slightly better idea from Larry Saylor's notes about what had worried him, I would be close to a place where I could make recommendations and hand the project over to the college.

It was late Tuesday when I handed the rental car keys to the young guy at the hotel's concierge desk. From my room, I sent Gabby an email to ask if we could meet in the morning, and thought how nice it would have been to have someone back home who wanted to know I had arrived safely. Being unattached is a mixed experience.

Flipping through my notes the next morning after resisting waffles for breakfast in favor of cold cereal and feeling massively virtuous for it, I turned my attention to the rest of the papers I had accumulated. I came across the copy of Larry Saylor's handwritten list with the international phone number. I promised myself I'd look it up although I wasn't sure I'd try to reach whoever it was. What would I say? This number was written by a man who later drowned on a golf course in a peaceful New England town in America, and do you know anything about it?

The financial reports I had in front of me only confirmed what I and Larry Saylor and everyone else knew. Margoletti got shares in the companies listed in Gabby's research as payment for legal counsel on intellectual property rights and patent law. Logic dictated, however, that since he was still walking around, smiling and being a big shot, whatever games he played apparently weren't criminal, or at least not provably so.

I realized Geoff Johnson's mistrust had colored this project for me too. My brief contact with Larry Saylor had reinforced the feeling that something was fishy about Margoletti, but the reality was I hadn't found a single concrete reason to recommend Lynthorpe turn down, modify, or re-negotiate what looked to be a tremendous boost for the college. I decided to recommend approval with a second valuation of the art once the ownership documents were in place. I'd contact Margoletti's office to get the missing documents proving ownership of the handful of important paintings and wrap up the job.

I hadn't heard back from Gabby, so I decided to go for a walk to add to my healthy morning. A little voice inside my head cheered, if only because that might mean I could have French fries with lunch. It was the same helpful voice that urged me to try the ginger and lime martini the other night after the green appletini, but which was silent the next morning when I woke up with a headache.

I wandered along a pretty street with shops selling collegiate merchandise and handmade paper goods, which gave way in a few blocks to more ordinary stores with signs for sodas and sandwiches, and then to a block of boxy buildings with signs for hardware and auto parts. Off to my right, down an abruptly residential side street, were some older apartment buildings, their brick façades shielded by tall, leafy trees whose roots were pushing up blocks of concrete sidewalk. A couple of moms were out with strollers and several young men with backpacks and cell phones walked quickly in my direction, passing me without seeming to notice I existed. From the conversation I overheard one guy having on his phone, I got the idea he was a university student, and realized this was probably where the graduate students lived who didn't or couldn't stay on campus.

As if to prove me right, I saw someone with a dark ponytail come out of one building. It was Gabby and I raised my arm to catch her attention, then dropped it when I saw Dermott coming out right behind her. She was frowning and talking over her shoulder, and he didn't look any happier. At the bottom of the entry steps she turned and faced him, still talking and shaking her head, her ponytail whipping back and forth from the effort. He threw up his hands in a jerky movement, stepped around her, and marched down the street away from the corner where I stood, anger making his body stiff.

She stood still for a moment, her head turned to watch him go, then lifted one hand and appeared to swipe at her eyes. Suddenly she turned in the opposite direction, almost as if she realized I was watching. Before I could shrink back around the corner, she had seen me. She lifted her head and waved. There wasn't anything to do except wave back and wait for her to reach me.

"I was wondering when I'd see you again," she said, but her voice was tight and she looked away after a quick glance at me. To determine if I had seen her arguing with Dermott? I wasn't going to bring it up if she didn't, so we exchanged information about our schedules. I would work in my hotel room on the draft report and would meet her when she was free to go over the gaps in my review of artworks included in the gift, and to talk one last time about what might have been worrying Saylor. I figured there might be a stray remark or notes somewhere that we hadn't found, so we agreed to meet in his office.

"My goal is to get a draft done by tomorrow morning, bring it to President Brennan, and revise it if he has questions or wants more detail."

"You haven't found any serious problems?" Gabby said, sounding more like herself as the minutes passed. "That doesn't make sense to me. He was so convinced...of something." She shrugged and shook her head.

"I promise I'll be super cautious, but, no, I've done a bit of background checking and I've seen the public reports of what you might call ethical challenges, but nothing illegal, or at least nothing labeled outright as such. Margoletti may not be the person you'd like to go into business with, especially with your money or your bright idea, but there are lots of people I'd feel the same way about, and I'm pretty sure some of them are admired and envied for their success."

Gabby wasn't satisfied, I could tell. "Some people have all the luck, don't they? The rest of us go paycheck to paycheck . . ."

"Working in the development office, you're going to see that a lot, the discrepancy in wealth. If it really bothers you, you may want to rethink the next career move you make." I tried to keep my tone light, but it was a truth that we working folk had to face up to at some point. Trying to look and sound sympathetic at a cocktail party while the women in a group compare notes about their vacations in Bali, or the men grumble about getting good tee times at Pebble Beach takes some mental flexibility. I once tried to bond with them by beginning a story about Fever's habit of spitting up hairballs on the carpet right after I had it shampooed, but it didn't seem to click.

"Oh, I don't mind so much. Dermott, well, it's all those student loans and so little chance for a tenure track job anywhere these days."

Money might have been the reason the newlyweds had been arguing on their doorstep, and my heart went out to her. Marrying a millionaire had not been a deliberate strategy, but at the time it had cushioned me from the kind of life so many new college graduates faced. I couldn't think of anything to say.

Maybe she thought my silence was a criticism of her. She shifted into professional mode and said, "I'll spend an hour in Larry's office before lunch, to organize what seems to be most important for you to look at. After that, I have some other work to do for Mr. McEvoy. Pretty soon I have to take all the papers over to the dean's office. I'm cheating, though. Don't tell him," she said, lifting her eyebrows. "I'm making copies so that Mr. Saylor's files are still useful for you."

I laughed. Whoever said computers would end the need for paper files hadn't given enough credit to the bureaucratic beast. "Fine. How about we meet in Larry's office at five?"

By five o'clock, my stomach was rumbling, which reminded me I'd had nothing for lunch except a smoothie. That might have accounted for the fact that I was a little light-headed as I parked the rental car in the lot behind the old red brick building where the late financial vice president and his staff had their offices. A dozen parked cars attested to the fact that people were still at work. One, at least, was highly paid, judging by the glossy finish on a black sports car that almost blinded me as the reflection of the sun bounced off the hood. A couple of middle-aged women in summer dresses and sandals were coming out of the building's back door, deep in conversation, and one smiled and held the door open for me with her free hand. In the other, she held a colorful paper plate with a napkin spread over it.

"Birthday cake," she said when I looked at it. "My husband loves it when I bring him home some cake."

I laughed and told her I knew what she meant.

The building was quiet except for some chattering that came from way down the hall, the site of the office party, I could guess. It got so quiet I could hear a fly buzzing against the window on the landing as I mounted the staircase. It was warm from the trapped heat of the day, and the printer in the small room on the second floor where Gabby had made copies for me the other day was making rhythmic sounds as it spurted out paper.

I poked my head in the late vice president's outer office, but it was empty. I called Gabby's name but didn't hear anyone in his office. To the right, the bigger workspace seemed unoccupied as well, but I could hear someone moving around even though I couldn't see anything. I crossed back through the reception area and into Saylor's office. The place looked like work was in progress. Open files sat on the worktable and the top of the file cabinets, and one of the desk drawers was open.

"Hi," a voice behind me said as I surveyed the room. Gabby made a face as she took in the mess. She tossed her bike messenger bag on a chair and closed the desk drawer as she passed. Looking at the file tabs as she flipped the open folders closed and stacked them up on the corner of his desk, she said, "I left the place neat when I finished, honest."

"Did you lock up when you left?"

"His assistant said she'd lock up during the lunch hour. This looks like student workers midway through a project, maybe organizing his files to distribute to the people who'll be handling parts of his job until they hire a new vice president. Don't worry, I can round up what you need."

We took seats at the big table near the window, where Gabby began to sort paper-clipped pages into short stacks. She stopped at one point, frowning at a piece of paper that was buried in one pile. "A note from Mr. Saylor asking me to find out what I can about a new IPO." She fiddled with her ponytail. "One of the companies Mr. Margoletti's involved with. I guess they went public recently."

"Did he send it to you?"

"This is the first I've seen it. I'm sure he meant to pass it along the next time we met. It's so weird. I can't get used to the idea he's dead, you know?"

"Did you go to the funeral? That sometimes gives a sense of closure."

"Yes, but it was sad. His staff came, and some of the faculty, but the president wasn't there. The church was half empty." Gabby shook herself, glanced at her watch, and said, "I only have an hour before Dermott comes to get me. We have to meet with his student loan advisor." She made a face, and sighed.

Shrugging off whatever was bothering her, she pulled over a file folder, and proceeded to walk me through the highlights of her research. Then, she held up something I hadn't seen, a copy of a page from a Christie's auction catalog with a color photo of a Sam Francis painting, estimated to sell between one and one and a half million. "We haven't talked much about the individual pieces of art," she said, "and this is one thing Larry was worried about."

"This piece? I didn't see much about the art in his files," I said. "There was a list in the development office material, though."

"Larry's notes are around here somewhere. This page should have been in the folder with everything else, but I had pulled it to start verifying that the donor still owns it. It's on the accountant's list but not on the gift list. He got a phone call and after that, he started looking at them more closely. He told me the lists weren't quite the same and asked me to check a few pieces, to see what might have happened."

"There are two lists? I saw one in the files I borrowed from Larry's office, but I figured it was a copy of the same one, the one that Margoletti's lawyers made."

"I did too until Larry explained that he received a second one, this one created by Mr. Margoletti's accountant."

"Do you have that list?"

She worked her way through some of the files that had been left on the table and on Saylor's desk, but couldn't find it. "Wait, I made myself a copy. I spent so much time here that I kept a work file handy in his cabinet. See?" She had stooped over a low lateral file and now pulled out a folder. "I labeled it with my name, under G." And rifling through it, she came up with a stapled set of pages and handed it to me.

"Let me understand," I said. "You were working off two different lists?"

"No, I was working with the lawyer's list, the one that had on it all the artwork Mr. Margoletti was including in the donation. Larry had the list Mr. Margoletti's accountant sent him to track where every piece of art was. Most of it was in storage in California."

"Do you remember the names on the two lists that didn't match?"

"Not offhand. Larry had highlighted the differences, but I don't see his copy here."

Rats, I had missed something. I hadn't flipped through all the pages on the other list because the entries on the first page were all the same and I had assumed it was a copy of the same list. Damn.

Gabby saw my frown. "It's easy enough to compare them once you have both lists. There are only a few differences."

"Does the documentation explain the discrepancies? Maybe these were pieces he intended to hold on to?"

"They're not marked that way, so I don't know. For some reason, Larry thought there was a problem. I'm sure that's why he needed to see the president. I picked that much up from his comments."

She had been flipping through the piles of papers left out by the student workers. "Aha," she said, raising her voice in triumph. "Here's something." She slid a sheet of paper over to me. It was another page from an auction sale catalog, advertising the upcoming sale at auction of a painting by Roy Lichtenstein, in the style he became most famous for. A stippled cartoon drawing of the close-up faces of an unhappy man and woman, accompanied by a dramatic text in a bubble. I looked my question at Gabby.

"I remember Mr. Saylor being especially interested in this. I had no idea a comic book picture could be so valuable. Read the provenance."

Sold by the painter to such-and-such gallery for a few thousand dollars. The gallery sold it to a reputable dealer a few years later for many thousands of dollars. The dealer sold it to a collector and the collector turned it around at auction ten years later for a million dollars. Each time the piece sold, the price went up exponentially until, at the sale last year being advertised in the catalog, a handwritten note in Gabby's writing reported, a new buyer paid twenty-one million.

"Art can be a great investment, but this isn't unusual. This piece is one of a series that pretty much defined his style. There's nothing here saying Vince bought it, however."

"It's not on the lawyers' list, but it was one of the ones on the accountant's list that I remember. All I know is we were working in here when the accountant from Mr. Margoletti's office called him. I only heard Larry's side, but he said something about how someone could have given Mr. Margoletti such a big gift, that you don't pay a lawyer twenty million dollars, no matter how good he is."

"Someone gave the Lichtenstein to him?"

"Apparently, although I'm only guessing that because of what I heard," Gabby said.

"It might mean that Vince Margoletti didn't mean to give it to Lynthorpe," I said, thinking out loud. "Either that, or the gift list was outdated, although, frankly, this is not the kind of painting one would overlook." I was thinking of the handful of pieces I had incomplete documentation for.

"If I can find his copy of the list, where he might have made notes, I'll get it for you to save time. In the meantime, you can keep this because I have another copy in my folder. I'll copy the Francis sell sheet for you. I'm guessing a lot of the art research has already been packaged up and sent to Mr. McEvoy's office, or to Dean Anderson."

Gabby had continued to flip through the papers in her "G" folder, and now she said, "Oh, good, here's another one I was asked to check on." She pulled out a copy of another auction house catalog page that was promoting a small oil painting of leaves in autumn colors by Georgia O'Keeffe.

Again, ticked off on an auction catalog page were tracings of the painting's past to show it was not stolen goods or a fake. The piece was valued between one and two million dollars and was painted relatively early in O'Keeffe's career, but the style was immediately recognizable. For this latest sale ad, the seller's name wasn't listed on the printed page, but that's not unusual. Not too many people choose to advertise the fact that they may have expensive art hanging in their living rooms. Security systems are good, but art thieves are sometimes better. High stakes auction purchases are frequently made through dealers, middlemen who act for the real buyer and are well paid to preserve their privacy. "The O'Keeffe belongs to Margoletti too?"

"I'm sure this is one of the ones that was on one list and not the other. That's why he would have asked me to do the research and get the sales information."

I searched and found the O'Keeffe on Gabby's copy of the accountant's list. "Interesting. It doesn't say how much he paid for it. It says 'acquired.'" I looked up at the young researcher. "If he didn't buy it, he has some remarkably generous friends or possibly a tax dodge going on, although if that were the case, surely he wouldn't have approved his accountant giving you the information."

There were oddities in what Gabby had told me, and I needed time to sort them out. I also needed to check the two lists against each other, maybe with Gabby's help, first thing tomorrow. I laid the catalog pages out on the table in front of me. Lichtenstein, Francis, O'Keeffe. All offered through reputable auction houses. Could they be fakes? "You said there were others?" I said.

"At least one more. I wish I could think of the artist's name. There was no auction sheet for it. Mr. Saylor just mentioned it and said he'd look into that one himself. All I remember is the style wasn't as modern, it was a realistic painting, if you know what I mean."

"Can you make me copies of these auction sheets?"

"Sure. By the way, there was another one that looked like it fit the same pattern, but Mr. Margoletti sold it two months ago."

"He confirmed that he'd sold it?"

"His accountant checked with him, no problem. We noted the update and put it in the back of the file to make sure the paper trail was complete. See? Here it is."

A small painting by Jim Dine, no doubt with a signature heart in it, although there was no photo of the piece included in the documentation Gabby had, only the handwritten annotation "Sold, per V.M." dated three weeks ago.

I nodded. "Good work. Without a note like that, some future curator could spend a long time looking for a painting that didn't exist in the collection."

"I'll go down the hall and make you copies of everything," Gabby said. "Won't be a minute." She smiled. "I'm relieved that you're going to help. I wouldn't feel right knowing how upset Mr. Saylor was, if I didn't make sure someone but us knew about this, someone who'd be able to make more sense of it than I can."

"No promises," I said. "I'm not a detective, and the college hasn't asked me to do more than help ensure that the valuations are correct, but I guess this fits under that heading, doesn't it?"

She grinned at me, her dimples blazing. "I guess it does. Be right back."

I thought again about the pages Gabby had shown me. Taken together, did they hold the answer to Larry Saylor's uneasiness? Maybe if I called the auction house, I could learn something, although they were notoriously close-mouthed. Might be wiser to call the accountant, whose contact information was probably on the list Gabby was copying for me. If it wasn't, I'd ask her for it before leaving tonight.

It was late and the building was quiet. I heard Gabby talking to someone, probably that cute husband of hers, their voices inaudible but raised over the sound of the office machine. I glanced at my watch. It was almost six and time for him to pick her up. I gathered up my notes and my briefcase. Outside, a car backfired somewhere. The copier was still churning, but she must be about done. I got up and walked to the office door, looking toward the stairs. Nothing but the copier's thrum. I figured I'd collect the papers on my way out, so I went back in, picked up my bag and headed down the hall toward the noise, which came from the small, open room right next to the stairs that I'd seen before.

The machine was cranking away, but the top was open. No sign of the young researcher or her husband.

"Gabby?" I said, raising my voice. Maybe she had gone to the ladies' room across the way. I pushed the door open, but no one answered. There was a room next to it with a frosted glass door and what looked like a chart of office hours on an index card taped to the glass. The door was partly open. The other doors along the hallway were closed. I walked over to the open door and pushed it, hoping I wasn't trespassing or interrupting a late-day student conference. "Hello?" I called, peering ahead at a wall of books stuffed to bursting. I took another step and my foot brushed against something at the same instant the door stopped in its swing. Looking down, I saw a hand resting on the floor.

"Gabby," I breathed, dropping to my knees beside the still figure crumpled near the door. Out in the hall, the copier stopped suddenly and the silence was shocking. In the sudden quiet, I heard a door close and the hum of an elevator somewhere. "Help," I yelled to whoever might be around.

"Gabby, can you hear me," I said, leaning down and reaching to touch her fingers. She lay on her back, turned slightly to one side, her ponytail splayed out behind her head. Her eyes were shut and there was no movement, no sound from her. One side of her chest was blooming red blood, which had already dribbled to the scuffed wood floor underneath her.

At that moment, a door slammed somewhere, and footsteps came up the stairs rapidly. I looked back to the hallway over my shoulder, ready to yell for help again.

"Hey, Ms. O'Rourke," Dermott Kennedy said, his mouth in a crooked grin, coming to a halt behind me. The smile evaporated and a crease appeared between his eyes. "Are you okay? Wait a minute—is that Gabby?"

He dropped down, pushing me roughly out of the way, and grabbed the unmoving hand I was hesitantly touching, the one whose third finger wore a narrow, still shiny, wedding band.

TWELVE

*T*he next hour was a blur. I remember Dermott on his knees, crooning Gabby's name. I was already dialing 911 when he hollered at me to call for help.

"She's been shot, I'm sure of it," I told the woman who answered the call. "No, no, there's no one else here. The two of us, me and her husband. No, of course neither of us has a gun. Hurry, she's bleeding a lot."

"Baby, baby, it's okay. I'm here," Dermott kept saying, even though it was obvious she was unconscious. It felt like forever, but was only a minute or two before I heard the amplified chatter of two-way radios at the same time I heard someone banging on the door to the building.

"I'll go," I said, and ran down the stairs, hanging onto the banister so I wouldn't fall headlong in my rush. I was shaking so much that moving fast was dangerous. The guy I'd seen on campus earlier, Macho Cop, was peering in the window, a gun in his hand. His partner was kicking at the door. The door opened from the inside when I yanked it and I pointed them up the stairs. "Outside," the macho one shouted at me, giving me a push to emphasize his instructions. "Get outside now." He slammed the door open so far it latched into a piece of hardware on the wall. The other uniformed policeman had already disappeared up the staircase. I stumbled out the door and leaned against a railing, my heart pounding and my stomach churning.

The police car, sitting at an odd angle to the sidewalk with its flashers on, was beginning to attract attention even before two more cop cars zoomed up. Two of the cops ran past me while two more fanned out along the building's front. After a quick, barked conversation on his two-way radio, the male cop turned door duty over to a female in uniform and headed up the stairs at a trot. I heard a siren coming from the back of the building, so I guessed they were trying to cover the parking lot in case whoever shot her was still inside. I didn't have time to be alarmed by the thought because Dermott was yelling as he was being almost dragged down the stairs.

He was begging the officer who held his arm to let him stay with her, pleading for them to stop the bleeding, and it broke my heart. A fire department ambulance pulled up and almost immediately a couple of guys in regulation gear and lugging large cases trotted up the sidewalk. The woman guarding the door spoke into her radio, then said, "Okay, all clear," and waved the firemen into the building.

From then on, there was a steady stream of responders. A fire truck and its crew, an ambulance and two EMTs, a couple of people in street clothes but with IDs that got them right through, a pot-bellied Lynthorpe College security guard, and a few faculty and students drawn by the commotion hung around. Dermott, banished to the lawn like me, peppered me with questions. What did I see? Did she say anything to me? What did I hear? It wasn't doing him much good since I hadn't heard or seen anything useful. At other moments, he would insist that he be allowed to go back upstairs to be with his wife, but the cop on door duty wasn't buying. Lynthorpe's uniformed cop kept trying to get in too, blustering about his responsibilities.

"Look," I heard the cop to him say at one point, "you're an old hand. You know better. It's a frigging crime scene. No one goes up except the investigators and the EMTs." The EMTs came into view through the glass, moving carefully toward the front door with their burden, a bright yellow gurney onto which Gabby was strapped and partially covered with a blanket. A mask covered her nose and mouth, and a fireman was close to her, holding up a clear plastic bag of fluids. They hadn't come down the stairs, because those were partially visible from where I stood, so they must have found the elevator I had heard.

Dermott leapt to the doorway as the EMTs reached it and bent over the free side of the gurney, saying her name over and over as the small band made its way to the ambulance. It drove off without him and he turned and saw me standing nearby on the grass, trying not to cry. I grabbed his hand to say something but he spoke first, panic in his eyes. "They won't tell me how she is or what happened."

It was heartbreaking to hear his pain and fear, and I couldn't think of anything to say that would ease it.

THIRTEEN

*P*olice stations are all the same, maybe not on the outside or at the front desk, but one anonymously furnished, enclosed room is a lot like the next when you're shocked, tired, and scared. I had to wait to give my statement. There isn't much violent crime in a small town, I guess, and Gabby's shooting had stirred everyone into action. A dozen uniformed cops and men in sports jackets and ties were clumped around the space in which I had been deposited, talking in groups, occasionally calling out to someone in another cluster, barking into desk and cell phones.

I had no trouble figuring out who the chief of police was because he was in uniform, a crisply pressed navy blue suit with shiny buttons and a cap to match, and was clearly the center of the drama in the room.

Finally a nice looking man came over to me and introduced himself as the detective who would be heading the investigation. I wondered if he was the only one in Bridgetown, which had less than ten thousand people if you didn't count Lynthorpe's student body. He started by asking me to let a clerk take my fingerprints, and perform some other test that consisted of rubbing paper pads on my hands and clothes, all of which was fine with me. Then, we went to the small room, where he offered me a bottle of water, and asked me what I knew. He was polite as I went back over the events from when I met the researcher in Larry Saylor's office at five o'clock until I found her on the floor at six. I didn't want to forget any small detail that might help find her attacker and his quiet questioning calmed me down. At one point I explained that I had a friend in San Francisco who was a homicide inspector, and that he would vouch for me if the police here would like to check. He wrote Charlie's name and phone number down and handed it off to an associate before continuing.

At some point, he told me what I already knew in my bones. Gabby had died shortly after getting to the hospital and no amount of heroics could revive her. Dermott was with her by then, having been driven over in a police car, and was completely undone. The detective, George Kirby, explained that because the town's police force was small the chief had called in the county's forensics team, which was still scouring the scene.

The same woman officer I'd seen at Lynthorpe came in and handed Kirby a note. He read it, nodded and told me I could go back to my hotel. Not home to San Francisco, though. When he had more information, he said, he'd want to talk with me again. Five minutes after I had retrieved my car, handed the keys to the valet parker, and splashed my face with cold water, my cell phone rang.

"Dani, are you okay?"

"No, Charlie," I said and started to cry. "This is a nightmare. The girl, young woman really, I was working with on campus, was shot and killed. She was so full of life. She had only been married six months. Her husband's a wreck. Charlie, she was murdered." I had to stop to catch my breath.

"Easy, Dani. Tell me what you know." I did, although it was pretty garbled. When I ran out of words, he said, "You don't sound so good yourself and you need to keep it together. Have they tested you for powder burns?"

"Huh?" I said. "Why would they...you can't mean they think I shot Gabby?" But I told him about having my hands and clothes rubbed with some kind of paper and he said that was the test for gunshot residue.

"Just a precaution, and they didn't hold you, but from what I heard, they're a little disorganized. The cop I talked to said they haven't had a murder in town for fifteen years, since the current chief took office."

"I told them everything I knew. Oh," I said, pausing.

"You didn't withhold something, did you?" I heard a warning in his voice.

"No, I promise, nothing about what I heard and saw today. It occurred to me while we've been talking that they didn't ask for any details about the project Gabby and I were working on. The project is the same one that the Lynthorpe College executive who died last week was working on. You don't think . . . ?"

"I don't think. I don't have a clue, but if I'd drawn this case, I'd be checking it out and soon. Listen, Dani, I'm a little worried. If the local cops don't catch a break soon, they're going to come back at you. I would."

"You would?" I said, my voice sounding forlorn to my ears.

"Well, not really, since I know you're only the world's unluckiest person when it comes to finding bodies. But if I didn't know you, sure. You were there, for God's sake."

"You've succeeded in scaring me half to death. Thanks for that." I wasn't crying any more. I was getting mad. It's not fair. I had been minding my own business, or at least my client's business, which was the same thing, sort of. So was Gabby, the voice in my head reminded me.

My hotel phone began to ring. "Charlie, can I call you back? There's a call coming in here."

He agreed as long as I promised to get back to him right away. "Don't talk to the cops again until you and I finish our conversation. Promise," he said sternly. I promised.

The new call was from Lynthorpe's president, Rory Brennan, his tone of voice even richer on the phone than in person. "Danielle, I was shocked to hear that Gabriela Flores has passed away."

"She was shot."

"Chief Cummings told me. He called me fifteen minutes ago. Frankly," Brennan said, "he was asking about you."

"Me?"

"He wanted to verify your story. That you were on an assignment with Gabby."

"I told the police that, at least three times. He didn't believe me?"

"Oh, I'm sure he did. You know how these things are, though. He needed to check. I know you're exhausted and upset, but I would like to impose on you a little further. I'd like to hear what happened directly from you. I'm wondering if you could meet me for no more than a half hour?"

"Tonight?" I said, wanting to say no, wanting to call Charlie back and then bury myself under the hotel bed's handsome covers and sleep for a week. What's that line from Hamlet? *To sleep, perchance to dream. . . .* I had a feeling I'd have nightmares. "I'm not sure I'm supposed to discuss what happened with anyone."

"I wouldn't dream of asking you to do something untoward," he said. A small corner of my fried brain registered his formal vocabulary, doubtless honed during many Parents Weekends.

"It's awfully late," I said, wondering if the president really understood that a member of his staff had died tonight. "Can we do this tomorrow? I have a monster headache and, truthfully, I'm shaky and a little queasy. Even a half hour is more than I'm up to."

I could hear in his voice that he wasn't happy. Maybe he was used to having everyone around him jump when he called. My body refused. In fact, it wouldn't even stay vertical for tooth brushing after I got off the phone with Brennan. I flipped off my shoes, pulled back the duvet cover, and flopped on the bed before I remembered I promised to call Charlie back. He sounded brisk when he picked up the phone in his office at the North Beach police station that seems at times like his second home.

"I'll call the local cops, Dani. I want to get a line on what's happening."

"Will they tell you anything?"

"Maybe not, but you never know. Your instincts are good. I want to find out about that guy that drowned playing golf. Two sudden deaths in the same little town, the two people who were working on the same project you told me about, it rings bells for me. If they are connected, and you're the third person on the project, well, I want to make sure you're protected 'til this is solved."

My stomach flipped, and I groaned. "Charlie, how could you do this to me? Are you trying to frighten me?"

"Don't mean to upset you, but I think you understand, even if you don't want it to be true, and it's best to be aware, right? Has anyone told you the cops are sure that guy, what's his name—"

"—the executive here, Larry Saylor?"

"Yeah, Saylor, did you ever hear back about his death? Did he have a heart attack or something, or is that investigation ongoing?"

I tried to remember what I'd heard. Not much. "His office was unsealed when I went there today with Gabby, if that means anything. I heard a golf course employee was the one who found Saylor."

He was silent for a minute. "Keep your cell phone on and remember what I said. Don't talk to anyone right now. I'll call you back when I have more information if you're not back here by then. Have you asked when you can leave town?"

"I'd like to come home tomorrow but the lead investigator doesn't want me to leave."

"See if Detective Kirby will let you go in another forty-eight hours. That would be a good sign."

"The way you talk makes me wonder if I need a lawyer."

"Wouldn't be the worst idea, Dani. Some cops tread more lightly if they know the person they're interviewing has legal backing. Know anyone there?"

Not likely since this was almost my first visit, and definitely my last if I had my way.

Charlie hung up before my brain reminded me I had agreed to meet Lynthorpe's president tomorrow. Was Charlie's warning so broad I couldn't talk with Brennan? My green-eyed protector had left me with a handful of unpleasant scenarios to consider, and I had a hunch sleeping was going to be hard tonight.

I woke up with the dull, disoriented feeling that comes from a sleep disturbed by bad dreams. I vaguely recollected something about being locked in a closet, or was it a car? Someone telling me I had to swim in a black pool where a shark lay in wait. A feeling of dread and a mouth full of spider webs. Ugh.

Three cups of coffee banished the nightmares but did nothing for my shaky legs. The reality of Gabby's death washed over me as I nibbled at a room service breakfast and all I wanted was to leave town as fast as possible. But I had to tackle the Margoletti gift recommendation first.

When the hotel phone rang, I hesitated before picking it up. "Ms. O'Rourke? We spoke last night." It was Detective Kirby. "We're still trying to reconstruct the circumstances around Ms. Flores' death. I'd like to meet with you again." I agreed, but asked how long it would take. I explained that I was hoping to leave Bridgetown in a day or two.

"Oh, I wouldn't plan on leaving yet," he said amiably. "Give us at least another day, please, before you make plans so we can make sure we've asked every question the investigation may turn up."

Said that way, it didn't feel threatening. I explained I had a job to get back to. He made understanding noises, but didn't change his request. After we got off the line, I pulled out my laptop and emailed Teeni and Peter, merely saying I had to stay a bit longer and suggesting they send along anything I needed to see right away. I didn't want to talk about Gabby, much less deal with Teeni's questions and concerns right now.

She immediately emailed back: "Will do. Your ex called yesterday to see where you were. BTW, that guy Burgess called from the law firm. Want me to try again with him?" We get calls like that fairly often. I felt bad for letting it go if some kind soul wanted to include us in his or her will, but I didn't have the energy or the focus to deal with it today.

Needing fresh air to clear my head and a change from my pastry and coffee routine, which had served only to jangle my nerves more, I decided to walk to the campus. I ended up at the student café where I ordered yogurt and fresh fruit in a gesture of apology to my stressed-out body, and spent a half hour on the patio breathing in the smell of cut grass and the elusive floral scent I now equated with Lynthorpe.

It was time to get on the phone and confirm a seat on a plane out of this place Friday, with or without Detective Kirby's permission. I was craving my own apartment with my cat on my lap and absolutely no drama, unless it was of the Fever variety.

Brennan and I hadn't set a time to meet so I headed over to the president's office, feeling a bit more like my normal self, under-exercised and overfed. His assistant pursed her lips and shook her head as her finger skimmed along the edge of his calendar.

"There's nothing, not even fifteen minutes," she said as the male student I'd seen before stood hunched over a corner of her desk answering a constantly ringing phone, murmuring discreetly to the callers and adding pink message slips to a growing pile. "I can't imagine when he thought he'd have time to talk to you. This place is a zoo. Press calls and alumni and parents, and we still have to schedule a campus assembly of some kind for everyone."

The great man was in his office, so she was able to check. He sent out word he'd appreciate it if I could meet him for a quick drink at the end of the day. He'd pick me up at the hotel if that was all right. I agreed. I'd have the day to work on the report, meet with the detective if he called, and do a little research on the paintings that had puzzled Larry Saylor. There were several other candidates for Saylor's concern, including Margoletti's financial health and his business practices, and my report had to refer to them all as diplomatically as possible. I had no idea which had turned out to be motivation for someone to kill Gabby and perhaps Saylor himself, but I was convinced with every passing hour their deaths were connected somehow to the Margoletti gift.

I was looking at the ground as I exited the building and didn't see the policeman until I had almost banged into him. It was Macho Cop, still playing hide and seek behind his Ray-Bans and sporting the short sleeve uniform shirt that showed off his toned biceps nicely. For the record, he had washboard abs too, if the snug-fitting uniform shirt was any indication.

On impulse, I stopped in the open doorway. "You were on the scene last night, weren't you? Is there any news?"

It's hard to talk to someone whose eyes are hidden. He frowned at me. "Luckily, my partner and I were close by on patrol." He drew himself up and hitched his gadget-heavy belt up with one hand. Did he think I had decided he was a stud and that I was striking up a conversation to catch his attention? The first part was true. He was hot. *You already have a cop boyfriend, remember?* my inner voice said.

"I was there when Gabby died," I said, standing my ground while assuring my inner self it was information, not a date, I was after. "I'm consulting with the college."

I saw why he wore the dark glasses. It forced me to look hard at him to try and figure out what he was thinking. I had the uncomfortable feeling that he was filing my face away in case another person wound up dead at Lynthorpe College. *You're projecting,* my inner voice said. *You feel guilty that you didn't rush down the hall and save that girl.* Probably true.

"Dani O'Rourke," I persevered, holding out my hand, and almost forcing him to respond.

"Officer McManus," he said, pulling out a fat wallet and handing me a card, "Clayton McManus." Someone came up to the door, so we moved aside slightly and he took my elbow almost protectively. When I looked up at him, he gave me a cute, crooked smile. "Welcome to Bridgetown, ma'am." *Isn't ma'am what they call older women?* I'm not interested in this guy, I pointed out to myself. He can call me Grandma Moses for all I care. *That's not totally true.*

Macho Cop was still smiling, although he had let go of my elbow, and now he plucked a toothpick out of his shirt pocket and stuck it in the corner of his mouth as he talked. It sounded like he didn't know much more than I did. What had I heard? Who had I seen when I arrived? He was eager, maybe trying to bring some fresh nugget of information to his boss. I had a hunch his looks didn't do as much for him in the police station as they did in the bar on Friday nights. In a small town, the high point in his workweek might be directing football game day traffic.

I didn't say much, but when he wound down, I got in a question of my own. "The gun?" I said. "Have you all found it?"

He may not have been the brightest bulb, but he hadn't flunked out of the police academy either. He didn't answer me, just nodded, pointed at the business card I still held, and invited me to contact him if he could be of any help while I was visiting his town. The harried student from the president's office came down the stairs and hustled through the door. I turned to follow him, with McManus close behind me.

"Hasta la vista, Ms. O'Rourke," he said, poking another toothpick in the corner of his mouth as he walked across the lawn to the patrol car, where no partner sat this time. Really? Had he cast himself as Arnold the Terminator? I shook my head. Nice bod, but really, we were so not on the same planet.

FOURTEEN

I walked back to the main street and shook off my mood for a few minutes by poking around in several gift shops, the kind you find in college towns. When I stumbled on a little arts and crafts gallery on a side street, I got lucky. A pair of hand-painted black and white paper earrings in jagged shapes that dangled three inches was perfect for Yvette. In fact, they were so like Teeni that I got her a pair too. Feeling that the day hadn't been completely wasted, I went back to the hotel and online to look up news about auction sales of works by the painters in Margoletti's collection. I ordered a hamburger, fries, and a glass of red wine from the room service menu and started in on the portion of the report that dealt with making a financial pledge binding on the donor and his estate.

But my stomach was taking orders from the part of my brain that insisted on replaying the scene in the office near the copier machine no matter how much I tried to distract it. Finally, I gave up and, after getting Charlie's message machine, flopped on the bed and closed my eyes. Of course, that was the moment Brennan called to say he was on his way, and would I meet him outside the hotel?

Rory Brennan was waiting, the passenger window of a surprisingly sporty, black car rolled down. He called my name and lifted a hand from the steering wheel, but didn't get out of the car. Executive discretion?

"There's a lovely restaurant and bar a couple miles out of town, quiet at this time of night, and a little too expensive for most of the faculty and all of the students, I believe." He chuckled as he put the car in gear and took off. He drove aggressively, an outlet for a man who had to make nice to scores of people every day.

Neither of us said anything for a few minutes. The town receded behind us and we were in the verdant countryside, skimming along under a roof of trees in full leaf, with occasional wooden fences popping up to mark the edges of private land. He turned onto a smaller road and in the twilight I saw the sign for the inn he must have meant. In another moment, the lights of a stately old colonial mansion shone at us and we were in a graveled parking lot.

Brennan was right. There were only six or seven other people in the bar area of the restaurant and the atmosphere was quietly elegant, with reproductions of horse and dog paintings adorning dark mauve walls, lit by brass sconce lamps. The waitress didn't blink when I ordered chamomile tea, although Brennan fussed a little. "Sure I can't tempt you with a very old whiskey?" he said. "They have quite a selection here." I didn't tell him that one very old whiskey and I'd fall asleep with my head on the table. I was sure the distinguished president of Lynthorpe College would not be pleased if that happened.

Brennan didn't seem in any hurry to get to whatever the real reason for our meeting was, telling me instead about the history of the building we were in, a Revolutionary War house and stone barn that had been used by American soldiers on their way to battle. There were trees in the courtyard, he said, almost as old as the country. At any other time, I would have been excited to learn that, would have insisted on going out to pat their ancient bark and take a few cell phone pictures. All I wanted to do now was get this over with, go to sleep, and catch a plane as soon as possible to go home. Finally, when I couldn't stand the chatter any longer, I spoke up.

"It's been a long couple of days, Dr. Brennan. What can I tell you that will ease any concerns you have?"

"Rory, please," he said in the false-hearty voice that was beginning to grate on me. The waitress delivered a double whiskey for him and a steaming pot of tea for me, and then retreated to the other side of the large room.

"I do appreciate your need to keep details of the crime itself to talks with the police, so I'll try not to put you in an awkward position. My only concern here is that Vince's name not be dragged into anything. Not only because of the gift, Danielle, but because he's an alumnus and a member of our board and because, well, frankly, it will cause anxiety enough among the parents and the students that a violent death occurred on the campus." He took a few sips of his drink, and looked at the amber liquid rather than me as he said, "It would create a circus atmosphere if Vince's name and reputation were in any way attached to the, ah, the proceedings."

My only excuse was bottled up stress, that and the picture of Gabby's hand curled slightly as it lay there in the open doorway. I felt heat flame into my face, my ears were hot, and my hands shook. "You've forgotten that Lynthorpe is already in the middle of what you call the proceedings, President Brennan," I said, my voice sounding brittle to my own ears. "Another of your alums, much more recent and a lot less financially endowed, was shot to death in a room in one of your buildings yesterday, a young woman with her whole life ahead of her. I expect there will be enough anxiety to go around when the word gets out." My voice broke, and I grabbed my spoon and began stirring the tea like crazy, which made no sense since there was nothing in it.

"Of course," he said. "I didn't mean to imply Gabriela's death was somehow less important. I am devastated about it, truly. She was an exceptional graduate, bright, upbeat, curious." He sighed. "This wasn't a good idea. I'm sorry. I'll drive you back to your hotel."

I didn't trust myself to speak after my outburst. He finished his drink in a single gulp, signaled the waitress for the check and we walked back to the car in silence.

My mind had begun to wander when, halfway back on the tree-lined road, he made a sudden right turn and started up a long hill illuminated only by the car's headlights. There were no lights of houses, even far off, and I tensed. Where was he taking me?

Near the top of the long rise, he pulled the car into a dirt space by the side of the road and turned off the engine, but kept the headlights on. I looked over at him.

"Since you were so curious when you asked us about that day, I thought you might like to see the golf course," Brennan said, swiveling toward me. "This is close to where Larry must have had his heart attack. Look, over there—that dark spot is the water."

I could barely make out a darker patch thirty yards away through some trees and beyond what must have been the mowed grass of the course. Even that was hard to see until the clouds parted enough for the moon to cast its cool light on the scenery.

"Are you a golfer, Danielle?"

"No."

"I love the game, although this job doesn't leave much time for relaxation. When I'm out here, I'm usually trying to convince someone to do something that will benefit Lynthorpe and am not paying near enough attention to my swing." He glanced at me and grinned ruefully, his fingers drumming softly on the steering wheel. He made no move to start the car.

I told myself to breathe deeply. Charlie's warnings about not talking to anyone about the crime scene were repeating madly in my brain.

"Look, this is a mess. Vince called me yesterday right before I called you." Brennan's tone had changed. We were definitely talking business and he sounded angry. "He says he might have to pull his gift, and even resign from the board if we can't settle this donation business quickly. He's beginning to wonder if we really want his money. And, as if that isn't enough of a concern, the fact that the press is quick to find fault with him is bothering him. He's afraid of gossip if his name is erroneously linked to trouble, as it might be if the fact that Larry and Gabriela were working on something related to him became public."

"Have you thought that there might be some truth to the idea?" I said, looking into the darkness. "The police haven't told me much, but I've heard enough to think they haven't decided for sure that Larry Saylor's death was an accident. Certainly, no one can claim Gabby's was anything other than deliberate. What else links the two?"

"Frankly, I think you're jumping to conclusions." I could feel him staring hard at me, but I kept my eyes on the darkness of the pond. "Until I hear otherwise, Larry died of natural causes, quite possibly a heart attack from what the police are saying, while out here on his own. And, sad to say, but in these times, Gabriela's killer could be a random nut case off the street. It happens, you know."

"If Larry was part of your foursome, why didn't at least one of you go to check up on him when he didn't return to the club house?" I said.

"I'm not sure I appreciate that." Brennan's tone was sharp. "Coe and I drove to the club together and it was natural for us to leave after our second drink. We both needed to get back. Vince left then too, since Larry had his own car. There's no mystery here. There was no reason to wait around."

The dark car was silent for a moment, the only sound the ticking of the powerful engine as it cooled. The explanation was logical on the surface, but I was remembering the tension in Brennan's office when I brought up the subject of the golf game. "Did you see Vince's car leave the club?"

"You told me you weren't a detective, Danielle, but I think you may have underestimated your professional curiosity. In fact, I'd say you're hinting that Lynthorpe's most generous donor had a hand in Larry's death." I jerked in surprise as his fingers tapped the hand I had rested on my bag.

"No," I said, wishing I hadn't done my thinking out loud. The idea had suddenly materialized in my head and there was no way I wanted to discuss it with Brennan. Charlie, yes, but not here and definitely not now. Margoletti would be furious, perhaps even publicly humiliated, if his alma mater turned down his offer because someone had found out he couldn't make good on some part of his pledge, if that was what Saylor had discovered. Could he have gone back, perhaps even driving up to this spot, to argue his case with Saylor, but lost his temper when the college's vice president stuck to his position?

Brennan leaned toward me far enough that his shoulder touched mine. I began to blather. "The project they were working on is the only thing I know about either of them, but the police haven't hinted that they're looking at Vince as a suspect. Have they talked to him or asked you about it?"

Brennan twisted his torso to turn and face me and there was another long pause. He looked more muscular here at close quarters than he had in his office, his shoulders filling up the car window behind him. I wanted this conversation to be over.

"Certainly not," he said, "and I haven't volunteered anything since I think it's irrelevant to either of the investigations."

It didn't look or smell like coincidence to me. I knew he wouldn't want to hear me say that, and wondered if it might be hazardous to my health in this dark, isolated spot to admit it. We sat there for a moment. A small animal popped out of the woods and scampered through the headlight beams into the cover of some bushes. Brennan's body was too close to mine, and I wanted badly to go home, or at least back to the safety of the hotel room. I was clenching my jaw so hard my teeth hurt.

"Is there a particular reason you wanted me to see this place?" I said, keeping my voice level.

"I thought it might ease any concerns you have. The fire department took this route to get to Larry fast. The club manager told me he gave them the directions when he called 911. No one else would think of this as a way to access the course. Even in the daytime, you can hardly see it through the trees."

He leaned farther toward me and pointed at the course. Was that meant to forestall my thinking that Margoletti could have waylaid Saylor by this route if he came up here by car? Was the president of the college threatening me, implying that no one would be likely to hear if I yelled? What did he want from me? Or rather, what did Margoletti want, since I had a hunch this whole meeting was his doing?

"I am curious," Brennan said, a little too offhandedly, the fine old whiskey slightly scenting his breath. "Did the police mention any speculations about what happened, anything other than a heart attack?"

"Not to me," I said.

"Did they say they found any signs someone had driven up here, where we are, I mean?"

"Not to me, but why would they?"

"I suppose they came up here and checked the scene."

If it weren't beyond ridiculous, I'd think he was worried his own tire prints were up here. "I have no idea."

"This would make a good lovers' lane, I'll bet." He chuckled, deep and insincere. "Running a college, you'd think I would know about every place in town that students visit."

Really? That sounded a little weird to me. Did the college president troll dark places at night checking up on his students? What kind of person was Rory Brennan?

"If Larry didn't stagger into the pond while having a heart attack," he said, "it could have been someone in the woods, a hiker or even a homeless person hoping to get some money from the last golfer through that afternoon."

His scenarios seemed improbable. This wasn't the likeliest place to find a homeless person. As for robbery, it would be like someone deciding the best place to catch a fish was in the golf course pond. Not hardly.

"They didn't discuss his death with me in any detail." I said again. "In fact, I wasn't specific about why I was meeting with Gabby and the detective didn't seem interested. I remember you wanted to keep the gift under wraps until you announced it, but I wonder if that's possible now. Shouldn't you brief the chief or the detective, even if you do it in confidence?" And then I wouldn't have to do it behind your back, I added to myself.

"No, at least not right now. If I think it's relevant later, I'll share everything they need to know, but, as you said, they don't seem interested."

Sooner or later, the connection between Saylor's and Gabby's death was going to be front-page news in this little town, and nothing the president or the big shot alumnus could do would be enough to keep the police from investigating. If Rory Brennan wasn't going to, then I intended to tell Detective Kirby what they had been researching the next time we met. With luck, my consulting job would be done by the time it became public, and I would be back in San Francisco. I might complain about the crime there when it kept me from spending time with my own green-eyed detective, but two mysterious deaths in the same week in a small college town was a full-on crime wave here. I wanted out.

A pause and then a slight straightening of his back, and Brennan said, "Best not to talk about college matters, especially confidential ones, right?" Wrong, but there was no way I was going to argue here and now. "Let's leave police business to the police, shall we?"

I seconded that and hoped we were done, but the president had one more agenda item. "Coe tells me he's concerned that there are too many copies of the Margoletti research materials unaccounted for. He recommends having you turn over your files, and work from a more manageable set of papers that his office can give you."

I sat in silence, not sure how to respond. In truth, there were a lot of apparently duplicative papers, at least a few of which might have sparked a murder. But who would decide which ones I needed? I left it that I'd check in with the dean and we'd straighten it out.

Brennan turned back to the wheel, seemingly satisfied. He started the engine and spun us back onto the road. He seemed to have come to a decision about this annoying woman who was a potential threat to the biggest deal he was likely to make in his career. "You understand my concerns. I'm trying to keep a donor happy, make sure we don't lose the gift, and keep Lynthorpe's name away from bad news. The last thing I want is to have Vince think twice about this gift and start selling parts of it in the hot market for contemporary paintings I read about in the newspapers. You realize the delicacy of these donor relationships as well as anyone could. That's really all I wanted to reassure myself about."

Gabby wasn't even a postscript in his reading of the trouble Lynthorpe might be in. I was silent as he shifted the car into a high, whining gear and we sped down the twisting road back to the main avenue. I asked if I could set up a meeting the next day to present a verbal draft of my report to him as the last step before handing in the formal version, and he agreed enthusiastically. A few minutes later he dropped me off in front of the hotel with an overly cheerful wave. As he turned out of the driveway, I shivered, wondering who Rory Brennan really was.

FIFTEEN

"*R*umors aren't good enough." We were meeting in Brennan's office again. I had a hunch he spent most of his waking hours sitting in his high-backed leather chair, listening to problems from everyone connected with this little school. *Of course*, my snippy inner voice pointed out, still wary after that spooky car ride with the man, *he may have created half the problems.*

I was uneasy sitting there, remembering how threatened I had felt. But that had been in the dark with no one around. Today, sun streamed in his window and the sound of voices in his outer office made last night seem almost like a fantasy. Brennan didn't mention our aborted drink at the inn, although he listened to my verbal report with a deepening frown, alternately staring at me and at the branches of a tree outside his windows. The coffee he had offered was cold in the mug beside me when I finished describing the stories that touched, but apparently didn't harm,

Margoletti seriously in the business world. "No one who makes as much money as he has or who is involved in legal wrangling as often as he is can avoid people's envy," Brennan said, playing with a pen on his desk.

"I agree, but it's enough to merit some further review, don't you think?" I said after ticking off the reports of ethical lapses and the side issue of the discrepancies on the two lists of artworks being given to Lynthorpe.

"Not in my mind." He shook his head. "Look, Silicon Valley is paved with lawyers, all looking out for their clients. Everyone out there is a little paranoid. The stakes are huge and it doesn't surprise me one bit that people feel their ideas have been stolen. I'll bet stories like that pop up every day."

"Perhaps, but magazines have lawyers too, and they aren't going to publish stories hostile to someone as powerful as Margoletti unless they feel they're on pretty safe ground. Your vice president and Gabby had pulled up media coverage that pointed to some possibly unethical business practices."

"I know about Larry's clippings. Believe me, he went over them with me in great detail. I wasn't convinced then and I'm not convinced now that this constitutes proof that an alumnus of Lynthorpe College, a member of its board of trustees, a brilliant lawyer and venture capitalist, and an art collector of taste and means is too crooked to give Lynthorpe the largest gift in our history." Brennan dropped his chin and looked at me through his eyebrows.

What, I wondered, did "too crooked" mean? Was there a "just right" crooked? Was a little crooked okay when twenty million dollars and an eye-popping art collection were at stake? Did Margoletti wield so much power even here, three thousand miles from his Silicon Valley fiefdom, that the president of the college would look the other way even if there was something fishy about the proposed gift?

"I agree that there's nothing firm here." I had told him Ethan's story without naming names, but Brennan dismissed it as partisan sniping. "Do you think hiring a private investigator might be a good idea?"

"I thought investigating is what you were doing for us," Brennan said, and there was no mistaking the annoyance in his voice.

"Not exactly. I'm looking at the ways to ensure that this wonderful gift doesn't have a public relations downside for Lynthorpe, that you and the board won't be criticized later for accepting a donation that might be tainted in some way, or might not even come through. I only have the public documents that Larry Saylor and Gabby have been able to find. For a deeper look, if it were the Devor, we might approach our own attorney to ask her to contract with a private—"

"No way," he said in a steely voice. "Look, I appreciate Geoff's concern that we do this right. I was happy to have you come take a look at this, but it's time to call a halt. Please stick with the terms of the gift contract and the valuation of the art which, as you said the other day, may need to be adjusted for insurance purposes, and let it go at that."

In his place, I'd be tempted to think the same thing, or at least I might if two people weren't dead. It was a glittering prize and unless there was something hiding in plain sight on those two lists, I couldn't tie anything illicit to the twenty million dollars or the art collection. There was no evidence that Vince Margoletti couldn't make good on his pledge, only a nagging concern that he wanted to close the deal awfully quickly, maybe before anyone looked closer at it.

"The only other specific issue I've come across that might be cause for concern is several discrepancies between listings of the art that is coming to Lynthorpe. You mentioned the other night that Vince might sell off paintings he could otherwise give Lynthorpe. Did Larry mention anything about that to you?"

"He said something about Vince possibly holding back a few pieces. We can hardly object to that without seeming to be grasping, can we? He said he'd confirm which ones with Vince directly."

"Do you know if he did that, and which ones they are?"

"I don't recall. That might be something for you to take care of, a better use of your expertise, I think, than looking for skeletons under the bed." He smiled at me as he said it to let me know he had forgiven my misplaced emphasis on trivial matters.

I didn't see what else I could do without Brennan's support, and his impatience was real, so I tried to fold as gracefully as possible. I agreed to write up my recommendation to have a second appraisal done on the art, to get the staffs of Margoletti's firm and Lynthorpe's to iron out any discrepancies on the gift lists that I could show them, and to suggest a few modifications in the contract to bring it in line with similar agreements I had collaborated on for the Devor.

I left Brennan's office relieved that the sense of some unnamed danger last night had faded, but feeling I had done a mediocre job for Geoff even though I had at least raised the issues necessary to be doing my job.

The day was sparkling and the air soft. I was a little stressed from the meeting, so I decided to take a walk around the perimeter of the campus to think about the next steps in my project before heading back to the hotel. After all, spending time in this part of the world in full-on spring was supposed to be a perk. Gardeners were clipping hedges, kids in shorts and sunglasses were lying on towels on the freshly cut grass, and I saw a faculty member sitting and talking with a circle of students on another lawn, punctuating his comments now and then with karate-style chops with one hand.

I thought about Dermott, so happy a few days ago with his teaching job, and about Gabby, so energetic and in love. I recalled what I'd heard about Larry Saylor, a man with integrity, and wondered, not for the first time, why fate and cruelty so often cut down the best among us. I stood for a long time looking at a sweep of blooming azaleas between the paved path I was on and one of the perimeter parking lots, sniffing the elusive scent that seemed to represent the season here at Lynthorpe. Too bad it would always remind me of death now.

While I was musing, a sleek black town car pulled into the parking lot near where I was standing and Vince Margoletti stepped out of the back door. He didn't look in my direction, but smoothed the side of his suit jacket and walked toward Brennan's building, briefcase in hand. For an instant, I fantasized the briefcase was full of money, like a crime scene in the movies. The town car pulled away slowly and, just as slowly, a sports car followed it out of the lot, undoubtedly cruising for a parking spot. There's never enough parking on any college campus and students usually get the worst of it, having to park in the farthest lots or on the street.

I turned and walked back to where I had parked my rental car in a visitor's section near the president's office. As I cut across the asphalt, the muffled sound of vintage Rolling Stones reached me. It was seeping from another idling sports car. It reminded me of President Brennan's car, although it couldn't be. Rory Brennan a Stones fan? *You're kidding, right?* said my inner voice. Some student had a car that looked like his, that was all. What was it with all these nice cars? I remembered that Dickie told me he got his first Porsche when he was accepted at Princeton. *Not all college students are strapped for money and some are even loyal to the world's oldest rockers*, my alter ego pointed out. *Get over it, scholarship student.*

Still slightly distracted, I made a wrong turn leaving campus and had to circle through several residential streets looking for the main one back to town. As I started moving forward at one four-way stop sign on a street where the trees made a lovely canopy, I heard a loud engine to my left in time to see a car come barreling through the intersection. It happened so fast. I slammed on the brakes but the other car smashed into mine and sent my car spinning. I did what every smart driver would do in a situation like that. I closed my eyes.

I smelled something at the same time the airbag came up and slapped me. The car stopped, and it was silent except for the tick of the engine. The bag had already begun to deflate, leaving a white powder on my clothes and in my face. I waited for the other driver to come and when he or she didn't, I peered out, worried that the person was more seriously hurt. No car. I opened my door and stepped out on shaky legs, walking a couple of steps so I could see the whole intersection. No car. A hit and run? How dare he?

Two other cars had come to the same intersection, and one driver stopped while the other drove slowly by, staring at me openmouthed.

"You okay?" the woman who had stopped asked. "I was at the other end of the block, so I didn't see much, but I sure heard it. Scary."

"I think I'm okay, just shaky. You didn't see the car then?"

"No. I was behind you," she said and pointed in the direction I'd come from. "Dark car ignored the stop sign, moving fast. It didn't even come to a full stop after it hit you, just slowed to stay out of your way while you were sliding around. Want me to call the police?"

The damage to my car seemed to be mostly a half-detached front fender. I asked her to wait while I checked to see if my car would start. When it did, I thanked her and said I had less than a mile to drive. She looked at her car, where a toddler in a car seat was beginning to fuss, and asked if I was sure. I was, sort of, but kept my reservations to myself. There was something I needed to process, something about the hit and run car, and I wanted to get back to the safety of my hotel room to do it.

What is it about room service that is so comforting? I eat out a lot, enjoy better food in livelier settings, but having salmon, grilled vegetables, and a little bottle of white wine brought to me on a tray in my very own room never fails to make me feel special, like Eloise, I guess. As I unpacked the silverware and set myself up to eat in bed, I pushed the blinking light on the room phone and promptly forgot anything I was going to think about.

A message, sent less than an hour ago while I was taking a hot shower to relax the stiff neck and sore shoulder I hadn't even realized I had until I walked through the lobby. The voice and what it said killed my appetite and my cozy feelings in a nanosecond.

"If you didn't like that, you won't like what comes next. Stop poking around and go back to where you came from. Now."

SIXTEEN

I didn't sleep well, not even after I checked the triple door locks several times. I had poked a hornet's nest, but the problem was I didn't know what or how. Was it about Vince Margoletti's shady dealings? I didn't have any information that wasn't already published, and the president of Lynthorpe already knew about that. Was it something about the two lists? I couldn't see how that could be because I only talked about it with Gabby. *Not so*, my inner voice reminded me. *You brought it up in your meeting with Rory Brennan, the meeting you had just left when your car was rammed.*

I tossed and turned with the implications of that for a few hours. When I finally fell asleep, I had unsettling dreams that left me more tired in the morning than when I closed my eyes at two a.m. After another hot shower at six, which only proved I was sore and achy, I got back in bed to watch it get light and to face up to the fact that I was in trouble. Whoever killed Gabby, and maybe

Larry Saylor, was literally aiming at me now. Did I have to solve her murder in order to save myself?

Okay then, my inner voice said, *we're in this for Gabby and for us*. Not that I planned to play cop, but from this moment on, it would be my highest priority to help Detective Kirby and the local police force find the bastard who killed her. The first thing would be to call Kirby and tell him what happened.

Of course, he wasn't available. My forward momentum banged up against reality, but I left a message that it was urgent, called down for coffee and a big basket of pastries because I needed strength, and focused on polishing the parts of the report for Brennan that I could do easily. I'd deal with the two lists later, when I could call Margoletti's accountant in California, assuming I could find his name and number in the bulging set of papers I now had. In the meantime, I called the car rental company. They didn't like it, but agreed to deliver a replacement and pick up the damaged one. There was a lot of talk about insurance.

Finally, I pushed everything on the hotel room desk to one side, stacked up my notes and sat down at my laptop to write my final report in sections. My boss, Peter, was right. I would include enough of my concern so that no one could come back later and complain I hadn't given them fair warning should this gift turn out to be less than it seemed. The consultant works at the pleasure of the person who hired her, though, and I'd heard Brennan loud and clear. He intended to run with Margoletti's offer in the absence of a screaming red flag. I dug in and only came up for air when the last of the room service coffee was cold and the phone rang.

It was Detective Kirby returning my call. He listened to my tale about the hit and run drivers, and asked why I hadn't filed an accident report. I told him I'd been too flustered and, anyway, the mystery car had long since disappeared.

"Traffic accidents don't usually get reported to me, even when I'm not on rotation as the lead officer in a murder investigation." He sounded impatient, even annoyed.

"I know that, but there's more." When I added the information about the anonymous call, he was silent for a minute, then said he was going to send someone over to get a full report from me and see if they could find out about the call from the hotel switchboard. Maybe the recording was still available.

"Did you recognize the voice?"

"No more than I recognized the car, although I have to say the car, or at least the kind of car, seemed familiar."

"Okay, you tell that to the officer I'm sending over. Any detail is worth giving us, seeing as how you've been threatened."

"May I go home soon?" I said. "I can be easily reached there and I don't feel safe. Whatever's going on around me is a hell of a lot more complicated than my simple assignment was."

"We'd prefer you stay in Bridgetown a little longer, Ms. O'Rourke. We've got a lot to sort out and you're pretty much in the center of it."

I started to protest, but he talked right through me. "I may need you to identify someone if we pick up the other driver, or to corroborate something a suspect tells us about the Flores shooting, and I know you don't want to have to turn around and fly right back if that happens in the next twenty-four hours."

He had a point. I hesitated, but realized I could stay locked in my room when I was alone and get the consulting recommendations done. I'd be relieved when I could hand the business over to Brennan and be done with the project.

When I got off the phone, I checked my email. Peter's assistant, Dorie, had emailed an hour before to say Peter needed to talk to me. Teeni had sent me a heads up that Dickie had called late yesterday to ask if I was back at Lynthorpe. I looked at my watch. It was ten in the morning here, only seven in San Francisco, but Dorie and Teeni were already moving at top speed.

My cell rang as I was polishing off the last of the crumbly pastry, and when I checked the caller I.D., I did a double take. Teeni might be up and functioning at seven, but no way would my ex-husband be. Unless there was something catastrophic he had to tell me. "Dickie?"

"Ah, sunshine, there you are. Actually, where are you?"

"At the hotel in Bridgetown, working on the Lynthorpe job. Is something wrong?"

"That's why I'm calling you. I heard someone got killed at Lynthorpe last week and I got to worrying. You do have a way of getting in the middle of things. Tell me you were far away when it happened, please."

"Actually, I was down the hall—"

"I knew it, I damn well knew it. Geez, Dani . . . are you okay?"

I wanted to say I was fine. I wanted to tell him I could handle this on my own and that he didn't need to hover. But instead I heard myself saying, "It's a mess and a tragedy. The police want me to stay here and..." My voice wobbled and I had to stop and swallow hard. I had been holding everything at bay, but yesterday's drama increased the stress more than I realized until that moment.

"I'll be right there," Dickie said.

"I'm in New England, remember? But thanks."

"And I'm at my school reunion. I arrived last night. Are you at the hotel right downtown? Stay put and I'll be over in thirty minutes max. Don't move."

I sat motionless for a moment on the edge of the bed. Dickie here. A shoulder to lean on, an ally in a strange place. That was the soothing part. Dickie, though. Overly protective, pushy, untrustworthy, mercurial, as likely to complicate things as to help. I sighed. I would maybe have lunch with him, tell him part of what had happened, not so much he would get ideas about how to help, because that was when having him around was too much like letting an untrained puppy loose at a pool party.

The hotel phone rang and Coe Anderson's assistant wondered if I could meet the dean of the liberal arts school for lunch. I told her I was already booked, and, after asking me to hold, she came on again to suggest a quick dinner tomorrow. "It will have to be early," the assistant said. "The dean has a faculty meeting later in the evening. The recent incident on campus has everyone in overdrive." I bet it did. I agreed and she said he would meet me at my hotel.

I'd hardly hung up when there was a knock on the door. The distorted image of my ex through the peephole was almost enough to make me laugh. Dickie is a handsome man, but these weird, tiny windows do funny things to foreheads and noses, and it cheered me up to see him staring back at me looking like a particularly geeky character in a sitcom.

He knew better than to hug me. A squeeze of the arm was as close as he got these days, which was good since I was still sore. I was glad for the friendly contact and for the physical presence of someone who was in my corner, and I told him so. "It's been awful," I said as he took the room's only chair and I plopped down on the edge of the bed. I filled him in on what I knew happened to Gabby, and explained the possible connection with her research on Lynthorpe's big donor.

"Is that why you were asking about J.P.?" he said. "I wish you'd told me everything last Sunday."

"No, actually that was entirely different. Peter's trying to work a connection to a collector's heir and thought the polo-playing Margoletti might do."

I shared the concern all three college executives had expressed about finishing up my consulting work quickly.

"I can't believe you're mixed up in another suspicious death," he said, having waited with uncharacteristic quiet while I ran through the details. "If I didn't know better, I'd think you were bad luck. Ah, don't cry, I was only kidding." He handed me a tissue and started pacing. "Okay, so no more talking to the cops. I'll call Jerry—you remember him, right? He's so networked it's crazy. He'll know the best lawyer in the area. We'll get him on the team right away."

"Lawyer? Why do I need a lawyer?" I said, blowing my nose. "Or a team, for heaven's sake. I didn't do anything, Dickie."

"You know how it is, cupcake. These small town cops want to close the investigation quickly and you're an outsider. What's simpler than to point at you?"

"Without a motive? Without a gun? Because she and I were meeting before it happened? I don't buy it, and, Dickie, wouldn't it make me look guilty to refuse to help and to hide behind a lawyer? I want them to catch the bastard."

"Only if you were guilty. I'm going to call Jerry right now." Which, being Dickie, a man well known for lack of impulse control, he promptly did.

While he was persuading his buddy's assistant to drag her attorney boss out of a meeting, I debated with myself. Dickie's perspective was a welcome dash of cold water. I had been muddling around in a daze, wanting to help but not thinking clearly about my own position. Charlie had warned me too. For once, I thought, I'm going to listen to their advice. I would call the police and explain my friends had advised me to lawyer up, not because I was guilty, but as a sensible precaution. I also needed to call the airline, to change my reservation again.

Dickie was talking, presumably to Jerry, when there was a sharp rap on the door. I went to the peephole again, but there weren't any laughs this time. It was my new best friend, Officer Clayton McManus, mirrored shades and all. I groaned as I opened the door.

"Hi there, ma'am. How are you today?"

"Busy, actually," I said without opening the door too far.

"Detective Kirby instructed me to escort you down to the police station so you can file a report on that hit and run."

"I'm not sure—" I began.

"Hold it, hold it," Dickie shouted, jumping up and waving with his free hand. "Not you, Jerry. There's a cop here. Don't move, Dani. No Jerry, she's not being forced. Wait a minute, you."

This last to McManus, who had transferred his mirrors to my ex and moved his hand to his utility belt, a maneuver I didn't like.

"Sir, who exactly are you?" Macho Cop said, taking a step into the room.

"I can explain," I said, but was drowned out by Dickie talking to all of us at once.

"He's in the room, Jerry, he's in the room. Dani, sit down. You, you, what do you think you're doing? My wife isn't going anywhere."

"Ex-wife," I said, but I wasn't sure anyone heard me.

"I'll ask the questions," Macho Cop said, dropping his voice half an octave as he went into what I assumed he picked up from TV as the role of the manly policeman. Or, maybe he was still channeling Arnold Schwarzenegger. "Ma'am, if you'll come with me—"

"Oh, no you don't," Dickie said, dancing over to stand between me and McManus. I was thinking that this room wasn't really large enough for three people to walk around in when a new head poked around the doorframe.

"Pardon me, but should I make up the room now?" said a thin, middle-aged woman with steel gray hair and a vacuum cleaner hose in one hand. She glanced curiously at the tall cop and Dickie.

"It's probably not the best time," I said from my position behind Dickie. She nodded sagely and backed away. The door swung shut behind her with a click.

Dickie was still on the phone with Jerry, explaining the situation in overly dramatic terms that made it sound as if the policeman had handcuffs and pepper spray out and ready. I did a double take. Actually, he was now holding a can of something and was trying to speak loud enough to be heard over Dickie.

"Sir, I'm going to ask you one more time to put the phone down and tell me who you are. You are interfering with police business, sir. Put the phone down." Macho Cop had a booming voice when he chose, and he had used it on Dickie, who stopped moving all of a sudden.

"Um, okay, Jerry. I will, but only if . . . okay. But . . . okay." A sudden quiet descended on the small space. Dickie looked from the pepper spray to Macho Cop and back to the can. "Okay, officer, no need to shout," he said.

I cleared my throat into the silence. "I can explain, officer. My friend was on the phone with a lawyer and . . ." I ran out of explanation.

"He says he's your husband," Macho Cop said, holstering the pepper spray carefully.

"Ex-husband," Dickie and I said at the same time.

"Uh huh. And he needs a lawyer?"

"Of course not, but Dani does," Dickie said. We were both sitting on the bed and I kicked his leg. "Well, she doesn't need one, really. She didn't do anything, but she should have one, just in case."

"In case? For a hit and run report?"

"What?" Dickie turned to me with a look of such horror that I couldn't help myself. I began to laugh and once I started I couldn't stop. Both of them stared at me in what I assumed, through my tears of laughter, was complete confusion. Twice, I started to say something, only to dissolve in involuntary giggles again.

When the fit had passed, I took a deep breath and let it out into a completely silent room. "Look, this has gotten far too complicated. Dickie, my rental car was hit at an intersection in town yesterday and this officer came to take an accident report."

Dickie opened his mouth, but I held up my hand. "It was a minor accident, I'm fine. Officer, are you sure Detective Kirby wants me to go to the station? That's not what he said when we talked."

"Yes, ma'am. He gave me the command personally."

I wondered if Kirby already had information about the anonymous caller, but thought I'd keep that whole part of the incident to myself, at least until I heard what he had to say.

"I'm happy to speak with the detective. After that, we'll see what legal help I do or don't need. Dickie, I promise I'll be careful, but the sooner I talk to him, the sooner I can clear this up once and for all."

I stood up. Dickie protested, saying Jerry would call back right away with the name of a local attorney. I said that would be great and that I'd be the first to holler for one if the circumstances merited it. I told Dickie to come looking for me if I wasn't back in an hour, grabbed my bag, and marched out without looking at Officer McManus, whose attempts to be important were beginning to get on my nerves. A great body was not enough compensation for his movie-cop dramatics. "Order me a cobb salad," I called over my shoulder. "Iced tea, no sugar. See you downstairs in an hour." There are times when action is called for, and I had reached the snapping point somewhere around the moment the pepper spray appeared. I was pissed, and Kirby was about to hear me roar.

SEVENTEEN

I was still in a bad mood thirty minutes later after sitting in the reception area filling out a three-page form that wanted more detail than I could dredge up. Detective Kirby was waiting for me. As we moved into the stuffy little room where they interviewed me before, Macho Cop swaggered away down the hall. Maybe it wasn't fair, but I could only hope that was the last time our paths would cross.

"We don't have anything useful about that call yet, by the way. Maybe someone can pry something out of the computer records, but it's not as easy as it looks on TV."

"But you'll tell me if you do get anything? I feel really exposed and vulnerable."

"Understood. Anything we do find will become part of the Flores investigation, but if it suggests you're in danger, we'll let you know right away."

Thanks, big help. I was hoping for around-the-clock police protection, but I just nodded for now.

"In looking over my notes, I have a few more questions. Probably nothing, but we're still trying to make sense of this. You don't mind doing it today, do you?" Kirby said, pulling up a chair. "I want to keep this investigation moving."

"Not if it won't take long and certainly not if it helps find the person who killed Gabby".

"One thing that I'd like you to try and think back on," he said, "is the timing of the events. As much as you can, can you put your story in the context of minutes passing? For example, how long was Ms. Flores down the hall before you heard voices?"

"I think five minutes, not much more or I would have noticed. She was making copies for me."

"How many copies?"

"Maybe a dozen pieces of paper. Wouldn't have taken long."

"Do you have any idea of the time?"

"When I heard the other voice talking to her, I looked at my watch. Her husband was to meet her at six, and I assumed it was him, so I looked at my watch to see if we'd been there almost an hour. It was about five minutes of six, I remember."

"And was it her husband, Mr. Kennedy?" he said.

I stopped to think. "I can't say. The voices weren't clear. It was a man. I've only spoken with Dermott a couple of times and I'm not sure I'd recognize his voice."

"Then they weren't arguing?"

I hesitated. Their voices had been raised, but I wasn't about to pass along something vague that could get Dermott in more trouble. "I couldn't hear what they were saying and it didn't jump out at me as a fight. You know, I saw Dermott come into the building later, after I found Gabby, so it couldn't have been him."

"Unless he left the building and came back in later."

"Dermott kill Gabby? No way. They were madly in love. You could see it."

"As you say, you only saw him a couple of times."

I was uneasy. Dermott, doubtless still in shock about his wife's death, and now a suspect in her murder? Even though I've heard the police always look at the spouse, it was ludicrous. If anyone needed a good lawyer, it was Dermott, not me.

"How long after the voices started did you hear the gunshot?"

"Not long. At the time I didn't know it was a shot. It was kind of muffled. I think I registered it as a car's backfire or some other noise from outside the building."

"And that's why you didn't come to Ms. Flores's aid right away?"

Go ahead, lay more guilt on me. "I didn't know she needed help."

"Then why did you come down the hall?" he said casually.

"Because it was time to go. Gabby told me she and Dermott had a meeting that night, and I didn't want to make them late. I had everything I needed, so I thought I'd meet her at the copy machine and head out."

"And did you pick up the copies?"

"No. I found Gabby and I never did get them."

"Are you sure she made them?"

"I could hear the machine."

"Was it still on when you got there?"

"No, it got quiet right about the time I got to the end of the hall. The whole building was quiet by then."

"So where were the copies and, come to think of it, the originals?" he said.

"I have no idea. I told you, I was looking for Gabby."

"Were there papers on the floor in the room or the hallway?"

"No, I'm sure not. I would have noticed."

"In the office where you found Ms. Flores?"

"No, I didn't see anything."

"Did you have any sense there might be someone else on the second floor?"

The thought chilled me and I went back to that awful couple of minutes when I tried to understand what might be happening, and that motionless hand lying there. "I don't think so. But, like I told Officer McManus, I don't remember much except seeing her."

"When did he interview you? The night of the murder?"

"No, when I saw him at President Brennan's office later. He asked me some of the same questions."

Kirby jiggled his pen against the little notebook he had open on the table, making a rapid-fire tapping sound. "Okay. We're almost finished, I promise."

"I yelled for help. If anyone was there, they would have heard me," I said, shrugging my shoulders to get rid of some of the tension from remembering the scene. "I did have a feeling someone was using the elevator, but I'm not sure. It's a big building and the elevator was out of sight. I can tell you no one showed up to help before Dermott came up the stairs."

"Can you tell me, as precisely as possible, where he was when you first saw him?"

"This is ridiculous, you know?" I said. "It's a waste of time." The detective opened his mouth to argue. I said, "Okay, okay, I'll tell you, but I hope you don't waste any time on Dermott as a suspect while the real murderer gets away. I was on the floor, trying to get Gabby to respond when I heard someone open the door downstairs and climb the stairs. I looked over my shoulder and saw Dermott as he got to the top of the staircase."

"Could you tell from the sound where he entered the building?"

"Which door? Not really."

"And you came in the back."

"The street in front is blocked off to cars and I had to park in a visitor's spot in the lot out back."

"Was there anyone in the parking lot?"

"Yes, it was quitting time when I got there at five, and several women were talking to each other as they left the building and went into the lot. There were at least a dozen cars in the lot. Isn't there a security camera you can check?"

"The camera that focused on the parking lot behind the building where Mr. Saylor had his office wasn't functioning properly. When our people looked at the tape, all they saw was a patch of ground near the door, tops of heads, too fuzzy to identify, mostly leaving, but a couple heading in toward the building."

"One of those might have been me. Could you tell?"

"Not really. The images are bad enough, but the camera uses black and white film. Your hair is kind of red."

"Chestnut. My driver's license says brown, but that's only because there aren't enough options when you fill out the form."

His gaze moved to my hair, which he examined for a moment with the same expression I imagine he would have had if I had said it was green. "Okay. Let's get back to Mr. Kennedy. What did he do when he came up to the second floor and saw you?"

"He didn't know what was going on at first. I think he started to speak and then realized something was wrong."

"Was he carrying anything?" the cop said.

"I don't think so."

He flipped to a fresh page. "I'd like to go back to what you saw in the copy room for a minute."

"There was a long counter in the room with lots of papers in stacks."

"What were the papers Ms. Flores was copying?"

A picture of Rory Brennan's face in the dark car popped into my mind, the vaguely threatening tone of voice telling me it wouldn't be in Lynthorpe's best interests for me to mention Vince Margoletti. My hunch was it had everything to do with Gabby's death, and Saylor's. Taking a deep breath, I proceeded to lay out the basics of the consulting project, Saylor's concerns, Gabby's involvement, and the puzzling aspects surrounding Margoletti's proposed donation. I didn't share the questions about his character that the magazine article ticked off because, as Rory Brennan had said, they were mostly gossip. I felt a weight lifting from me as I spoke. I knew this was the right thing to do, consulting protocols or not. When I was finished, Kirby was silent for a full minute.

"I'm trying to see how the gift you described could be the trigger for this mess," he said, "unless it's the amount of money. Twenty million is a hell of a lot of cash, at least in my world. I don't know much about donations like this, much less art. Was there something potentially illegal in the papers Flores showed you?"

"Not that I saw. There were some small irregularities. What we didn't know was if they were clues to something we hadn't spotted."

"Anything confidential in them—Social Security numbers, bank account information, wills, stuff like that?"

"No, all public information, some of it on the provenance of paintings."

He raised his eyebrows in a question.

"Provenance? It means the formal history of who owned and traded a painting or other piece of art. It's common to keep a record of buys and sells as a way of assuring owners the work isn't fraudulent."

"Did you think these works were frauds?"

"Nothing that I could see suggested forgeries."

"I'm struggling here, Ms. O'Rourke. The anonymous call you got would seem to point clearly to something in your work with the college that's got someone scared. But you don't know what it is. You're telling me everything, right?"

"Believe me, if I understood what was so terrible in those papers I would tell you, I'd tell the president of Lynthorpe, I'd tell my attorney."

"You have a lawyer?"

"I will by the end of the day, at the suggestion of a couple of friends. Just as a precaution." My face probably reflected my feeling that even wanting a lawyer made me feel somehow less than innocent.

"Well, where do you think the papers went, if you don't have them and you didn't see Mr. Kennedy holding them?"

"I have no idea," I said. Until he started asking me to reconstruct the scene, I hadn't thought much about the papers as the key to all this. The question burned inside me now. Whoever killed Gabby must have taken the papers. They must have hoped to cover up something deeply wrong signaled by those few sheets, but who other than the man who owned the art described in them would understand their significance?

EIGHTEEN

*T*hey let me go soon after. I was itchy to get away from Lynthorpe and the mess in which I had landed. I was even ready to smile and listen to the fight song at Dickie's old school if it would get me out of town.

McManus, standing in the hall talking to another uniformed policeman, crossed his muscular arms and tightened his teeth around his toothpick as I passed by on my way to the door. With biceps on display, he tipped his head and smiled at me from behind his mirrored shades. I smiled back, entertaining a mental image of him walking into a wall in a dark room because he was too vain to remove those glasses.

Dickie was waiting for me in the reception area. The lawyer Jerry recommended was in court until two, but would meet us at his office soon after. Around bites of salad, I filled Dickie in on my session with Good Cop.

"Don't call him that, Dani. No cop is a good cop. He's trying to trick you."

"Compared to Macho Cop, he's a sweetheart," I said.

"Who?"

"You know. Mr. Cool, the uniform with the shades."

"Oh, him. I don't trust the guy."

"I wouldn't go that far, but he's probably not the brightest bulb on the force. I think he likes to hang around on campus and be—what do they say?—studly for the coeds."

Dickie rolled his eyes. "I have an idea. Let's get away for a bit after the meeting with the attorney, head over to my alma mater and watch a lacrosse game. It's the traditional big rivalry game, and I hear there's a hell of a forward on our team."

Lacrosse is that thing with little baskets on the ends of poles and there's lots of running around and very little scoring. My high school had a team. The one time I went to cheer for a boy I had a mad crush on, I was so confused that I immediately transferred my affections to a clarinet player in the band. My vow to embrace Dickie's homecoming activities melted away.

I had another idea, one I didn't want to share with my ex. I couldn't get Larry Saylor's supposedly accidental death out of my mind and I wanted to look around while it was still light, and definitely without Dickie. Maybe if I saw the area with my own eyes, I'd be able to accept the notion of the two deaths as a freak coincidence, which would ease my own fears. There would be golfers around, so it couldn't be dangerous. I was bothered by the idea that no one saw the college executive fall into the water, and wondered how that could be. If a friend were here, I'd ask her to come with me, but the only friend around was Dickie and I knew if I told him what I wanted to do, he'd be insufferable unless I let him come along, and then he'd be insufferable anyway.

"No, I need a nap after we meet the lawyer. You go to the match. In fact, there's really no need for you to come with me to meet this guy. After all, it's my problem. You go and have an evening with the St. Stephens' alums and I'll try and make sense of my notes for this donation report, which I want to finish so I can get out of here and go home. Anyway, don't you have to check in with Miss Rome?"

As soon as I said it, I wished I could take it back.

"Well, that's a bit of a *non sequitur*, isn't it?" he said, looking up at me from his Boston cream pie.

"Sorry, it's the fatigue. I only meant you have your own social life, and I don't want to keep you from it."

He went back to his dessert without saying anything, which annoyed me. Not that I was prying, but he could at least say something. It occurred to me suddenly that the charming Isabella might be right now sitting in a hotel near ye old prep school waiting for my ex to meet her. I felt the beginning of a blush and willed the blood to back down.

Finally, parking his fork, he said evenly, "Okay. You've had a rough time. As long as I know this lawyer will look after your interests, I guess I can head over to the school. I'm at the inn where parents usually stay. Here's the number. Call me there or on my cell if anything comes up, promise? And I'll come over first thing tomorrow to see how your meeting went."

"You don't have to do that."

"I know, but I'll feel better if I do." He got up, took a few bills out of his wallet, leaned down to rub my cheek with one finger and left.

I sat there, waiting for the other shoe to drop. It wasn't like Dickie to agree to anything he didn't suggest, to accept what I wanted to do instead of his plan, and to do so quietly. I fully expected him to come flying back in with a new set of arguments about how I needed protection, or an escort, or something. The minutes passed and the only attention I got was from the waiter, wondering if he could clear the table. The more I thought about it, the more I was convinced Isabella was waiting for him. Throwing my napkin down, I headed for the elevator, hoping she hated lacrosse as much as I did.

Quentin Dalstrop was as eccentric looking as his name, about five feet tall, with a large head and short arms. He wore a brightly patterned vest under his suit jacket and had rimless glasses that perched, Santa-like, at the end of his pug nose. It took me only a minute to realize he was exactly the person I wanted on my side. He couldn't sit still for more than a minute, and was pacing around like a compact tiger calculating its next meal before I was halfway through my story. When I told him about the hit and run and the anonymous call, he erupted in a burst of profanity, for which he immediately apologized.

"The good news is the chief of police is an upstanding guy and has no town-gown chip on his shoulder. He'll be straight with us on this."

"And the bad news?" I said, hearing it in his voice.

"Well, there may not be any, but from what you've told me, you're not going home soon."

I groaned.

"We don't know what their canvassing may have turned up in the way of witnesses on the first floor of the building or outside. This is a very small town and I wouldn't bet on them having access to great forensics assistance. You may be the closest they can get to the killer, which the anonymous call proves. Are you sure you didn't see or hear anything that could help identify someone?"

"A man's voice, Gabby's, talking to him. That's all."

"And absolutely no one—not even the smallest glimpse—in the hallway or on the stairs when you went looking for her?"

"Definitely not."

"And no face in the car that hit you?"

"I was still fighting with the airbag as he drove away."

"Well," he said, "maybe something'll come back to you in the middle of the night. If it does, you let me know. Now, if you want me to represent you, I'm going to do two things right off the bat. One, instruct you not to talk to the police again without me being present, and two, go over and meet with the police chief to see what I can learn. I'd like to know if they plan to keep an eye on you for your own protection."

We shook hands on it, exchanged cell phone numbers, and I left, relieved. I found a gas station that sold maps of the town and surrounding countryside, and located the golf course and the winding road that bordered it. That must have been where Rory Brennan had taken me. I circled the spot and decided I'd wait until late afternoon, the same time of day that Larry Saylor had gone up to that spot. In the meantime, I would reconstruct the lost materials as best I could from my last conversation with Gabby. Thinking about the final minutes of her life made me feel sick. I tried to shake it off as I waited for the elevator in the hotel.

"Ms. O'Rourke," someone called. I turned at the same moment the elevator doors opened. It was Dermott Kennedy. "I'm so glad I caught up with you," he said. "Can I talk to you for a minute? Please? I need to find out . . . to try and figure out . . ." His voice trailed off and he ran a hand through his hair. His face was pale and blotchy and he looked disheveled.

"You don't look so good," I said. Not the most polite thing to say, but an understatement. I was worried about him.

"I feel spacey. I've been at the police station a lot of the time, but on the phone with her mother, and at our apartment with the cops too."

"What did the police want at your apartment?"

"They wanted the clothes I was wearing. I know they're looking for some sign that I killed her, but why? It's crazy."

"It may not be that, Dermott," I said. "They're eliminating every possibility. It's routine. You and I both touched her. They're asking me lots of questions too. By the way, have you eaten?"

"No, and I'm not hungry," he said.

"You'll think more clearly with something in your stomach other than coffee," I said, leading him into the hotel's restaurant, empty at this hour. He protested some more but I ordered him a sandwich to pick at and iced tea for both of us.

"Did you talk to your family too?"

"I don't really have one," he said, poking listlessly at his meal. "No sisters or brothers. My dad died when I was ten and my mother when I was in high school. The only grandparent I have left is in a care facility. She has dementia and doesn't know who I am."

"I'm sorry."

"Gabby was my family." His voice cracked and he swallowed hard. "They asked me if I owned a gun."

"Do you?"

"No," he almost shouted, then lowered his voice. "I wouldn't ever have a gun. Ms. O'Rourke, they think I killed my own wife." His eyes filled with tears and the fork dropped onto the plate with a tinny clatter.

"Please call me Dani. We've been through a lot together and we both knew Gabby was wonderful." I touched his hand briefly, but had the feeling he was so brittle right now that anything more might cause him to dissolve completely.

Suddenly he blurted out, "It's the damn life insurance policies. When we got married, we each took one out with the other partner as beneficiary. It's what the articles we read advised newly married people to do."

"How did the police even know?"

"They looked around while I was changing and found the insurance policies and some financial stuff on the desk. We were supposed to meet with an advisor in student services when I came to pick her up. I'd had the folder with me in the car and left it on my desk."

"Don't they have to get a search warrant? Or is that just on TV."

"I don't remember. I think they asked if they could look around, and I didn't see why not. Now they're suggesting I killed her for the money."

"But you're not in jail."

"Not yet, but they're trying."

"Is there anything I can do?"

"Your listening helps. I feel like I've fallen in a hole and everything's upside down."

"You're not sleeping much, I guess?"

"No, and when I do, I wake up in a panic. I think I hear noises, or Gabby calling me. It's horrible."

"There's nothing you could have done. This was an ambush."

"I wasn't there when you found her." He looked at me with eyes that blazed. I pitied him, but his intensity was making me uneasy. "But you were. That's why I came looking for you. I have to know. Did you see anything? Did Gabby say anything to you?"

"Gabby was unconscious when I saw her on the floor," I said. "The police have been asking me the same questions. There wasn't anyone there when I got to the copier room. You were the first person I saw. Did you see anyone leaving the building?"

"No, but that doesn't mean anything. I explained to the police that the main entrance isn't the only one. There are exit doors at each end of the first floor corridor, and another at the back of the building behind the stairs. If someone wanted to get away without being seen, any of those doors would be better bets."

"What about the pathway from the building to the sidewalk?"

"No, no one close enough to have come from the building. I don't remember details, but it was six o'clock. Most of the students are finished with class and back in the dorms or at the cafeteria, so the sidewalks are quieter than during the day."

"Cars?" I said, unsure what I hoped to find out but determined to learn what I could from the only other person who was around. Other than the murderer.

"No, I'm telling you, there was no one in view when I came in."

"Dermott, do you know of any reason why someone would want to hurt Gabby, to kill her?"

"It must have been a random thing, someone hoping to grab her wallet, or thinking some of the offices were unlocked and panicking because she saw him in an office."

"Why do you say that? Was her wallet missing?"

He shook his head. "They showed me what they found in Mr. Saylor's office—her bag and her briefcase, a sweater. Nothing was missing that I could tell. Whoever it was might have been hoping to force her to go back to the office with him and she resisted. She was like that." The ghost of a smile crimped his mouth. "Not easily intimidated for all that she was friendly and positive."

His face fell and he covered his mouth with one hand. "Oh god, I can't believe she's dead." This time the tears spilled out, and he wiped his face savagely with the napkin. He jumped up. "I have to get out of here. I'm going crazy. Sorry." He rushed out of the restaurant and was gone before I could get out of my chair and follow him.

I stood looking out into the street, wondering. Was Dermott right? Was it a robbery gone bad, a simple case of being in the wrong place at the wrong time? Certainly, the college president favored that explanation. It would let me walk away without the nagging sense of responsibility I was feeling. Then I remembered the papers Gabby had been copying. What kind of robber grabbed esoteric research material like that? What robber took both the originals and the copies?

NINETEEN

*I*t was too early to head up to the golf course if I wanted to see how busy it was when Larry Saylor had gone back up to that spot. I went upstairs, retrieved my cell phone from its umbilical cord to the outlet on the wall, and checked. Three messages, one from Suzy, one from Charlie Sugerman, and one with no caller ID listed.

"Would it help if I came?" Suzy said when I explained I was stuck in Bridgetown. "I will, you know. At least you could unload on me. I don't like the idea of you sitting around by yourself."

"I have a lawyer now," I said to reassure her, "and Dickie's here."

"Dickie? I should have known. You told him and he flew out immediately, without a toothbrush, I'm sure?"

"No, no. His prep school's annual reunion is this weekend."

"You're at a college, aren't you?"

"Right. His school's in the next little town."

"Hey, that could be a good thing, right? Still, you want me to come? I know he can be a curse as well as a help."

I thanked her but explained that I expected to be back in San Francisco before she could finish packing. I have seen her take two weeks to pack for a long weekend, so I know how she operates. "I have to get out of here. I'm going crazy, but I need to do everything I can to make sure the police don't decide to prosecute Gabby's husband."

"Why would they?"

"They haven't got a clue who really killed her and you know how the police always say the killer is most likely to be a relative? Well, he's her only local relative."

"I hope they have more than that. It would be shocking. Does he have a lawyer?"

"I meant to ask that when I saw him a little while ago. He was so upset he jumped up and left before I had a chance."

"Don't get any more involved," Suzy said. "You have a way of getting excited and finding yourself in nasty situations you can't get out of."

I opened my mouth to protest, but shut it with a snap. In truth, my curiosity about things that didn't add up had gotten me into a few awkward situations in the past. All the same, I decided against telling her I was going to drive up to the golf course. This wasn't the same thing. I was only going to look around, but I had a feeling she'd be all over me no matter what I said. So I thanked her and promised to call from the airport before my plane home took off.

✑

Charlie had left a message: "I do think you should hire a lawyer out there to make sure the cops don't get ideas. I had a good talk with the local chief. No cause for panic. I'll fill you in when I reach you. Take care of yourself." If Dickie was too free with words of affection, Charlie was the opposite. It was as if he thought his messages might be posted on Facebook or something.

I debated calling him, but decided to wait until I was back. I knew Charlie would not approve of my idea to check the place out on my own any more than Suzy would have. Anyway, I had taken his advice on two counts. I had told Detective Kirby about the research and had hired a lawyer to protect my interests.

The third recent call was an unknown number and I never return those, especially if my inner voice says they might be anonymous threats. I stuck the phone in my bag, and turned to the computer to finish the part of my report having to do with making a pledge binding. As I flipped the pages of notes I'd taken in my meetings at Lynthorpe and in San Francisco, I came across a name that rang a bell. I pulled out the single copy of an auction page that Gabby handed me before she went down to make me copies of the others.

There it was. Bart Corliss. He was the man Geoff had mentioned, the one who had jumped under a train. And here it was in a faint penciled note, "Corliss," scribbled in the margin of the copy, almost off the page. So, had he been so grateful to his lawyer that he had bought him a present, a Roy Lichtenstein cartoon-style painting for twenty-one million dollars plus the broker's fee? That's a lot of gratitude.

Before I could explore the connection, I noticed out the window the golden light that signaled late afternoon. I needed to get out to the golf course. I jumped up and grabbed my bag, remembering to sign off the Web and flip the computer closed. As I was waiting for the elevator, I remembered I had a dinner meeting with the college's dean at seven. I'd be pushed to drive out and back. No time to waste.

I swore at my easily distracted self when I realized I'd left the map in my hotel room. But I had internalized my destination when I traced it on the map, so I was okay. I looked in my rear view mirror a dozen times as I left town and climbed the road, but there was nothing at all suspicious. At first, there were a couple other cars, but they dropped off at side roads, and I was alone when I got to the place where the golf course was visible through a thin cover of trees. I parked in the same dirt pull-off where I'd had that awkward nighttime conversation with President Brennan. This time there was plenty of light and when I walked toward the course, I could see the pond, not at all menacing looking now as it reflected the blue and gold of the clouds and sky.

Four women were laughing and chatting as they hit off the green and away into the distance. They piled into two motorized carts and zipped down a graveled path and out of sight. So they must already have played through this hole. I waited to see if they appeared again, but they didn't. Wondering if I was about to be hit on the head with a ball, I ventured through the trees and closer to the green that lay between me and the pond. There was a group of men far off but pointing in my direction with their clubs, so I retreated to the car to figure out what to do. I might be sitting here for a while, until it was too dark to play. That would make me late for dinner.

Happily, there was cell phone coverage. I called the dean's office and explained I was on an errand and might be later getting back to the hotel. If he could wait, terrific, but if he couldn't, I'd try to reschedule at least a phone call.

Meanwhile, the men had arrived on their carts, two of them smoking fat cigars. They glanced toward the woods at one point, but I wasn't sure they could see me. I used the time to check emails and to respond to a couple of questions Teeni forwarded from the fundraising staff at the Devor. Mostly, they wanted me to approve expenditures, which I wasn't likely to do unless I could work my way out of the department's tight finances. One of Teeni's emails caught my attention. *"Burgess says he must talk to you directly at Geoff's urging. He's the lawyer for a company called Loros. Said he'd been trying to get you on yr cell. Shall I set up appt?"* I hoped it wasn't the call I had just erased, and responded that she should give him my cell phone number again ASAP with my apologies. I doubted very much it was a bequest.

Time has a way of disappearing when you're looking at a screen, and when I looked up, the sun had set, muting the landscape. I checked my watch and was glad I'd left a message for Coe Anderson. Putting my handbag in the trunk and locking the car, I made my way through the trees again, picking up a dry fallen branch that was long enough to serve as a probe if I decided to venture to the pond. There was no one in sight in either direction as I stepped onto the manicured green.

I stood there and turned in a full circle. The dips and rises on the course meant that someone here might be visible to people farther away, then lost in the middle distance before becoming visible again when the golfer got close. That was if they were standing. I reminded myself that my question was whether or not anyone could have seen a man on the ground in the throes of a heart attack? Much less likely, even when the sun was still above the horizon, I realized.

I walked over to the pond where Saylor had died. It was bigger than I had thought, certainly no puddle. There was a narrow strip of sand around the edge, scuffed but too fine and dry to show any footprints. I couldn't tell how deep it was at the center, but the edge where I poked the stick was quite shallow, maybe two or three inches deep. I looked around. Hoping no one would catch me being such an idiot, I slipped off my shoes, turned the bottom of my slacks up a couple of folds, and stepped into the edge of the water cautiously, poking in front of me with the stick. How far out did you have to go before it got deep enough to drown while lying flat?

Surprisingly, the sand gave way almost immediately to a muddy bottom. I shuddered at the feel of the mud between my toes. I've never liked wading in rivers. Give me white, sandy beaches anytime. The stick went a little deeper and I moved forward again. Suddenly, I jumped and cried out. An animal with a hard shell had moved under my foot. I scrambled backward, flailing with the tree limb. Was it a biting animal? Was it coming after me under the dark surface of the water? I lost my balance and sat down hard in four inches of water, and then it was underneath me. My hand brushed it as I scrambled to get my balance and stand up. Calm down, you fool. It was almost smooth, with a slightly pebbled surface. It was a perfect half circle. It was a golf ball, buried in the mud.

Soaked and dirty, I stood there, tree branch in one hand, golf ball in the other, darkness falling, and wondered if Saylor had tried to retrieve a golf ball, lost his balance, and suffered a stroke or a heart attack while trying to stand up again in a panic. If he fell farther into the pond, he might have been in a foot of water, which would be enough to drown him, poor man. No mystery, really, a freak accident. The dean's comment about there being no lake might have been true, but it might as well have been one when Saylor's head lay flat in it.

I heard a high-pitched whine coming from the course, and looked around as I hopped from one foot to the other to put on the sweet little ballet slippers that would now be ruined, and climbed to the green. Dark had almost fallen, but I could see a golf cart headed in my direction, still far off but clearly coming this way with one occupant. The last thing I wanted was to be seen in this condition, so I trotted back across the green as furtively as I could and picked my way through the trees, dropping the branch and the muddy golf ball in the fallen leaves. I retrieved my bag, shook out my pant legs and ducked into the car.

The electric cart stopped on the green and a man in a white short-sleeved shirt and dark pants jumped out. I got nervous when he turned on a flashlight and headed toward the pond, but after a minute, he came back, got on his little cart, and continued toward the next green. Ah, the groundskeeper, maybe the same guy who found Larry Saylor. I bet they made a special stop at this green every day now.

My wet slacks were uncomfortable and my watch said I had to hurry if I was going to change and meet the dean. I was alone on the way down until a car turned out from a side road. I was driving slowly since there were a lot of sharp turns in the road. No place for it to pass, and it was closer to my bumper than I liked. I eased to the right, hoping there was room for it to pass, but the driver didn't take the hint. I sped up a bit to put some distance between us, but the car closed the gap immediately. I began to get nervous but told myself I was almost at the bottom of the hill, where the main road met this one and where there was bound to be traffic.

Of course, my luck, there were no other cars as I signaled and turned toward town. All I could see were its headlights creeping closer to me. Then, the driver turned on the high beams, almost blinding me. By now, we were racing along together and I was scared. Ahead of us I could see a lighted strip mall with a gas station sign on my side of the road. Good. I clicked my turn signal on, tapped my brakes repeatedly, and held my breath. The car behind me didn't give an inch.

"Okay, buddy, this is it," I said to the rear view mirror as the brightly lit station loomed. Getting as far to the right as I could without leaving the pavement, I swerved into the driveway and braked, peeking around my shoulder as soon as my car stopped moving. Nothing. The taillights of the car were rapidly receding from view.

If someone had meant to hurt me, he had plenty of opportunity on the winding road or even on the flats. Bratty teenagers fooling around? All I had was another case of the shakes and a strong instinct to get back to home base and lock the damn door. I was beginning to think Bridgetown was the spookiest place I'd ever been, pretty college campus or not.

TWENTY

*T*he dean had been and gone, the desk clerk told me. "He seemed a little put out," she said, eyeing my damp slacks. I could imagine what "a little put out" translated to, and didn't envy the clerk. A maid had been in the room, picked up the mess of papers I had scattered in my rush to get going, and turned down the covers. No chocolate on the pillow, alas. No call from Dickie either. I guessed the lacrosse match was a thriller. After a hamburger and fries downstairs that I didn't enjoy as much as I had a right to, I fell into bed and slept fitfully again, replaying the wild ride down the hill, and woke up with a jerk from dreams of falling through black space. When I gave up and took a hot shower at six the next morning, I told myself to get a grip. If I wanted to get back home where I would feel safe, I had to see what the dean wanted that was so important, return the call from Geoff's contact, drill down into the short list of undocumented art purchases, and give Brennan a report of some kind.

I wanted to lead with the Lichtenstein painting that Bart Corliss gave Vince for services rendered. The first hint I had that something was wrong was seeing the laptop lid raised. Surely I had closed it when I left the day before, and I hadn't used it last night because I'd been so tired. The auction sheet should have been on top of the pile of papers on my desk, but after a five-minute search I knew for a fact that the page was gone. It couldn't have been the maid.

My neck and shoulders protested as I stood up after looking under the bed. I was going to feel the after effects of the accident for days, even if the damage was only superficial. But I had to accept that someone with a specific objective had been in my room while I had been on the golf course. Someone who could have looked at the map and guessed where I was going. I was obviously close to finding something important.

The day manager assured me that none of their housekeepers would have touched my papers except to move them to make my bed. Was anything else taken, jewelry or valuables? I said I wanted to talk to whomever was on duty at the front desk last night. She was gone too, but the manager was able to get her on the phone. She had seen nothing, heard nothing. My only announced guest was the dean of Lynthorpe, but she had reported that to me right away.

"Did he go up to my room?"

"No. He sat in the lobby for about fifteen minutes, then got up and told me to say he'd left."

"Did you see him leave?" I persisted.

"Well, sure, at least I assume so. I mean, I don't remember seeing him go out the door, but after he left the message, he didn't sit back down and I'm sure he didn't head to the elevator. That I would have remembered."

"Could anyone talk their way into my room?" I said to the manager. "Your receptionist seems pleasant, but maybe she's too nice, and tried to be helpful? And now she doesn't want to admit it?"

He got a little huffy and insisted that would never happen. He told me I could fill out a report and describe what had been taken, but suggested I search one more time.

"It's easy to overlook something, especially in a strange room. If you like, I could come with you."

I thanked him but said I was sure and would get along without the missing paper. I debated calling Detective Kirby, but there wasn't anything concrete to say about the car that tailed me for a few minutes, certainly no useful facts about make, model, license plate, or driver. Charlie was on my side. Dickie was in the vicinity, although that was not necessarily a benefit. I had a lawyer. But now I was on my side too.

I was too nervous to wait around for the police to figure out what was happening. The phone call proved I was a target, even if the tailgater didn't, and the missing page cemented my conviction that I was on a criminal's radar. I was going to get to the bottom of the puzzle surrounding Vince Margoletti's proposed gift, no matter what President Brennan wanted.

I looked at my watch. Plenty late in the morning to call Charlie in San Francisco. I wanted to tell him what happened, and ask him what I should do about it.

"For one thing, forget about driving. Stick close to your hotel room if you have to stay in that town another day. Cabs only, and let the bellman call them for you so the dispatcher doesn't have your name. Keep your cell phone with you all the time. Promise you won't get any fancy ideas, and I'll get there as soon as I can."

"I prom . . . wait. Get here? What do you mean?"

"This is the last straw, Dani. One hit and run could be anything. The car tailing you could just be kids, but on top of the threatening phone call and someone getting into your hotel room, I'm not ready to dismiss it. To tell the truth, I don't like the way this investigation's going. Kirby's honest but he's not very aggressive."

"But what can you do? You can't investigate on your own."

"No, and I don't think they'd like me showing up in any official capacity, but I can't sit around and watch while you're in danger. At the least, I can keep you company. That car thing sounds fishy. I'm going to get someone to cover for me and fly to Boston tonight."

"Charlie, really you don't need to. I have a lawyer, and I will take your advice and stick to cabs. I intend to get the hell out of here tomorrow or the next day with the lawyer's help. By the time you got here, I'd be at the airport. Honest, I'm not taking any chances."

His job barely gave him enough free time to go to a movie, and coming all the way to Lynthorpe would mean several days off with no advance notice in a police station decimated by budget cuts and high case loads. We compromised. I would call him every evening and morning I was still at Lynthorpe to check in. I also agreed to give his name to Quentin.

I didn't tell Charlie that my ex was staying nearby. For one thing, it would hardly ease Charlie's concern. Dickie saved my life once, even if it was sort of by accident, but he's not cautious where danger is concerned. For another, I wasn't sure that Charlie would understand how disinterested I was in Dickie, with or without the presence of his new girlfriend.

An hour later, the hotel phone rang. After a moment's hesitation because I didn't want to hear proof that the car that followed me was driven by the same man who threatened me, I answered. It was Coe Anderson. I explained that I'd gotten lost while exploring the area, leaving out my trip to the golf course and leaving out my speculation about him worming his way into my room to steal the documents that held the clues to Gabby's death.

"I'm sorry to hear that," he said, although his tone of voice suggested there was some fault involved on my part. "When can you come in for a brief meeting?"

"Your office? But it's Saturday."

"Welcome to the life of an administrator."

"You can't tell me on the phone?"

"The president and I met with Vince. There's no time to lose."

It sounded urgent. I was, after all, a paid consultant here, and I was curious to see what could possibly have ratcheted up the pressure beyond what it already was. Maybe I was simply a glutton for punishment. I agreed to take a cab over in an hour. Setting my concerns about Coe Anderson aside, I turned to the list of tasks still waiting for me. First, I called Quentin's office, expecting to get a recorded message. To my surprise, his assistant answered. She explained there was a trial beginning Monday morning. "We're all in," she said, resignation strong in her voice. I asked if the lawyer could see me, and she said she'd check when he got out of his conference, but it would be tough unless it was urgent. I told her I wasn't sure how urgent it was, but a short conversation with him might answer the question. She laughed and said she'd try and I should call back later.

Then I sat down to think through the tough part of the Margoletti gift memo. What do I include, I asked myself? Describe the problem attached to the auctioned paintings given to Vince Margoletti? Explain the two lists and recommend they be reconciled before the gift was finalized? No one would want that delay, but I'd be derelict not to point it out. Mention Margoletti's mixed reputation as a P.R. issue to be faced and planned for? Given Rory Brennan's stern rebuke, there wasn't much sense including it. He'd just tell me to ax it before he signed off on the report.

My other assignment, born out of the tragedies and underscored by the threats against me, was to collect, interpret as best I could, and hand over to Detective Kirby the clouded, dark aspects of this situation. Gabby's face when she told me that Larry Saylor was dead flashed in front of me. She had turned big brown eyes on me, the kind that are hard to refuse, and asked me to help make sense of the executive's findings. Even then, a little voice inside my head had warned me it might be sticky. Now it was too late to back away.

By the time I had to leave for campus, I had figured out how to get the important stuff into the report with the goal of letting them sign off on the basic gift with a set of stipulations. I outlined it well enough so I could finish the text pretty quickly from my notes and the material that had piled up since day one. I didn't know what to do about the auction sheets, since I didn't have them and they obviously hid a clue about the puzzling issues, other than to describe what I could and list the artists' names. I set that problem aside for now.

Coe Anderson was twitching as he escorted me into his office. He jumped right in. "Rory and Vince want this business settled now, no more delays. Vince will make a stock transfer to Lynthorpe that will net enough cash to hire an architect and get started. We need your report today." He leaned across his desk and emphasized his point by lifting his index finger in the air.

Something about finger pointing sends me into resistance mode every time. "It might be hard to get it to you today, although I'm aiming for Monday morning. My plan is to send an email draft to the president tomorrow at the latest. I need to add a section about some specific works of art, and I'm missing some information for that." *Hint, hint, you wouldn't have it by any chance?*

He rocked back in his chair. "How hard can this be? A man wants to give us a lot of money, he's not a crook, and you keep bringing up imaginary problems." He looked mad enough to bite a hole in the table. I was surprised into silence, and he went on. "Frankly, I don't care if it upsets Geoff Johnson or not. We want you to turn in what you have by the end of today, along with the materials you worked from. Vince is set to bring in his P.R. team Monday morning."

"'We' is you and Vince, or you and Rory?"

"All of us. It wasn't your fault that Larry died, or the development assistant, but if you had finished your report sooner, perhaps . . ." He let his implication sit there while my face got hot.

"You can't mean you think I am somehow responsible for Gabby's death," I said, fighting to keep my voice as cool as his.

"No, but I don't think any of us realized that having someone outside the college involved would complicate the process so much. I'm sure your report will be valuable, will give us some pointers going forward. And I'll be happy to recommend you to my higher education colleagues, of course." His smile was as phony as his gesture of professional courtesy. At least to my ears, his voice was patronizing and dripped with insincerity.

"And if I report a problem with the gift, something that may be related to Larry's and Gabby's deaths?"

"God forbid. You can't do that." He jumped up and started pacing the small space behind his desk. "Let me be quite candid here." More finger pointing, this time at me. "Vince sat in that chair early this morning and said we either accept the collection now, or he withdraws the offer. So you see, my hands are tied."

Interesting, that choice of words. Tied? He couldn't do, or had to do, what? "Then let me be candid too." The dean sat down again, so hard his chair squeaked. "There's something wrong about a few of the artworks, something that's related to Gabby's death. I will have to go to the police with what I've learned if it's at all possible that it's related to the events around here."

"The police?" he said, his eyebrows almost reaching his hairline. He looked frightened.

"They know about the project Gabby and I were working on. They may not think it's relevant but I decided after talking to an attorney that I couldn't withhold it."

"You weren't supposed to divulge our confidential business," he said, his voice rising. "How much did you tell them?" Without waiting for a reply, he continued, "Rory and Vince will be unhappy to hear about this. Send Rory your report, and make your plane reservations at the same time."

His words were tough, but the expression on his face didn't match. Yes, he was afraid of something. If he was trying to cover up his involvement, this might be my only opportunity to force him to show his hand. I kept my voice pitched low. "What do you know about a Georgia O'Keeffe painting?"

His brows contracted and he became very still. "What?"

"How about Roy Lichtenstein?"

"I don't know what you're talking about. Artists, I know that."

"Do you think Lynthorpe is going to receive major works by them? Is it on the list you've seen?"

"I don't remember. Are we supposed to?"

Not believable. Of course he knew. Two major American artists and two extremely expensive pieces of art, and the dean of the college that would get them didn't know? Give me a break. "Good question. There's one in storage. The accountant lists it. But it's not on the master list."

Coe Anderson looked carefully at me. "You realize there are more than fifty pieces in this gift, and that Vince may not be giving us all of his collection? And, that he has accountants, not curators, in charge? With that set-up, it's easy to lose track of one, another reason to nail this transaction without more delay."

I was interested. "Do you think Vince's accountants have lost a twenty million dollar Roy Lichtenstein? Is that even possible?"

Coe shrugged and continued to stare at me. "Was that one of Larry's suspicions?"

"I need to talk to Vince Margoletti."

"That's a very bad idea," Coe said.

"I'm not sure I have a choice. We're talking about extraordinary assets that either are or are not coming to Lynthorpe. Surely you want to know." Are you baiting a tiger? my inner voice cautioned. No, but it was that or walk away from Larry's and Gabby's deaths. I couldn't turn the issue over to Kirby until I knew enough to help him investigate.

"It sounds as though you have some ideas already," he said, punctuating his disapproval with a sharp exhale. "If it's because some of these damned duplicate lists you looked at are inaccurate, I can understand why it may have confused you. That's one reason I wanted to get all the paperwork into one place."

In his office, where he could control what I saw? He went on, underscoring every word, his eyes riveted on my face. "But you absolutely cannot speak to Vince. You will be responsible for Lynthorpe losing this once in a lifetime opportunity." He forced a smile. "Ultimately, we can only go with what Vince's lawyers provided, right?"

Coe knew there was something fishy. Was he pressuring me on his own behalf, or on Vince's? I stood up, putting my hands in my pockets so the dean couldn't see they were shaking. "I have to get back to the report so I can meet my deadline. I'm genuinely sorry the consulting hasn't been what you all expected."

"Will you recommend we accept his generous gift?"

I didn't answer.

Coe looked up at me and I could see him weighing my silence. He escorted me to his outer office door without another word and stayed in the doorway watching me as I walked away. Had my mention of the two paintings set off some kind of alarm with him? I didn't have much time, and I didn't like the tone of Coe's voice. At least, if he was behind all of this, I'd drawn him out.

I eased myself into the hotel's desk chair, feeling a small stab of pain in my neck, the only physical reminder of the hit and run attack. I wanted to get to Vince Margoletti before Coe Anderson did, but as I searched for his business card, my cell phone rang. It was the California lawyer who had called me several times at the Devor, and he got right to the point.

"I've been trying to reach you for more than a week," he said, impatience in his voice. "Geoff Johnson is a friend of mine and he said you needed to hear from me. I thought you'd call me back since it was so important."

I opened my mouth to explain, maybe apologize, but he wasn't in a waiting mood. "I'm the lead attorney for Loros and Geoff says you need to know if Vince Margoletti or his firm is currently providing the company with legal services. The answer, Ms. O'Rourke, is no, emphatically no. Loros changed attorneys a few months ago. I'm not in a position to say more, but I promised Geoff I would confirm that for you."

Loros. The company started by Bart Corliss, the man who went under the train, the man who gave Margoletti a magnificent work of contemporary art he had purchased at a glitzy art auction house. "Can you tell me anything about the decision to change law firms?"

"As I said, I can't tell you anything more except, perhaps, to say that my firm handled everything to do with the company's IPO from the moment the board decided to go public. Margoletti had absolutely no role from that date on." IPOs, or Initial Public Offerings, move companies from private to public, shareholder-owned status. If the company looks strong, investors swarm all over it, running the initial share price up fast at the opening and making the people who owned pre-public shares rich, at least on paper.

"Wasn't he on the board? Was he at that meeting?"

"He was not at that meeting. The board's actions regarding his role as an outside director were made in executive session and I cannot comment on that except to say he is not on the board now."

"Did he profit from the company's decision to go public?"

"I suppose so. The company bought back his preferred shares at the estimated price per share they would fetch in the IPO."

"So he would have walked away with . . .?"

"A few million dollars. That's more than I should tell you, but Geoff's a friend. I have no idea why you're asking, Ms. O'Rourke."

I wasn't sure I did either. Not fifteen minutes before she was murdered, Gabby had come across a note Larry Saylor meant to give her, in which he asked her to check out an IPO related to his research. She hadn't told me then, but it must have been Loros, and Saylor had figured out what connected Loros—or its founder—to one of the donated paintings. Something that tainted Vince Margoletti's gift enough to distress him deeply.

"I hate bringing this up, but Loros Corporation's CEO died recently. Geoff may have told you I'm consulting with a small college that will be the beneficiary of Vince Margoletti's art collection." I was talking fast because I could sense that the attorney was impatient, probably because he didn't have a client he could bill for the minutes. I had a vision of a gigantic clock with a bright red arrow clicking off each wasted instant. "I've been reviewing the history of some of the pieces he's donating in order to make sure the assessed value is correct. I came across the Loros founder's name as the previous owner of a very valuable painting, which he bought through a New York auction house."

"Of course I know Bart Corliss died. I wouldn't know anything about his private purchases, however. I am the attorney for the company, not Mr. Corliss's personal attorney," he said, cutting me off.

"Yes, but I wonder if he ever said anything about the painting. You see, it looks as though he gave the painting to Mr. Margoletti."

"Gave?" The lawyer snorted. "I rather doubt that, Ms. O'Rourke. Relations between Mr. Corliss and Mr. Margoletti were strained, shall we say, for the past four months at least. Unless the gift was long ago."

"No, I think it was recent. It's worth quite a bit, about twenty million dollars," I said.

"Twenty million?" Burgess was incredulous. I'd broken through his impenetrable veneer with that number. "And bought at Sotheby's or Christie's? Well, you've got hold of some bad information there, Ms. O'Rourke. As I said, I'm not Corliss's personal attorney, but it strains credibility to think that Bart Corliss would buy, much less give away, a major work of art. I seriously doubt he knew more than the names of the art auction places back East."

"Why?"

"Look, the Loros corporate offices are downscale spaces in a slightly run down building on New Montgomery Street. They're decorated with framed photographs of their products. Cheaply framed photos. Bart Corliss was a brilliant, intense, ambitious man, but he never showed an ounce of interest in anything cultural in my presence and certainly not to the tune of twenty million dollars. I've been to his house, and, believe me, it could use a little upscaling. He sank every cent he had into the business and didn't even draw a salary until after the IPO." He barked a laugh into the phone. "I'd bet real money your information is wrong."

Puzzled, I tried a few other angles, but Mr. Burgess wasn't a lawyer for nothing. He had said all he intended to and within a minute (that's sixty seconds in billable time) he informed me briskly that he had another call waiting, asked me to let Geoff know he had returned my call, and was off the phone.

So now I had the Lichtenstein that Corliss had given to Vince and the O'Keeffe that was lost or not to investigate, and I wasn't going to get any help from the college. My inner voice pointed out there was a more immediate concern. Had I just stirred up a killer's instincts?

TWENTY-ONE

*E*than had left me a message and he sounded apologetic when I returned his call. "You got me thinking. You know Bart Corliss, the guy who started the software company but committed suicide?"

Timely, since I had been talking to his company's lawyer of record ten minutes ago. "A board member at the Devor mentioned him to me."

"Right. Margoletti's firm handled his start-up, so how come he fired Margoletti weeks before the IPO was announced, and then killed himself?"

"You're saying Vince Margoletti had something to do with his death?"

"I'm not saying anything other than Margoletti and Corliss intersected, broke up dramatically, and now Corliss is dead."

"Tell me about his company."

"Corliss built a beautiful product, one that filled a specific and expanding niche in tech. For the past several years, there were rumors Loros was about to go public, but they always pulled back from the projected IPO dates when the time got close."

"Any rumors about the back off?"

"Officially, they decided to wait out sluggishness in the economy, or to deal with some internal product issues first. Always a reason, but backing off three times makes you wonder. Then Corliss held a press conference to say they were definitely doing it on a certain date and the market got excited. I placed an order for damn near as many shares as my broker could get his hands on."

"And?"

"And nothing. Went off as promised, I got a decent piece of the action, the price ran up, I sold half and held onto the rest. Made a little money. Corliss and the rest of the founding team, and the board members, made a pile."

"Margoletti did too." Loros's lawyer had confirmed that for me.

"I heard he didn't agree with the rest of the board about going public. He and Corliss butted heads on it. The rest of the board sided with Corliss."

"Why?"

"You got me. Probably a combination of control and money. The fewer shares that exist, the greater percentage you have, right?"

"It doesn't make sense. Neither does the timing of Corliss' death. Why, when he's made a fortune on the new stock, would Corliss kill himself?"

Ethan agreed it didn't compute.

"This is going to sound like a crazy question, but do you know if Bart Corliss liked modern painting? Did you ever hear about him buying art?"

"Sorry, Dani, I didn't really know the guy, only bumped into him a few times. Seemed quiet, nerdy, not sociable. That's about it."

"Okay," I said. "I'm trying to connect some dots that refuse to make sense." I realized I trusted Ethan for the same reason he trusted me, and that was because Suzy trusted us both.

I sat for a few minutes after ending the call, willing my imagination to clue me in as to why someone would kill anyone who knew about the IPO and the gift. Vincent Margoletti was at the heart of it, whatever it was, he wanted me to stop looking at the missing artwork. Did that mean he had hired someone to scare me off? I must be getting close to the heart of the secret.

Dickie had left a couple of messages while I was on the phone, and the house phone had rung too. I didn't want to get distracted from the task at hand, so I let them go for now. My heart rate was elevated as I punched in the numbers from Margoletti's business card, but I could have saved myself the stress. A bland assistant's voice told me firmly that Mr. Margoletti was not available and that she did not know when I might reach him. I could only leave my name and cell phone number and ask him to call at his earliest convenience.

I turned back to my notes. As I sorted through the material, I noticed something I hadn't seen when I first scanned everything from Saylor's office. Without context, it hadn't caught my attention, but now I wondered. It was a photocopy of a computer-generated note on plain paper that was mixed in with some IRS charitable instructions.

Margoletti—It's been delivered to the warehouse in San Francisco. The papers will be sent directly to you as you instructed. At the top of the paper, a handwritten note: *This is what I mentioned. He has no idea what it means. Maybe you'll have better luck.*

The handwritten note wasn't signed. The paper had fold creases as if it had been inside a business envelope, but there was no date, no address, nothing to help me understand it. I was ready to bet the "it" was a piece of art. No business letterhead, so it wasn't a communication from an auction house or a gallery. Maybe this was simply the tail end of a much longer conversation. Maybe.

I looked at my watch. I needed to catch Quentin for a minute if only to update him on events. I picked up the room phone to ask for a cab when there was a series of rapid knocks on my door in some kind of rhythm. A frowning face peered at me through the peephole. I opened the door warily.

"There you are," Dickie said. "I was getting worried. You didn't answer your room phone or your cell. You shouldn't scare me like that."

"How's the reunion going?" I said, stepping aside to let him in.

"Oh, you know. A lot of bragging about how well they're doing, and a lot of complaining about taxes and college tuitions for the kids."

"I can never figure out why you come to these things if you don't enjoy them."

He gave me an apologetic look. "They're the closest I have to brothers. I know that sounds dumb, but an only child sent off to boarding school has to take what he can get."

In my family, closeness wasn't hard to find. My memory is of standing at the door of the room I shared with my kid sister and yelling to my mother at the top of my lungs that I wanted privacy and would she please tell my sister to go somewhere else for a while so I could listen to my music. I realize Dickie's childhood wasn't perfect, even with a father who loved him dearly. His mother loves him too, I guess, in her way, which is more about preserving his status and his money against people who would sully one and take the other, specifically me with my obvious—to her anyway—goal of "marrying up."

"Okay, it's not dumb," I said, grabbing my bag and ushering him out of the room and toward the elevator. "Even though it's Saturday, I need to meet with Quentin. Ouch." I had reached too far for the elevator button and my neck let me know.

"Are you hurt?" Dickie asked, the question I had hoped to avoid.

"No, not really," I said, relieved that the elevator had been right there and I could beg off talking to him further while we descended in the company of a young guy carrying golf clubs.

"Oh, Ms. O'Rourke," a voice called as we walked toward the door. It was the bellman, hurrying across the lobby. "I heard about your accident. The hotel manager asked if you needed help with your rental company?"

"Accident?" Dickie looked from one of us to the other.

"No thanks. They'll send a new car if I need it."

"What happened to your car?" Dickie was glaring at me as if I had done something wrong, which was grossly unfair. The young bellman nodded unhappily and beat a hasty retreat, something in my face signaling him that maybe he had made a mistake. If I hadn't been so physically down, if I had had anyone else to turn to, I wouldn't have caved so quickly. In the moment, however, there were so many questions and so many threads I was chasing, and I had no friends around or even work colleagues to talk things through with, and Dickie was right here, and, well, I gave in.

"We can't talk here. I need to see Quentin. If you want to help, you could call his assistant and see if he has a few minutes."

"It's Saturday, babe. He's far, far away."

"He's there. I already left a message."

"Okay, I'll call right now." He pulled out his phone. "But what's this about? Your accident?"

"You can go with me to Quentin's office and I'll fill you both in." I didn't want to discuss it in the lobby of the hotel. "What about the reunion, though?" *And Miss Roman Holiday*, I added mentally.

"Nothing I can't miss this afternoon. Golf, mostly. I don't play, remember?"

I did. It had been one of his attractions for me in the early days. He didn't say if Isabella played, but I was guessing not or she would have invited him to caddy. "You have a car, right?"

Dickie gave me a thumb and forefinger sign as he spoke into his phone and went to wait for his car to be brought around. The bellman was still subdued as he handed the car keys to Dickie. I thought he might be feeling bad for his lack of discretion until

I saw the car Dickie walked to, a brilliant yellow Ferrari, so low slung that I had to hang onto the car's roof as I bent to get in. Truth was, the bellman was in awe. "This is your rental car?" I said, gritting my teeth as I tried to get comfortable.

"Yeah, well, sort of. I thought I'd try it out so I . . ." He got busy with the seat belt.

"Don't tell me you bought it? You didn't."

"I kind of did. I mean," he said, rushing to get the words out before I could comment. "I can take it back. These things are always on approval. They're not for everybody, you know?"

You can say that again. I didn't, mostly because the noise a Ferrari makes as it leaps forward, straining the bounds of gravity, begging to go from zero to one hundred miles an hour in six seconds, precludes normal conversation. When we had made a couple of turns and were cruising along in second gear, attracting every eye we passed on the street, Dickie started asking questions. I had to shout if only to get him to stop. "Hold on. I said I'd tell you everything, but I don't want to run through it twice. Do I have an appointment with Quentin?"

"Yes. We lucked out. He doesn't have much time, but he said if we could be quick, he'd see us. Is there anything he shouldn't know?"

I thought for a minute, trying to make sense of Dickie's question. "Of course not. What do you mean? Are you asking if I've done something wrong, like something illegal?"

"Not exactly," he said in a placating voice that meant, yes, that's precisely what he meant.

"No. I need to tell him about the accident, and some other things I'm learning. I need some advice."

"You mean you've gotten yourself mixed up in a dangerous situation again? How do you do it, Dani?" His voice rose. "I mean, think about it. How many people outside of war zones find themselves in the predicaments you do?" He pulled the car up to the curb outside the law office and turned off the ignition.

"That's not fair," I said into the sudden silence. "I can't help it if some of the people I meet get into trouble, or turn out not to be nice. The girl who got shot the other day was sweet, but I didn't even know her two weeks ago. I hardly even met the man who drowned. I only want to make sure I do everything I can to help in the investigation."

Dickie made a noise I remembered from my years of living with him. Part snort, part gargle, it meant I had said something he thought was open to interpretation and that his interpretation was that I wasn't being completely logical. Irritated, I turned to open the door.

"How do I get out of this thing?" If there was something as old fashioned and ordinary as a handle on the doorframe, I couldn't see it. To make my embarrassment complete, when I looked out the window, my nose was about as high off the street as the nose of the little poodle staring at me as he pranced past on the end of a leash. I wanted to explain to the smiling passersby that it was only because of my sore neck that Dickie had to haul me out of the Ferrari's passenger seat.

TWENTY-TWO

*S*oothed somewhat by a mug of tea and Quentin Dalstrop's leather conference room chair, I tried to organize my thoughts while we waited for him. If Gabby was one topic, Coe Anderson's hostility and ultimatum another, and the accident was the third, how much could I say was connected? In my gut, I knew they were. To explain why, I'd have to share everything I knew about the Margoletti gift. What I wanted most to know was when I could leave Bridgetown and get back to the relative calm of San Francisco.

Quentin answered at least part of the question by telling me that the chief of police was a smart man and knew I had no motive for killing the young researcher. My biggest value might be supplying a motive for someone else. In fact, when he spoke with the chief, he learned they wanted me to come in yet again, this afternoon. I protested but Quentin said he'd go with me and let his junior attorneys handle some of his pre-trial research.

It was time to talk about my project, the key to everything that had happened. After all, I was the only person who knew what papers had been on the copier, and could testify that whoever killed Gabby had been careful to take all of them when he bolted. Taking a deep breath, I plunged in. I must have talked for fifteen minutes straight. Dickie tried to interrupt a couple of times, but Quentin held up his hand in a stop sign, and my ex bit his tongue. Quentin scribbled notes to himself now and then, but mostly listened, his eyes fastened on my face. When I wound down by recounting my conversations with Suzy's cousin, the Loros attorney, and the dean, Quentin shook his head.

"That's some story, Dani. I think you're right. There have to be connections and you were right to tell the police about Margoletti. If I'm getting it straight, though, you're not sure what's so damaging in the research that anyone would kill to keep it from coming out?"

"That's the problem. For a while, I thought perhaps the paintings that aren't accounted for properly had been stolen before they wound up in his hands, but I researched online and there aren't any stolen paintings by these artists that show up in stories."

"Maybe they're fakes," Dickie said.

"I wondered about that too, but the auction catalogs are detailed. It doesn't mean they couldn't be fooled, but these are experts and I'd bet against it."

"Anything else jump out in the research files?" Quentin said, chewing on his pencil.

"Only that Margoletti has a somewhat shaded reputation and that he has huge positions in investor stock at a handful of private companies. If any or all of those companies fail, his asset base will be seriously undercut. If there's anything he took part in that leads to a scandal, his name on the building might not be such a good thing, PR-wise. Someone tried to scare me, the dean's mad as hell at me right now, and they're prepared to go ahead without a recommendation from me even if that upsets the college's board. These guys are rushing to get this deal done before I dig deeper."

Quentin worried his lower lip with his teeth. "Did you come across information about Margoletti having a criminal record? What I'm getting at is that if he has any history of physical coercion or violence that brought him to the attention of the police, the cops here will see him as a person of interest."

"No, nothing." Even as I said no, however, an idea began to take hold in my brain. Could the paintings given to Margoletti by the company founders have been a way of laundering money? Maybe Margoletti was moving illegal funds for a client through his art collection. Dickie liked the notion but Quentin was dubious. "I'm not saying there aren't attorneys who get involved in illegal activities, but it doesn't compute for this guy. He's already rich, famous, and from what you say, immensely powerful."

Dickie was up and pacing the room. "Do you really trust the cops here? Would they take on the local college president or a rich man? You know what I mean."

"I do," Quentin said. "In a small town, not every policeman is going to be as unmoved by status as one would like, but it's what we have, Richard. My job is to see that Dani is in no way pulled deeper into this than the circumstances warrant, no matter who else they should be thinking about."

"Look," I said, changing, or rather returning to, the topic of Vince Margoletti, the man at the heart of all this. "I have to talk to Vince. He may be behind all of this, or he may be totally in the dark, focused only on making a splash with his gift."

"You think he could be innocent?" Dickie said, surprised.

"I don't know. Coe Anderson is pushing me like crazy and I think he's nervous, something about paintings and the exact tally of what's included in the gift."

"But you've said you suspect Margoletti," my ex said. "I'm confused."

"So am I. Quentin, what do you think? Is it dangerous?"

Quentin nodded. "It could be. You're stirring up the weeds, hoping to flush a bird. But you might get a rattler instead. If you have ideas about the kinds of questions that might help solve the crimes, bring them to Detective Kirby. Let him ask them."

I had to be content with that, at least until I had a better plan and a perfect question. I begged for an hour of quiet time at the hotel before my meeting with Kirby, and Quentin and I agreed to meet at the police station. Dickie insisted on driving me back to the hotel in the yellow Batmobile. He pulled away from the curb with a roar, and zoomed up to the next traffic light. When it turned green, Dickie turned left and had not shifted out of first when an amplified, disembodied voice came in the window. "Pull over here, sir. Pull over right here. Now."

"Damn," Dickie said. "This is ridiculous. A traffic cop. Well, this'll be short. I wasn't speeding. I'm guessing he stops everybody in a Ferrari." Like there are others of you, I wanted to say.

The police car drew up behind the Ferrari and the uniformed officer sauntered slowly to the driver's side of the Ferrari. No, no, let it not be him. The mirrored glasses, the muscled arms displayed to advantage in a short-sleeved uniform shirt. Yes, the person least likely to form a positive bond with my ex-husband.

Macho Cop leaned way down to peer into the car. "Well, how about that? Hello ma'am. Is this the loaner for your rental car?" He laughed and straightened up before I could ask him how he knew about my traffic accident. Probably the stranger from "Frisco" was good for a little gossip.

"Not him," my ex groaned. "I would get stopped by the village idiot." Fortunately, McManus couldn't hear Dickie over the sound of the engine.

"Excessive noise," Officer McManus said five minutes later, for the third time. The first two times, Dickie had been insisting that there was nowhere in the world where going twenty miles an hour would be illegal, and was too passionate in his self-defense to hear what he was being stopped for. The only reason he heard it the third time was that he stopped for breath. The explanation didn't sit well with him when he did hear it. But, then, I wouldn't have expected a man whose vanity license plate is FAV4DSN to buy into the notion that he could get a ticket because his engine sounded like a small jet.

I was getting pissed. "Enough, Dickie. Stop. Right. Now. Okay, Officer McManus, give us the ticket. We need to be somewhere soon." I didn't say we were headed to the police station to meet with his boss.

"Well, I wouldn't want to make you late," he said, and laughed again as he straightened up and slapped a hand on the roof of the Ferrari.

Big mistake. Richard Argetter III was having none of this car slapping. He struggled to open his door and get out, which probably appealed to him because he would look less like a small child once his long legs were upright. Officer McManus obviously didn't approve of Dickie getting out of the car because he said, "Do not exit the car, sir. Do not exit the car," in the sternest monotone he could muster while trying to hold his ground. By now, the testosterone was almost visible, swirling around the yellow Ferrari, and passersby were slowing to watch, maybe hoping for a fight.

Neither of them noticed when I got my own door open, leveraged myself out and onto the sidewalk, and walked away. A cab let someone off at the next corner and I grabbed it and gave the driver the hotel name. When I got to my room, I took the phone off the hook, took two aspirins, called the reception desk for a wake-up call in forty-five minutes, and pulled a pillow over my ears. I didn't sleep, but at least it was quiet.

When I got down to the lobby, Dickie was waiting, seemingly relaxed, reading the local paper. I hadn't been married to him for four years without learning to read his body language. This was a man loaded for bear.

"Hey, feeling better?" he said with a big smile as he jumped up. "Ready to meet Quentin at the police station? My chariot awaits." He carefully folded the paper and replaced it on the lobby table. Dickie never folds discarded newspapers. In fact, he never picked up his socks or his jackets, or the dog's leash. This was a clue to how tightly wound he was at the moment.

"So, did you get a ticket?" I said as I kept walking toward the door.

"Oh, yeah, I guess."

"You guess?"

"Two, actually. That idiot small town cop gave me two tickets." He laughed, not convincingly.

"For?"

"Stupid stuff. No big deal. The bellman told me this guy gives tickets to college students all the time. Chip on his shoulder, big time. He's kind of a campus joke."

"You checked with the bellman?" I couldn't see Dickie sharing an embarrassing moment with a kid.

"He saw the tail end of it. Said the cop wanted to get a close look at the Ferrari. They don't get many, well, any, around here, he said."

"Oh brother. Guys and cars."

"Here's the car. Hey."

I walked past the Ferrari's door, held open by a young valet whose eyes were caressing it, and up to the other guy on duty. "Can you get me a cab?"

"Uh, sure," he said, looking back at the Ferrari. "But, I mean, wouldn't you rather ride in that?"

"Nope, whiplash," I said, unwilling to explain to a kid why my ex-husband was going to drive me crazy if I couldn't get away from him.

Dickie was glaring at me from the driver's side of his car. He did not like to be ignored, another trait I remembered all too well. While I waited for the cab, he revved his engine, noise abatement be damned, and roared up to me, reducing both bellmen to abject awe. "I'm only trying to help, you know," he said, looking up from his seat, "but if you don't want me around, that's fine. I should be getting back to the reunion anyway. I'm already late, and I left...."

As in left my sophisticated, trouble-free, self-reliant Roman girlfriend waiting for me to return in my show-offy car. "Fine. I have a lawyer and we can handle this now. I wouldn't want you to miss any of the fun."

He stared hard at me for a moment, then wished me luck in a curt voice and roared off.

TWENTY-THREE

Quentin was waiting on the front steps of the police station, and briefed me on how this would work before we went in. They'd ask a question, I'd look at Quentin and only if he nodded yes would I answer. Even then, if I didn't want to talk about something, I was to shake my head and he'd jump in to remind them I was there voluntarily and only to help where I thought I could.

The chief himself met us in the reception area, although he explained he wouldn't be at the interview. We walked together to a plain room with a painted but scuffed concrete floor, white walls that had seen better days, and an ugly metal table with four metal and plastic chairs grouped around it. The chief shook hands and told us Kirby would be along in a minute.

As we waited, I looked around at the depressing décor. One wall had a dull mirror that obviously was two-way glass. There were several laminated signs taped to the walls, but none were readable from where I sat, Quentin at my side. The room made me feel like a criminal. *Duh, you think that's an accident?* said my inner voice.

Just when I was getting impatient enough to speak, the door opened and Detective Kirby hurried in. "Sorry to keep you waiting," he said, "but I was pulling together some faxed information."

The chief left and we settled into our chairs. Over the course of the next thirty minutes, I was walked through my vague suspicions about the documents that Gabby had been trying to copy for me.

"I still don't get it," Kirby said. "The paintings weren't stolen and weren't fakes, so why would the material motivate anyone to kill the victim? You think they're supposed to be given to the college? So who owns them now?"

"That's a problem. I don't know who owns them or where they are, only that there are two lists that don't match and Larry Saylor and Gabby Flores apparently were asking the same questions."

"And they're dead," the detective said, tapping his pen on the table.

Thank you for that. "May I ask if you're looking at Mr. Saylor's death as suspicious now that Gabby's been killed?" I said, looking over at Quentin to see if he thought I was overstepping. He was looking at the detective curiously.

"The investigation is open. Since Ms. Flores was shot, we need to re-examine the circumstances of Mr. Saylor's death. Now, I'd like to check out a few things, Ms. O'Rourke." He held up several sheets of paper, presumably the faxes he had been gathering before we arrived. "You work for an art museum. Do you buy paintings like the ones you're investigating?"

"I don't buy anything. I'm involved in raising money and getting people to give their artwork to the museum. The curators buy art." I was trying to read the fax sheets upside down to find out if he had made my life harder by going to Peter for information.

"Do you do this sort of consulting a lot?"

"This is the first consulting job I've been offered. I was flattered at first." I sighed and when he looked a question at me, explained. "The chairman of the Devor Museum's board recommended me for it. It seemed straightforward at the time."

"You didn't know any of the players before this—Saylor, Margoletti, Flores, anyone at Lynthorpe?"

"Only Geoff, the Devor contact. He's on the board here."

"He knows the big donor?"

"Slightly. They both graduated from Lynthorpe in the same class and they both live in California. But Geoff told me he doesn't know Vince well." No need to say he didn't trust Vince.

"I don't believe in coincidences," the detective said.

"Neither do I," I said. "But if you mean the two knowing each other, wealthy people tend to be recruited to alumni volunteer positions. That's nothing unusual."

"Okay, I hear you," Kirby said. "At the risk of seeming to beat a dead horse, can you think back to the time period from when you got up to leave Mr. Saylor's office until Mr. Kennedy joined you on the second floor? I know you've said you can't recall anything specific, but I'm going to run you through it again and I'd like you to close your eyes and think carefully as I ask you each question."

"I can't see how it will help," I said.

"Try to put yourself back into that office. Ms. Flores has left, carrying the papers. You're sitting there. What do you hear?"

I was sitting there again, with the quiet sounds of the campus at the end of the day coming in the open window, birdsong, maybe an air conditioner somewhere, a car. "It was quiet except that the copier started up. Then, it was noisy the way these machines are, you know?"

"And was anyone speaking?"

"I thought I heard Gabby's voice, talking with a man."

"And you didn't recognize his voice?"

"I hardly recognized hers. I'm sure it was a man's voice, though."

"And then?"

"I walked toward the stairs. The conversation had stopped. The copier was still pushing out paper and it drowned out everything at first. When I squatted down at the open door, when I saw her hand—"

I shuddered. This was getting too real.

"Yes?"

"It's possible someone was still in the building. I've been trying to remember what I was thinking when I called out for help, but it's hard. It was a jumble, you know?"

"What was it that made you think you weren't alone?"

"I heard a sound from down the hall. At least I thought I did. But I never saw anyone. There were several women staffers leaving the building when I got there, but that was an hour before."

"We've interviewed everyone who worked there that afternoon. No one noticed anything unusual except you looking for Mr.

Saylor's office. A few workers were still gathered in a room on the first floor far away from the staircase, celebrating a colleague's birthday. Apparently, they were making enough noise to cover up anything they might have heard." He flipped back through the pages of his notebook "Try to bring back that few minutes. You told me before about an elevator?"

"Oh, yes, I'd forgotten. I thought there was someone in the other wing of Saylor's office suite when I arrived. It's a long space with a handful of cubicles that I couldn't see around. But the sound was indistinct, you know? Then, nothing until I was trying to get her to respond. It might have been an elevator door pinging as it opened or closed. I couldn't see the elevator from where I was, inside the faculty member's open door."

Quentin spoke up from his side of the table. "That might be useful, don't you think? It could suggest someone was in Mr. Saylor's office before my client arrived, and that the killer exited the second floor by way of the elevator."

Kirby grunted. "We'll revisit the office and the elevator, although I expect it's too late to find any fingerprints or other evidence."

"My memory of the entire nightmare is getting fuzzier as time goes by." I remembered the feel of her fingers when I touched them, though. That I'd never forget. "I was confused, and I was in a strange place, and then in shock. And now, I think I'm a target." I knew my voice was rising. I looked over at Quentin, signaling my desire to get out of the airless room and away from the grilling.

"We don't know that yet," Kirby said, "although we take the chance of it seriously. Certainly the anonymous call suggests someone wants you to go away." He sounded sincere, but not as motivated as I was to find out what had happened.

"One more thing. Please describe Dermott Kennedy's behavior and appearance from the moment he arrived on the scene."

"I'm not sure what you mean. Upset, shocked?"

"I mean before he understood what had happened." The detective flicked the pages in his little notebook until he came to something that he stopped to read. "You told me that when he first approached you, Mr. Kennedy didn't seem to know what had happened."

"That's right. He was coming up the stairs and when he got near the top step, he saw me, I guess, and started to say something like, 'Oh, hi.' He was cheerful and when I looked at him, he was smiling."

"And then?"

"I guess my expression stopped him. He started to ask me what was wrong, but when he got close and saw...and saw his wife's hand . . ." I gulped. "He dropped down next to me and began saying her name."

"When did you first know he was there?"

"When he got near the top of the stairs."

"And his clothes? Did you notice anything?"

I looked at Quentin. He nodded. I hoped I wouldn't get Dermott in trouble. "Like what? He had on a sports jacket but no tie. Chinos."

"His shoes? Leather, sneakers? Flip-flops?"

"Not flip-flops, regular shoes I think. I was focused on a bleeding woman, not on footwear."

"One more question. Was there anything that might have been blood on his clothing? Chinos are light colored. You might have noticed, and I assume he was wearing a shirt."

"Of course he was and, no, nothing like that. His jacket was dark, so I wouldn't have seen blood on it, but he looked perfectly normal."

"He had blood on his pants and his shirt when the police examined his clothes."

"Well, sure. I mean, he got right down on the floor when he saw her. I had some blood on my sweater and on my knees, which I'm sure your officers reported. We were crouched over her, trying to help her."

"Okay, let's confirm what happened next. After Mr. Kennedy arrived, who was the next person on the scene?"

"Your men, two uniformed policemen. I only know the name of one, McManus. The other one was with him."

"And they came upstairs?"

"Yes, but only after I opened the front door. They were banging on it."

"So you went downstairs, leaving Mr. Kennedy alone with his wife?"

"Yes, but only for a minute. The cops ran up the stairs."

I might have continued, but Quentin interrupted me smoothly, reminding the detective he had said he was finished with his questions and that my injury from the car crash was catching up to me.

"I wanted to ask you if the security cameras for the building have been checked," I said, curiosity trumping the desire to be gone. "Wouldn't that tell you who came into and left the building?"

"They don't have many of them on the building and none were particularly helpful." Kirby snorted. "Just grainy images. Probably didn't seem like a high priority to install better units."

With that, he stood up, signaling that the interview was over. As he walked Quentin and me toward the reception area, I started to ask him a question, but was interrupted by an oddly familiar voice. "Detective Kirby? Inspector Sugerman. Thanks for making time to see me. Hi Dani, you okay?" A hand reached out to squeeze my arm gently as I spun around. I wasn't hallucinating. It really was Charlie.

He looked a little tired and his tie was twisted to one side, but the green eyes were twinkling a little as he registered my surprise. Before I could do more than stutter, Charlie had turned to the detective and was agreeing to meet him in his office in five minutes, as soon as he'd seen me off.

"But, how . . . I mean, why . . . ?"

He laughed. "It was worth a long day and two plane changes to see your face. Seriously, though, what you've been telling me isn't adding up. I had a three-day break coming to me in rotation. Weiler even blessed it. Said he wouldn't know what to do for entertainment if you wound up in jail a continent away."

Quentin murmured something about jail not being a likely option and I introduced them. Charlie suggested we three have dinner to go over the case and said he'd meet me at the hotel in a couple of hours. Quentin surprised me by agreeing, saying he'd use the time to sort his notes for Monday's court case. "You're a much better pair of dinner companions than a rerun of 'Law and Order' and a frozen chicken pot pie."

I left the police station feeling more optimistic than I had in days.

TWENTY-FOUR

*C*harlie had found out the town had an Italian restaurant cops loved, so we met there. The mouth-watering smell of garlic and olive oil that blew out of the open door was enough to convince me. We were silent while we dug into bowls of ziti and penne drenched in fresh tomato sauce and laced with salty calamata olives, tender little meatballs, and a snowfall of Parmesan cheese. Comfort food, something the hotel restaurant hadn't been able to supply.

It also was comforting to hear Charlie's crisp summary of what he'd learned, and to know he had been as forceful as professional courtesy allowed in urging the police to focus on connecting the dots between Saylor's death and Gabby's, and to see that the "accident" with my car had to be part of the same case.

I started to tell them about my meeting with Coe Anderson and what sounded like a veiled threat when Quentin wiped the last of the tomato sauce off his mouth, reached for his beer glass, and said, "Good thing Dani's ex-husband got me involved, given that there aren't a lot of viable suspects so far."

The rest of the people at Tomaselli's Italian Restaurant, Family-Owned Since 1932, were laughing and talking, but it was silent at our table. I chased the remains of a mushroom around my plate, not wanting to meet those green eyes.

"Really?" Charlie's voice was neutral, slow. "That's good to know. I wouldn't have credited Richard Argetter with knowing a lawyer in Bridgetown, but, then, I wouldn't have guessed he'd even be here at this time. Fortuitous."

Since Charlie didn't talk like this in real life, I knew I was in trouble. To Quentin, Charlie sounded like a lawyer, and he smiled his approval. The mushroom gave up and when I had popped it into my mouth, I had no choice but to look up. "His prep school alumni reunion is this week," I said. "He went to boarding school in the next town. Quite a coincidence, isn't it?"

"Yes, indeed," my handsome homicide inspector said, a big and completely phony smile on his face. "Major coincidence."

"Look, guys," I said, eager to change the subject. "I've been circling the facts I know, adding details, piling small bits together in piles, but getting nowhere. I'm frustrated and over my head. I'd like nothing better than to hand this over to the local authorities and go home. Can I do that? Help me understand the big picture, please."

Quentin frowned. "I wish I could say go, but I'm still getting signals they won't be happy if you leave, and if you insist, they might pull some legal strings to keep you here."

"Agreed," said Charlie, shifting into professional mode, although the look he gave me suggested we'd return to the subject of coincidence later. "The lead detective seems like a good guy, smart, and clear-headed. They don't have much to go on yet, and you're the best witness he has. As long as that's the case, there's no way he'll be satisfied with you promising to come back later."

I looked at Quentin. There would never be a safer group or a better time, so I returned to the wild idea I'd been entertaining that Margoletti was involved in a money-laundering scheme. There had been rumors in the art market once paintings by famous artists began fetching stratospheric prices at auction from unnamed buyers working through unknown agents. That could explain paintings coming into his possession in lieu of payments for service, or a painting being bought quickly and sold with sketchy details. Both men sat silent, each looking off into space as if trying to picture the attorney as a crook. "Could be," Quentin said, "but if it's the answer, we're in over our heads. That's an investigation for the feds."

"Agreed," Charlie said. "Let's suggest it to Kirby, just to make sure the idea doesn't get lost. It would make some sense, given the lengths to which someone's going to get rid of every scrap of evidence about the artwork that's ringing your bells."

Quentin promised to call Kirby Monday, and we left it at that.

The cab ride to the hotel was quiet. Charlie paid the driver and walked me briskly into the lobby. No questions, no recriminations, only silence. It wasn't until we got on the elevator and I pushed the button for the third floor that I realized I didn't know what Charlie's plans were for the night.

I cleared my throat. "It really was a coincidence that Dickie was in town, and other than finding a lawyer for me, which you recommended, he hasn't been involved." Much. "Are you staying with me? You can," I said, then heard my voice, which sounded doubtful to my ears. "I mean, I'd like you to if you want to."

"I booked a room." He sighed. "Look, this is complicated. I figured I could read the cops better than you could, and could ease their minds if they didn't understand your way of getting mixed up with murder."

The door opened and we stepped out. An elderly couple was waiting to get on, so I held my comment until the door had closed and they were gone. As we marched along the wine-colored carpet to my room, I whispered, "Not my way. I don't want to have a sore neck, a wrecked fender to explain to the car rental company, and my very own criminal lawyer. You think I like this?"

We entered my room. "I'm sorry if I'm in a lousy mood. Blame it on pain, but I really am glad you're here and you're right. I need help." I started to put my arms around him. "Ow," I said, stepping back and clutching my collarbone.

He looked at me, startled. "How bad are you hurt?"

The hotel phone rang before I could answer, and I picked it up, hoping it wasn't Dickie. I had had enough awkwardness around men for one day.

A voice I didn't recognize slurred my name. "Ms. O'Rourke, help me please. I don't know who to call. Please . . ."

"Who is this?"

"Dermott . . . I . . . someone broke into my apartment. Surprised me. When I tried to turn on the light, he shot me."

"You've been shot? Dermott, where are you?" I said, signaling Charlie frantically to come closer and listen.

"In the apartment. I must have fainted. . . ." He sounded weak.

"Have you called 911? Can you call for help?"

"No, can't. The police think I killed her. . . ."

He was fading and I panicked. "What's your address? I can come right over—"

Charlie shook his head and pulled the phone away from me gently. He spoke calmly to Dermott while I scrambled over to the table next to my bed and searched for a speaker button on the phone console. "We're going to call 911 for you. You need to get to the hospital. We'll find out where you're being taken and meet you at the hospital. It's okay, I'm Dani's friend." He listened for a minute, then looked at me. "I'm going to call 911 now. Yes, we'll find you."

Charlie tried to convince me to let him go alone, but I wouldn't hear of it. Dermott had called me for a reason, even if I didn't know what it was. We got directions, and on the way over to the hospital, Charlie quizzed me about Gabby's husband. I realized I didn't know anything beyond what he or Gabby had told me. Clearly, he didn't trust the police, which I could understand if they were determined to see him as a suspect.

The local hospital was only a mile or two from the hotel and we got there just as the ambulance pulled up. I tried to speak to Dermott as the EMTs unloaded the gurney and wheeled him into the building. "We're here, okay?" He looked awful, pale, disheveled, confused, what I could see of him as he was hustled past.

He grabbed my hand and said something to me, but it was slurred and too soft to hear. I would have gone into the examining room with him if Charlie and one of the nurses hadn't both put their hands on my shoulders. I went back to the dreary waiting room with its TV set, on but soundless, and a score of heavily rumpled magazines in piles on a low table.

A minute later, one of the EMT team walked over to me. "You're the sister, right? He said to return these to you." He handed me a set of keys.

Without an instant's hesitation, I plunged into what was probably perjury. "Yes. Thank you so much. I left them there and I need to get in to feed my cats. You know how it is," I babbled, smiling idiotically while I jammed the keys into my pocket. Two uniformed policemen had arrived and were in and out of the emergency room door, their equipment-loaded belts clanking and their black shoes squeaking as they took turns going outside to presumably report back to the station. Without identifying myself, I waylaid one, someone I'd never run into before, to see if Dermott could have visitors. He said no deal. "We have an investigation to conduct before we know what Mr. Kennedy will be doing when he leaves here. Who are you?"

I opened my mouth, but Charlie had joined me and squeezed my elbow hard. "Officer, I'm Inspector Sugerman, S.F.P.D. I've been consulting with your department's homicide team on the Flores case." He held out his hand.

After getting a look that meant he would do better without me close by, I drifted away while the two talked. In a few minutes, Charlie came back to me and said, "Come on, Dani. There's nothing we can do for Dermott right now and it's getting late. Let's get you back to the hotel."

I didn't argue, but as we walked into the parking lot I said, "I feel like I abandoned the guy when he asked for help, Charlie. What did the cop say?"

Charlie didn't answer until we got into his rental car. "There were no signs of a break-in. He told me Kennedy may have tried to commit suicide, chickened out and invented the intruder story. He shot himself in the shoulder. He did say they found something at his apartment that raises a lot of questions."

"Shot himself? That makes no sense. It's more likely the same person that went after me and killed Gabby, and maybe even Saylor, is now after Dermott. Oh . . ."

Charlie's loud sigh filled the car. "What? There's something you've been keeping to yourself, am I right?"

"Actually, I started to tell you over dinner but we got off the topic." I filled him in on Coe Anderson's hostile behavior and the so-called crank caller. "I'll feel rotten if I made Coe so worried about being caught at something that he felt he needed to get into Gabby and Dermott's apartment."

"And shot one of his faculty members?"

"Agreed, it sounds ridiculous, if only because we don't know what's got everyone so riled up."

"Unless your Gabby was a pack rat or a blackmailer, I can't see why she'd bring sensitive papers home, and the way you describe her, she wasn't like that. It's possible someone doesn't want any of you to figure out what's behind the big gift to Lynthorpe College.

But it's also possible the husband could try to take his own life if he had killed his wife in a fit of jealousy or rage. It happens."

My head was spinning. I had been ready to go to bed hours ago, and I was slightly dizzy. Charlie must have seen something on my face because he peered at me. "You okay, Dani?" I wasn't. I was so tired I could have lain down on the sidewalk and slept.

Charlie hustled me back to the hotel, escorted me to my room, and made sure I wasn't going to faint. Then he told me his room number, kissed me on the forehead, and left. After squirming around for a few minutes to find a position that would be easy on my neck, and finding there was none, I collapsed into a restless sleep.

TWENTY-FIVE

I woke un-refreshed and groggy. Someone was knocking on my door. "Room service," a man's voice said. The clock next to the bed read nine-thirty a.m. and my first emotion was guilt. So late, too late for work, too late on a weekday to be lying around. Then I remembered last night's trip to the emergency room and everything else that had turned this tidy little assignment into a first class circus.

Another knock. "Dani? You there?" The voice was muffled and as I pulled on my robe and shuffled to the door, wincing at the movement, I congratulated myself on having dug my way into another hole. I didn't know if it was Charlie or Dickie. Sooner or later they were bound to meet, maybe even outside—or inside, heaven forbid—my hotel room and I'd have to explain one guy's presence to the other. Great. Even if Dickie and Miss Rome were a couple, I knew my ex would be particularly interested in whomever I was seeing.

I peered out through the keyhole. Charlie, looking as though he'd been up for hours. I opened the door, knowing I looked like I'd been at a college binge party that ended at dawn.

"Hey, I brought you coffee and a Danish," he said, sweeping past me and setting down a couple of Styrofoam cups and a paper bag. "Hope I didn't wake you up." He examined me standing in the center of the room, robe pulled around me, hair doubtless in tangles, squinting. "Oh, I guess I did. I'm sorry." He came over and tipped up my chin with his hand and kissed me on the forehead. "Sorry." But he seemed wired and preoccupied.

"I just spent a half hour with your detective, who shared a new wrinkle with me. They arrested your friend Dermott Kennedy. They say they found evidence that links him to his wife's death."

"What?" I said as I perched on the side of my bed and blew on the hot coffee. "What kind of evidence?"

"You're not going to like this. A gun, the same caliber that was used on his wife. They'll do tests, of course, but they seem pretty confident it's the same gun he shot himself with."

"Why would he call me if he wanted to kill himself?"

"Second thoughts. Happens all the time."

The caffeine was starting to work, which only made me madder. I unclenched my jaw and, remembering what I saw in the mirror when I opened the door, sidled over to the bathroom to find a hairbrush. "How seriously is he wounded?"

"The bullet went into his shoulder. He's lucky. It could have ripped an artery. He'll recover but he's too groggy to be interviewed right now."

"That makes two of us," I said, splashing water on my face and hoping it made my eyelashes look plump rather than my whole head looking like I'd been drenched in a rainstorm. My annoyance, I had to admit, was not only about Dermott's bad treatment, but about being caught without at least minimal makeup on. I can be superficial. "It doesn't make any sense," I said. "Does it ring true to you? You do this stuff for a living."

There was a moment's silence. "I would be asking a bunch of questions and kicking myself for not testing Kennedy for powder residue after he showed up at the scene of his wife's murder."

"I think they collected his clothes later. He told me that."

"From what Kirby told me, the Flores crime scene was seriously compromised by having so many people barging around. The medical examiner's staff didn't get there fast enough and county forensics couldn't get much that was useful by the time they arrived. There's fresh powder residue on Kennedy's hand now, but no way to tell if there's older residue too. Kirby's pissed that some of his cops don't know how to follow procedure."

"They shooed us out of the building fast enough, " I said, remembering the rush to get us out in case there was a murderer hiding nearby. "Dermott was on the lawn with me. Charlie, do you honestly think he could have killed his wife?"

"I couldn't say without investigating. I mean, what was their marriage like on the inside? Was there a big life insurance policy out there? Was she pregnant and he was complaining it would stall his career?"

"You're depressing me," I said, taking a bite of the super sweet pastry and willing the sugar to get me going. Eating also gave me a moment to remember Dermott's explanation of why he had a life insurance policy on Gabby and Gabby's concerns about his heavy student loan burden. Reluctantly, I told it all to Charlie.

"Might be something, but I agree it's thin, unless the guy had huge debts or was involved in something illegal and needed payoff money."

"Hah. He's a mild-mannered history professor, Charlie, and his wife adored him. Hardly the secret gambler." But I could almost hear Gabby telling me about the student debt Dermott had from grad school.

"You know what I keep coming back to?" Charlie was frowning at me, or rather past me at nothing in particular. His green eyes weren't so warm and sparkly. "The supposed break-in to his apartment. If he was burgled, and shot when he surprised them, what were the bad guys after?"

"Bad guy, singular. But, Charlie, if he shot himself, did he toss his own apartment first? Would he bother with that if he were committing suicide? If Kirby says the place had been searched roughly, it seems to me to prove his statement that he surprised an intruder. Am I making any sense?"

"Kind of, although nothing there is proof, only suggestive. Kirby said the police did find signs of a disturbance. Dermott was in the apartment the whole time and says the intruder surprised him while he was sleeping. Kirby had a team at the apartment early this morning, and I know he's working the case hard. They're not going to tell me much more and they won't let me talk to him, Dani."

A picture of the distraught husband I met with at the hotel restaurant came back to me forcefully. "When I saw him the other day, he was adamant that he's never had a gun, never even fired one. He must have been framed. It's the only thing that makes sense."

"By someone who planted the gun? That would be your friend's killer."

"There might be security cameras in the neighborhood, or other ways to check it out." The caffeine and sugar were beginning to hit my brain.

"This isn't a sci-fi world, at least not yet. There aren't security cameras everywhere. This is a small town. I could believe some traffic cameras, but buildings on a residential street?" He shrugged. "The good news is if they've arrested Kennedy, they're not interested in you as a suspect. We might be able to get you out of here and home again. Feel up to traveling?"

"Right now, all I feel like is a long, hot shower, and several more cups of coffee. Thanks for this, by the way," I said, holding up the cup and the remaining bit of the pastry. "I look like hell and I need time to recoup." He started to protest, but I held up my hand. "Half an hour, in the restaurant downstairs, okay?"

While I was showering, an idea came to me. Not precisely a great idea, maybe not a thoroughly legal one, but something I convinced myself was worth trying. Question was, would Charlie squash it? After all, he was a sworn officer of the law.

While Charlie had been bringing me up to date on the trouble Dermott was in, I had noticed the set of keys sitting on the desk. As soon as he was gone, I went over and confirmed they looked like house keys. I remembered where I'd seen the couple coming out of an apartment house and knew I could find it again. The right thing would be to hold onto them for Dermott or turn them over, but to whom? The police? They already had access. No, he wanted me to have them for some reason. *You want to see the apartment, don't you?* my inner voice said. *Look for a clue about who shot Dermott?* Well, yes, I admitted. Or some mysterious piece of paper that would explain the Lichtenstein, the O'Keeffe, and the other paintings that were the big question marks for me.

Fate took my side in the matter. While I picked at some scrambled eggs and tried to come up with a plausible reason for ditching a handsome, green-eyed lover who had flown all the way across the country to protect me, and Charlie demolished a tower of pancakes drowned in blueberries, butter, and syrup, his cell phone rang. His S.F.P.D. partner is a perpetually depressed and irritated veteran of the homicide squad, and this is why. He was calling to see how much longer his partner would be gone, given that the mayor was freaking out about a murder that took place in front of a tourist attraction, wounding several civilians as well as a teenage boy who was being convicted by the media of being a drug runner before any evidence of that had surfaced. The mayor, gearing up for a re-election run, was demanding immediate results. The police department was—surprise—short-staffed. Charlie turned those amazing eyes to me in apology.

I was magnanimous, understanding, and grateful for everything he'd done. I agreed with him that I'd do everything I could to be on a plane myself tomorrow. I went up to his room with him and we kissed a bit, hampered by my stiff neck, before he threw his meager belongings into a duffel bag.

"I'll catch the first available flight out of Boston, but I want to know you're going to get out of here tomorrow. I swear I'll come after you otherwise."

"Promise," I said, and meant it.

"If I thought it would help, I'd call Richard myself and ask him to deliver you to the airport."

No, no, I thought. Let's not go there. "Oh, I think he's busy with what's her name, the woman from Italy. She's his date for the prep school reunion."

"Ah," Charlie said, and didn't add anything. As he ducked into his car, where I had walked with him, he said, "Do not drive. Use taxis. Call me the minute you get back to the city."

"You'll probably be busy in a shootout."

"I get involved after the shootouts, Dani. I'm the good guy, remember?" He kissed me on the nose, and I smiled as the car pulled away.

Realizing the police might still be at Dermott's apartment, I went back to my room to make my flight arrangements, trusting that Charlie was right and the police would let me leave now that they had a suspect in custody. The agent warned me a big storm was headed toward Boston and I should check for delays before heading to the airport.

Then I flipped open my laptop and summarized the handful of questionable assets from the unmatched donation lists, and what I could report about each. I made no assumptions, suggestions, or implications. Just facts. I read the whole document once more, then added a cover note and emailed it as a draft to the president of Lynthorpe. Let them figure it out. I was focused on the human costs of this gift, Larry Saylor, Gabby Flores, and Dermott Kennedy, and I was pretty sure the answer was too twisty and foggy to put into the kind of report I had been instructed to write.

Teeni had left me an email with all caps in the subject line "THEY CALLED P FOR REF," which should have made me happy for her but only pushed me further into a low level depression. My friend and ultra capable sidekick at the Devor would disappear soon in a blaze of glory. Charlie was gone again, the urban sheriff running off wherever he was needed. Dickie was too busy with his new girlfriend even to bother me. Geoff was sure to be disappointed with the weaselly report I submitted to President Brennan. My neck hurt when I moved.

My watch said it was still morning and I didn't want to venture over to Dermott and Gabby's apartment for at least another hour. This was as good a time as any to try Vince's number again. What I wanted to probe for couldn't be distilled into one smart question, and I didn't think Kirby knew enough of the backstory to be sensitive to what Vince might say. I fiddled with a pencil for a few minutes, rehearsing. *You wouldn't happen to have a Georgia O'Keeffe stashed in the trunk of your car?* No. *My, that Lichtenstein was expensive. Did you take up a collection from your closest friends to pay for it?* No. *Did Larry explain what was bothering him when you last saw him alone?* Possibly. I had never tried to ask him point blank.

My hands were a bit sweaty as I dialed the great man's office. I knew he was here in Bridgetown, but not how to reach him locally.

I knew better than to ask the president of the college or the dean to give me his phone number. But I needn't have gotten so worked up. His office was closed and the recorded voice said to leave a message. I wanted to confront him without giving him time to come up with a smooth lie, so I didn't.

With nothing more to delay me, I decided against lunch, and, figuring the police must be finished going over Dermott's apartment, headed there. A cab deposited me in front of the brick building in Bridgetown's small downtown business district where I'd seen Gabby and Dermott. There were no police cars parked in front of the building, no yellow tape, no one skulking around. The cars I did see were almost all about as worn looking as the buildings. The only new car looked out of place, which said something about the salaries non-tenured history professors and junior fundraisers were paid, I suppose. I looked around furtively, although I doubted anyone would know who I was even if they did see me. I was nervous. I didn't know what I might find in the apartment, but I was convinced it wouldn't be proof of Dermott Kennedy's guilt.

"Flores/Kennedy" was written on one of the buzzers in the unlocked foyer. I rang it for form's sake and when nothing happened I climbed stairs that brought me to a landing and a dim hallway with doors facing each other. There was noticeable gray smudging around the door handle and frame of Number 21, undoubtedly left over from the attempt to find fingerprints. The hall was silent and dark, with one window at the end that faced a light-blocking tree. Listening for noise first and peering back down the stairs, I tried a couple of keys from the set Dermott had left for me at the hospital before finding the one that opened the door.

I hadn't expected to be hit with reminders of Gabby, but her presence was everywhere, bringing surprise tears to my eyes. A pretty sweater was draped over the back of a chair, framed photos of her with other smiling people sat on top of a crowded bookcase, and I recognized the slight scent of perfume in the air as what she was wearing when I last met with her. Dermott must have both wanted and grieved these intimate reminders.

Not all the books were in the bookcase. Half a shelf's worth had been swept off and onto a pile on the floor. Some from another bookcase were scattered on the rug, as were papers that might have been on the dining room table nearby. A small desk stood in one corner of the room, and its drawers had been pulled out and emptied onto the floor. A framed painting hung crookedly on the wall, and the couch cushions had been pulled off and thrown around. Had the intruder done this, or the cops?

I picked my way through the mess to the small kitchen that opened off the living room. Here was a mess of another kind. Dirty dishes were piled in the sink, and the trash container had been dumped on the floor, leaving coffee grounds and odd bits of food scattered around. Yuck, but I realized it was a great rationale for me to be here. I would explain, if I needed to, that Dermott gave me the keys and I came to help clean up the mess. This would be after I finished snooping around, of course.

The apartment was small. A bathroom opened off a short hall and across from it was the bedroom. I could see a painted dresser in the room with its contents half out of their drawers, and an old-fashioned dressing table that looked untouched. A closet door was open, more gray smudges around the doorknob, and the hangers pushed to one side, exposing several neatly matched pairs of women's shoes. The bed was unmade and I started around the end, thinking to look more closely at the dressing table.

Suddenly, I gasped and pulled my foot back from where I was about to step. "Oh yuck," I heard myself say.

The rumpled bedspread had fallen partway down to the floor, and along the portion that touched the bare floor, a smear of darkened, dry blood was visible. I now saw that the mattress had no sheet on it and that it, too, bore dark stains. My stomach did a slow flip. So it was here that Dermott was shot, while he was in bed, or getting ready for bed. Or, if the detective's cynical suggestion was possible, here's where Dermott sat and deliberately shot himself. What a ridiculous idea. I could no more shoot myself than I could walk across a tightrope thirty stories up, and I was sure Dermott wasn't a masochist either.

I stood on the side of the bed opposite the signs of Dermott's wounding, and grabbed the bedspread so that I could pull it gently back up to hide the bloodstained mattress. My goal was to look under the bed, but as I tugged the fabric, something flew up out of a deep fold and then fell back into a crevice. Curious, I poked around with a clean tissue until I found the object and lifted it up. A sliver of pale wood, pointed at one end and slightly fuzzy at the other. A toothpick. The picture of Macho Cop rolling a toothpick around in his mouth rose in my mind. *Probably dropped it while he was helping to search the apartment this morning,* my inner voice said, *and we should get out of here.* I dropped it back onto the bedspread, wondering.

Where had the intruder been, and had he been in the apartment before Dermott got home, rummaging around for whatever he thought Gabby's husband had in his possession? Maybe more copies of the missing art gift papers, if that was what had unleashed this violence? Would the cops have recognized the papers as important if they had seen them?

I left the bedroom and went back to the living room, picking up typewritten pages from the floor and glancing at them as I did. Student papers, by the look of them, now scattered so thoroughly that it would take someone who knew more than I did about the French revolution to reassemble them. Nothing even remotely connected to Margoletti or art that I could see. Same with the papers that hadn't hit the floor.

Stacking what I'd picked up on the center of the desk, I moved over to a closet near the front door. The hangers here also were pushed to one side and held outdoor clothing. I dragged a box from the shelf above the coats down to the floor and squatted in front of it, but it yielded only voluminous research notes, possibly for an academic paper on someone named Guillaume Marie-Anne Brune, who, with all those female names, was actually a man, if my quick scan of a page or two was accurate.

I was standing up to put the carton back when my heart missed a beat. The front door knob was rattling. I had no time to think and, suddenly, my reason for being in the apartment sounded too flimsy to convince a preschooler. I heard a key scrape in the lock. There was no time to do anything but step into the closet, pull the door shut behind me and quietly move the hangers to form an inadequate curtain of coats and jackets in front of me. The box of papers sat in center of the closet floor, with my size ten feet squished behind it.

"I saw her come in," someone said in a tense whisper near where I stood pretending to be a raincoat. "She" could only mean me, which meant someone who knew who I was had been following me or had happened to see me and be bothered enough to tell someone else.

I heard shower curtain rings rattling open a few seconds later. Then, whoever it was moved back toward the living room. "Not here, bro," said the same voice, and since I didn't hear another person answer, I guessed he must be talking on his cell phone. "She must have left by the back door to the alleyway."

A series of grunts, then, "You told me she was at the hospital last night. She knows the husband's been arrested."

The voice had been drifting closer to the closet while my heart made such thudding noises that I was certain the man in the apartment could hear me. Suddenly, the closet door swung open and my heart nearly stopped. Someone spoke practically in my ear. "Maybe we should just forget about her . . . "

A booted toe reached in and kicked the box of papers lightly. It bumped against my foot. It was a lousy time to realize it, but the lack of food in my stomach was not the best preparation for hiding in a closet while a bad guy looks for you. The smell of tweed and wool coats was making me dizzy, and I was afraid I would faint and fall forward. My ears were buzzing so loudly I could hardly hear what he saying. *Hang on*, my inner voice counseled. It's not like there are options, I pointed out to myself.

He must have moved to the kitchen. I heard what sounded like someone kicking the trashcan. Something rolled across the floor. Between my pounding pulse and being half buried in the folds of dense fabric, I couldn't hear everything. But then he walked back in my direction. ". . . but if anyone saw the car, they might remember it."

Who was talking, and who was he talking to? If I could see him for an instant, I'd know who hit my car at the intersection. *Do not look*, my inner voice admonished.

"Okay." He had stopped near the closet and his voice dropped to a hissed whisper. "You made sure his prints are all over the gun, right, and they can't connect you to it? We get her to stop looking, Brennan and Anderson sign off fast, and then we're out of here."

And, with that, my would-be killer pushed the closet door closed and the footsteps retreated. A few seconds later, the apartment door clicked firmly shut. I heard footsteps taking the stairs down at a jog. Only then did I slide down the wall to the floor on legs that had turned to soft noodles.

My breathing was so ragged that I worried I was hyperventilating. As much as I wanted more air than the closet provided, I was too terrified to open the door. What if he came back? The guy in the apartment, and whoever he was talking to, had a deal with Coe Anderson and the president of Lynthorpe College, and they knew who I was, a bad sign.

TWENTY-SIX

I sat in the dark, hot closet for as long as I could stand it. Then, my ears quivering to catch the slightest sound, I eased the door open and stood up, holding onto a wooly coat for balance. The only plan I had was to get out of here as fast as possible. Or, was it? What if they were still outside?

I should call for help. I couldn't call the police because they wouldn't be happy that I'd been in the apartment, especially if I told them their chief suspect gave me the keys and asked me to clean up. Also because, for whatever reason, Dermott didn't trust them. Part of me itched to call Dickie, but not the smart part. First, he was mad at me, and explaining my hiding in the closet while someone who had tried to kill me stood a few feet away wasn't going to improve his temper. Second, he had Isabella to take care of, and I didn't relish the idea of him telling her how I'd gotten into this mess. I had the feeling she and her dimples didn't get cornered in closets. By now, Charlie was out of reach and would be until he arrived in San Francisco.

Maybe I should wait until dark and sneak out, but I was too stressed to stay here much longer, even though the bad guy was unlikely to come back if he believed the place was empty. My heart was returning to normal operations and my head was clearing. As long as I was in the apartment, I'd take five more minutes to look around. What I'd overheard proved Dermott not only didn't stage his own injury, but that he was being framed for Gabby's death. Charlie had been told it appeared the same gun was used for both shootings. *Okay, connect the dots.* Easier said than done.

Could the driver who rammed my car be someone hired to scare me off, someone who wasn't otherwise involved and, therefore, someone I wouldn't be able to connect with Lynthorpe? Based on his side of the phone conversation, it didn't sound as if he was the shooter. His voice didn't sound like a criminal's, though. Whatever that means.

What about his mention of Rory Brennan and Coe Anderson? The president of Lynthorpe was tough under his smooth surface, but I was blanking on what payoff could possibly tempt him. Maybe he and the dean knew the pieces weren't legitimately Margoletti's to give away, but they were such prizes that they were willing to help cover up some evidence of that. Could it be that Margoletti was being tricked into signing off on List A while someone else intended to substitute List B in the final document? But you don't earn the reputation as one of Silicon Valley's top lawyers if you can be fooled that easily.

Was the man in the apartment sent by Vince Margoletti? What if the college leaders were all in the dark about something and Margoletti was using Lynthorpe to hide a theft, or cover up a money laundering scheme that went wrong, or foist off some high quality fakes?

I pulled out my cell phone, noting with another lurch of my heart that the ringer had been on the whole time I was in the closet. Thank you, Dickie, I thought, for not picking that precise moment to call and bug me about something really significant like whether or not I'd like to take another test ride in your new car.

Quentin, my lawyer, was the logical person to talk to. I dialed his office but the call went immediately to voice mail. I tried again. Same thing, damn. This was hardly the kind of message I could leave on a recording device.

I had to tell someone and Charlie was it for now, even if he couldn't help right away. My finger hovered over his number. I had promised him I would avoid doing anything rash, and what was going to Dermott's apartment if not rash? Maybe I could kind of skip over how I got here, and give him the basics. I hit the call icon.

Of course it went directly to voicemail, but that was all right since I didn't want to answer any awkward questions about how I wound up in this situation. I told him that I'd come in, that all I'd seen was Macho Cop's toothpick, and that I'd heard some scary talk that made it clear someone was looking for me, someone who had maybe tried to kill me already and who was trying to frame Dermott for his wife's death. I finished by saying I was going back to the hotel and calling the detective, then tossed the phone back in my bag, already unsure I should have confided in him. I would call Kirby but not from inside an apartment where I had no business being.

By now, a half hour had passed since the mysterious man had left, and I tiptoed down the stairs to the first floor. Going out the front door still felt too exposed, so I explored the rest of the first floor hall. Sure enough, there was a door at the opposite end, a single one with no window. I opened it partway and peered out. A large Dumpster occupied part of a wide driveway that merged with a paved alley. A couple of cars were parked along the alley, but no one was in either one. A flicker of something tickled my memory. What? I couldn't bring it into focus and I couldn't stand around much longer. I could see the tree-lined main street at one end of the alley only five hundred feet away, with car traffic moving normally. I walked as briskly down the alley as my shaky legs would allow toward the stretch of small stores. Nothing seemed out of place.

I had almost reached the end of the alley when a hand came from somewhere behind me and slammed over my mouth and nose. I was so shocked I couldn't think, plus my nose hurt where the hand had banged against it. Tears stung my eyes as my brain scrambled to make sense of what was happening.

A man's voice said, from behind and far too close to my ear, "I have an idea. Why don't you come for a ride with me?" The last time I heard that voice, I was standing behind a rack of clothes in a stuffy closet. I tried to turn to see what he looked like, but his other hand was on my arm, holding me tight to his body, turning us both around and away from the street.

I couldn't breathe. I grabbed for his hand, desperate to pull it away from my face, but he was strong and I couldn't do more than move his fingers slightly so my nose was clear. My legs were buckling under me. I dropped my bag, which was getting in the way of my attempts to pull him off me.

"Hey, we can't leave that lying here," he said, yanking me to one side as he leaned down to scoop it up. I lost my balance and would have fallen, but he pushed me up against a car. I was looking at a shiny black roof. It flashed on me then. This must be the new car I saw out in front of Dermott's apartment. Hadn't I seen it somewhere else before that? It couldn't be the college president's car, could it?

No time to think. "Yell and I'll use this," he muttered in my ear at the same time I felt something hard poke into my ribcage. He let go of my face as he reached for the car's door handle and I sucked in a ragged breath of air and yelled, "Help" as loudly as I could. It sounded like a soprano frog croaking. I hoped someone in the apartment building might hear. I took another breath to try again, and then something went crack against the side of my head. The world went black.

TWENTY-SEVEN

*M*y first thought was that I had the world's worst hangover. What else could it be? A painfully dry mouth, hammers pounding my temples, dizziness and, when I tried to raise myself on one elbow, instant nausea.

I was on a bed, a mattress with no sheets or blankets. Through half-closed eyes, I noticed the walls were bare of decoration and needed a fresh coat of paint. The door across from the bed was closed and the only window was high on the wall next to the bed. I tried to sit up, but the stomach wasn't having it and I fell back on the pillow and closed my eyes against the shifting room. Only then did what had happened sink in. I had been kidnapped, hit with something hard, and brought to this room.

There was a plastic water bottle next to the bed. I reached for it without raising my head and inspected it close up. It's easy to be paranoid when you've been kidnapped, but I tried to be logical. Sealed cap, brand name. My body was begging me to risk it and I did, forcing myself to sip slowly, the way people in movies were always admonished to do when they were rescued from terrorists or deserts. Even so, I gagged and had to settle for letting some dribble down my throat as I looked for a way out.

When I could, I struggled to a sitting position and swung my legs over the side of the bed, telling my stomach to behave. Maybe I was in a motel. If so, there would be other people around who could help me, unless they were all Norman Bates clones. Involuntarily, I glanced around for a bathroom. No other doors. It would be hard to rent motel rooms that didn't have bathrooms. So, not a motel? An apartment?

No one who went to the trouble my kidnapper did to get me here in the first place was going to leave the door of the prison open, but I had to try. I could see Charlie's face later if I had to explain I'd been unlocked up and couldn't get out. Sudden tears blurred my vision even more than the crack on the head. Would I ever see Charlie's green eyes again?

I pulled the door toward me inch by inch until a voice—the same voice—said, "I wouldn't do that," and an arm with a gun appeared in the doorframe. I jumped and let go of the door handle as if it were on fire.

"Let me go, please," I said, my voice wobbling. "I don't know who you are or what this is about, so you can let me go and I won't say anything."

"Back on the bed." The gun barrel waggled up and down. I swallowed hard, retreated to the bed and pulled the pillow up against the backboard. The door slammed shut.

Think, think, I urged myself, useless advice because I was already thinking, just not clearly. Okay, I could yell and beat on the door, although that only made sense if Bruce Willis was nearby and itching to come to my aid. I could get on something high and look out the window, maybe even open it and climb out, but there was no chair. There was no anything except the bed and the table next to it. Thinking the table might work as well as a chair, I rolled to one side to check it out. My feeble spark of energy leaked away when I realized it wasn't a table, but part of the headboard that extended out a foot on either side of the bed frame. I yanked on it to be sure. Damn.

He'd taken my bag, of course, and my phone. It would have been too easy to have a lipstick to write, "Help" on the window, and other handy Nancy Drew tricks. It must be almost dark. Charlie might be off the plane by now. If so, he'd call the detective and alert him to my latest folly.

The door opened. A man stepped through it quickly and closed it behind him. The first thing I noticed was that he had a gun, after which it was hard to focus on much else. I had to know, however, so I looked up from the barrel and saw Vince Margoletti's son glaring at me.

"I know you. You're J.P., the polo player, Vince's son."

"That answers one question," he said and marched over to the bed, grabbing my arm with one strong hand, and yanking me upright. "Does your head hurt? You aren't seeing double or anything? That's all I need."

"Yes, of course it hurts like hell. Thanks for asking." I couldn't be too badly injured if my snark was still operational, I realized, and in fact my head was clearing.

"I need to know what you found out." He dropped my arm and stepped back.

I squinted at J.P. It was hard to see him as a desperate criminal. He looked and sounded preppy, expensive haircut, tanned, wearing a fitted, black leather jacket that must have cost the moon. It was as if he was trying to act a part in a student film. "Found out about what?"

"Tell me what you learned about my father."

I swallowed. "Are you doing this for him?"

He looked at me as if I were an idiot, which pretty much matched how I felt. "Don't play games with me. You're telling them whether or not to accept my father's proposal."

"I'm verifying the gift contract he's setting up with his college. What's so bad about that?"

"You talked to his accountant."

"No. Look, there's some kind of mistake here. You have to let me go. Everyone will be looking for me."

"Like who?" he snorted. "The maid who cleans your hotel room? Let's face it. You're a long way from home."

"I have to call my assistant. She'll be expecting it."

"It's Sunday. I don't think so."

"My boyfriend. He'll try to call me."

"The Ferrari? He's not staying with you. I checked."

"No, but—"

"We have some things to talk about and there's not much time."

Weird, but his preppy accent took the evil force out of the words. I half expected him to start laughing at any moment, and tell me it was all a prank. *People don't smash other people in the head with real guns for fun.* I opened my mouth and he raised the gun. I closed my mouth.

"First, what do you know about the paintings?"

"There are a lot of them. Which do you mean?"

"Don't mess with me." He lurched toward the bed.

I scooted down and away. There's something about seeing the firing end of a gun aimed at you that paralyzes the brain. "I was hired to review your father's gift contract and to make sure the artwork was properly accounted for. I swear, that's all."

"What about the ones his clients gave him? Did you see the papers for them?"

"Papers?" I repeated numbly. "There's no special documentation for gifts he received in what we have. Wait, is that what the auction papers were?"

The ones that were on the copier? So it was something about the handful of expensive paintings for which the paperwork was incomplete or unusual that was wrong. Was whatever we couldn't see in them enough to make Bart Corliss jump under a moving train? Larry Saylor must have figured it out or gotten close. "J.P., I'm in the dark. Is your father selling those pieces because he can't make good on his pledge?"

"My father has more money than God." He laughed suddenly, that same whinnying sound he had made when he was talking to me at the polo match. "But I don't."

"I thought—" I stopped but not in time.

"What?" he said, leaning over me, the gun close to my cheek. "That daddy would make sure his only son had a decent income?" He pulled himself upright with a jerk and started to pace. "You know how much it costs to keep a stable? Ten ponies, two grooms, trailers, saddles, everything? And to stay with the team in Argentina, never mind keeping the loan sharks at bay?"

Argentina. The international phone number I found in Saylor's notes. "Did Lynthorpe's vice president call you? Is that why you surprised him at the golf course?"

"Surprise? No way. He agreed to meet me there so I could explain my problem, the sleazeballs who want a hundred thousand like yesterday, and why I had to have the rest of the money." He rubbed the back of his neck as if he were struggling to focus. "When I met him that night on the course, I thought he'd see that it was a matter of life or death and, since there was so much else the college was getting, he'd look the other way."

"So he did find something, but he didn't agree?"

"He got all pious about the evils of gambling." J.P. was pissed. "Look, I didn't kill the old guy. All I did was push him into the pond to make my point that he'd better keep quiet. I guess he wasn't too healthy."

"He drowned while having a heart attack your threats brought on, and you didn't try to save him, so you did kill him." Maybe not the wise thing to point out at this precise moment, but making excuses for murder bugs me.

"Yeah, well, I didn't know that when I left."

I bit my tongue so hard that I felt and tasted a speck of blood. Entitled rich brat. "So your father's cash gift to Lynthorpe is money he could lend you to pay gambling debts, is that it?"

"Lend? No matter how much he spends, my father has more every year, like magic."

"Then what? You want it all? Fair enough." Not really, but talking might calm him down. I hitched myself up on the bed and wiggled to one side a bit. If there was any chance to run out of the room, I was going to be ready.

"Of course not, just my share. There's nobody else, and he's always saying how proud he is of my polo, so why not invest in me?"

J.P. was looking at me as if I were the judge on Family Court. I wanted to tell him to grow up, but now wasn't the right time. I remembered someone telling me J.P. was a playboy even in college and hadn't done very well in his few semesters at Lynthorpe. I could believe it. It was obvious the son didn't have his father's smarts.

He was still talking. Apparently, I was his therapist at the moment. "Such a big shot. I'm sure he's hired the best P.R. firm already, and the slimy little president of Lynthorpe has worked up some ass-kissing statement about the great man, benefactor to mankind stuff. What do you think, Miss Do-Gooder? Is my father the biggest hero since Bill Gates conquered malaria in Africa?" His voice dripped with bitterness, but something else too. Fear.

I had a mental picture of the senior Margoletti's manner as he looked me over with those cold eyes, measuring me. Did J.P. not quite measure up? One of Dickie's friends at the polo match said Vince was proud of his son, but it seemed like J.P. didn't feel the love. Another image of Vince surfaced in my head, the tightly wound big shot who pushed hard against any holdups in the deal to transfer a fortune in art to the little college he had been only slightly involved with previously, but whose hand opened and closed spasmodically during our meeting.

"You're not doing this with someone from Lynthorpe?"

"Are you kidding? They tossed me out a few years ago. And anyway, how could they help me?"

So Coe Anderson's ultimatum had nothing to do with Margoletti's son. "So who's in this with you?"

The toothpick. The man J.P. had been talking to who could make sure the apartment didn't hold any clues for the police. The cop who had been on the scene right after the shooting. The cop Dickie had instinctively disliked. The name clicked into my head smoothly, like it belonged there. I breathed rather than said his name. "McManus—is he involved?"

"Shit, how did you know?" J.P. shouted. "I didn't tell you! You remember that when he gets here."

Bad news. "Why would he do something illegal for you?"

"He's helping me get through this mess at Lynthorpe, that's all. I did him a favor once, when I was in school here, and he's paying it back."

"A favor?"

"Some drugs. I could get them and he could sell them. Nothing major, mostly pot and pills."

Ah, the innocence of college days among the privileged. But, hey, nothing major. I was beginning to understand why daddy dearest was not willing to bankroll his polo-playing son for the easy life in Argentina. But I had to get out, and fast. "Why am I here? You aren't thinking you can ransom me? Your father wouldn't pay ten cents for me, never mind a year's stabling costs for your horses."

"When I saw you come out of the building, I knew you'd heard me, so you know too much. McManus is on his way as soon as his shift is over. He'll take care of you."

The cocky small-town cop who seemed to be around all the time, who watched from behind dark glasses, who liked showing off for college kids and, apparently, liked selling them drugs? Who was among the first responders when Gabby was shot, come to think of it. The image of Gabby lying on the floor, a pool of bright blood forming under her head, came back to me. Before I could stop myself, I gasped. "He killed Gabby. Or, did you?" I blinked and looked up at him.

"No," he said, sounding startled, "I didn't kill her. Who thinks that?"

My ears were buzzing and I was feeling faint. "You killed Larry, and it was either you or McManus who shot Dermott."

Not me, he said sharply. "You make me sound like some serial killer. I don't even own a gun." I looked at the gun in his hand. "This is McManus's."

So J.P.'s job was to hold me there until McManus arrived to deal with me. That meant I had a few minutes or maybe longer, depending on what the crooked cop was up to right now, to get out of here. I needed to make this count.

"J.P. listen to me." I made my voice as soothing as possible. "You're a decent guy caught up in something that got too complicated, aren't you? You would never kill someone deliberately, but bringing McManus in has raised the stakes. Maybe too high? What was your original plan, before McManus went rogue and killed the researcher?" I tried to sound reasonable, as if we were not having a conversation that might be the last one I'd ever have.

He didn't exactly calm down, but his shoulders slumped a bit and he leaned against the door, the gun in his hand still pointed at me. "I told you. I need money. There's no not paying these people, especially because they know who my father is. He has over a hundred expensive paintings just sitting in a storage facility. All I wanted was to take one or two, sell them, and head back to South America. No big deal."

"The ones Larry and Gabby couldn't find on the list sent to them by your father's accountant? They were pieces you stole, the auction purchases?"

"I only took one. I haven't got it yet, but I will as soon as I get out of here." He ran a hand through his hair.

"I didn't get it and neither did Gabby. We were just trying to come up with a tally for insurers."

J.P. licked his lips. "Good try. You know those paintings were payoffs. Why else was she copying them?"

"Payoffs? Wait, you're saying they were payoffs to you?"

J.P. glared at me. "Of course not. Dear old Dad made sure the CEOs knew they had to keep him happy if they wanted to avoid being investigated for stealing intellectual property."

"Are you serious?"

"Sure. His way of making money. High risk, high reward, he told me. Except when I did it."

I remembered Ethan Byrnstein using the same words, the Silicon Valley mantra.

"So," I said slowly, "your father's squeezing the clients he helped by having them buy the paintings at auction, a way to launder the payoffs. You figure it out, and now you want to blackmail your father." I looked at my watch. "We don't have much time. McManus is a loose cannon. We can figure out how to present this so you don't get into too much difficulty—"

"No way. You know too much." The gun snapped back up to point at my chest.

"So do you, as far as your corrupt cop is concerned."

"I need to finish this last deal."

"J.P., trust me, I am not as dangerous at McManus right now. Sitting here waiting for someone who isn't going to want either of us as witnesses isn't smart."

"McManus doesn't get his share of the money until I'm safely in Argentina. In fact, his plan is to go with me."

"Someone will figure this out, especially if I'm dead, you and McManus have disappeared, and there are two unsolved homicides at Lynthorpe. There will be a full-on investigation and someone will remember you had access to the family storage facility, even if it was high security."

When Margoletti Senior found out the Hopper painting was gone he'd have the FBI and Interpol all over looking for the trail. Whoever bought it would either ditch it or get caught and go to jail.

"And," I continued, talking fast as I pieced it together, "if the auction items that were listed as gifts were lumped together, he'd be worried about his own exposure, so he was eager to get the gift booked and the documents accepted without question. But Bart Corliss enters into this somehow. Was your father pressuring him for a painting too?"

J.P. gave me a hard look. "Why should he get all those pieces? If I just asked for one, I'd be set. In his name, of course."

Vince must have figured out that J.P. got to Corliss, and wanted desperately to shut down the deal. He couldn't call in the police, but when Corliss committed suicide, the threat of discovery was imminent. Vince had to get all the remaining paintings out of his—and therefore his son's—hands before J.P. tried anything else. If any of the missing art was noticed, J.P. might be linked to it. But with their relationship so poisoned by J.P.'s fear and sense of entitlement, Vince couldn't talk to him directly. So, he decided to give it all away.

"So far, your mistakes are all in the area of what is called 'white collar' crime," I said, Larry Saylor's heart attack aside for now. "It's McManus who's in deep trouble. And, J.P., think about it. He plans to kill me because he thinks I know more than I do. But he can't let you go. I think we should get out of here right now and go to the police. Well," as J.P. stirred and pushed off the wall, shaking his head violently, "maybe not the local police. I know a San Francisco cop I trust."

He glanced at the door, and then at the window. The gun, still aimed at me, was unsteady. I was right. J.P. was afraid of McManus. The way he handled the gun, like it was a prop, and the fact that he hadn't simply taken me to an isolated place and shot me when he grabbed me in the parking lot, told me he wouldn't kill me.

A flush darkened his face. "I haven't got much time. We have to get out of the country before my father figures it out and calls the cops."

If he didn't have time, then I didn't. I forced myself to stop thinking of the gun and concentrate on getting away from here fast.

TWENTY-EIGHT

I needed my phone. I swung my legs over the edge of the bed. "I have to go to the bathroom."

He had been about to speak and my simple request stopped him as suddenly as if I had screamed. He looked at me as if seeing me for the first time and realizing I spoke only Urdu.

"I've been here a long time. Please." In movies, the female spy doesn't have a bladder and can stand pressed up against a concrete wall in her remote desert jail cell, knife drawn, for hours waiting for the bad guy to walk through the door. I'm not her and this wasn't a movie. I hadn't been thinking about it, but now that I had said it to J.P. it was real. The bathroom thing was the only way I could think of to get my phone, sure, but I didn't have to fake the need.

"You can't. I mean, not without the door open," he said, although he sounded a bit embarrassed. I hoped the idea was as unappealing to him as it was to me. I hoped he wouldn't decide to shoot me because it was simpler than maintaining good manners.

"Open? No way. Where am I going to hide? Come on," I pressed, whining a little. "It's urgent, J.P. You have my word I won't try to escape."

"You can't escape," he mumbled. "There's no window."

Damn, one option gone. "Okay then. What's the problem?" I stood up, raising my hands in the air to reinforce that I had nothing hidden in them.

He stood there, gun still aimed at my chest, and thought. By now, I understood he was a slow thinker. There were beads of sweat on his forehead and his hair looked damp. I felt the stifling heat in the room, the result of the closed window and door and two highly stressed occupants. Cold water on my face would be nice. Get a grip, I told myself. This isn't really a bathroom break.

He was saying something and I jerked my attention back to the room. " . . . two minutes, no locking the door. I warn you, I'll come in if it's any longer."

"It might be three."

"All right, three," he said in a sharp voice. "But I'm counting and that's final. Let's go."

"I need something from my bag." I tried to look embarrassed. I knew he had it somewhere, and I needed to get my phone back.

"What?"

"You know, my time of the month."

"Oh, geez," he said. But his upbringing prevailed. He grabbed my arm and marched me out of the room, to the doorway into a living room, where he scooped up my bag and jammed it into my chest before hauling me down a short hall. We stopped before an open door and he shoved me in, pulling the door closed behind me.

"I'm counting," he yelled through the door.

Nature called so I multi-tasked, digging the phone out of my bag and turning it on. Six messages, probably all Charlie. I didn't dare listen since the sound might be picked up by my captor. Instead, I hit "call back" and prepared to whisper while flushing.

"In or near Bridgetown," I hissed. "Margoletti's son grabbed me but someone else killed—"

"Three," yelled the voice outside. Frantically I pulled up my slacks, pushed the phone back in the bag, and was buttoning the waistband when the door opened.

"Can I wash my hands?" I said, turning to the sink without waiting for a reply. Hastily, I threw some cold water on my face. It was still dripping off my chin as J.P. dragged me back to the bedroom, yanked my bag away and tossed it on the floor without noticing that the phone was in there, or that I hadn't turned it off. If there was a heaven, Charlie would be able to make something of this, like they do in the movies, and send in the Bridgetown police.

"Where are we?" I said, as loudly as I could for the microphone.

"What does it matter?" J.P. said. "You won't be calling a cab."

Not a happy thought, but I ignored the implications. "J.P., let's call your father. I bet if he knew how tough your situation was, he'd come up with the money you need right now."

"It's way too late."

"I don't believe that. I saw how proud he was of you at the polo match. Come on, we can solve this problem if we do it together now." Now, as in before some cold-blooded dirty cop drug dealer gets here. "Look, your father can help with any police charges too. He has pull, and if you're telling me the truth, that you didn't shoot anyone—"

"I didn't," he burst out. "It wasn't me."

"Okay, I believe you, but you need to tell the police. If you keep me here, if anything happens to me, it'll be too late and even your father won't be able to protect you. Let me go and I'll call him myself."

"Shut up and let me think." He was darting around the room, so jittery that I was afraid the gun would go off if anything made him jump. It occurred to me I didn't know enough about guns to know if the safety was still on. My inner voice reminded me that J.P. might not know either, which might have been comforting but wasn't. He was mumbling. "It wasn't supposed to happen, but he said she recognized him."

"And because of that, he killed her. Think about that, J.P."

J.P. wavered, uncertain of his best move. But then he pulled a cell phone out of his jacket pocket and tossed it to me. "You do it. Get my father over here, but nothing else. No cops. I'm locking the door and the windows."

Good. We were on the same side now. I had to keep him thinking like that. I found Vince's personal number in J.P.'s directory and punched the glass face of the phone so hard I almost dropped it. Vince answered. "Son, where are you?"

I began to talk so fast I was panting. "Call the Bridgetown police. We need help, your son and me." Oh, shit, I didn't know where we were. "J.P.," I yelled, trotting to the bedroom door. "Where are we?"

Margoletti senior wasn't buying. "Who are you? How did you get my number? This is absurd."

"Not absurd. This is Dani O'Rourke. I'm with J.P. and we're in danger."

"My old apartment," J.P. said, appearing in the doorway, licking his lips and looking back and forth between me and the living room. "The complex is being torn down, but I was able to use my key to get in."

"A crooked cop named McManus is on the way to J.P.'s old college apartment, where we're hiding. He's going to kill me, and your son too. Sooner rather than later." J.P. darted back to the living room, waving the gun around so loosely that I might have told him to watch it if I hadn't been consumed with getting through to his father.

"You're insane," Vince Margoletti said in a cold, hard voice.

"Listen, there's no time to waste. J.P. has a gun. He's in big, big trouble and he'll need all your influence to avoid going to prison. But first we need you to call the chief of police in Bridgetown, now. Do you know where this place is?"

He wasn't impressed. "You expect me to believe this?"

"J.P. seems to think I know something worth killing me for. He let Saylor die—"

"This is ridiculous," Margoletti said, sputtering. "Is this extortion? Have you kidnapped my son? Is that why you called my office?"

I could have wept, or beat the phone against the wall. "Listen to me. Your son kidnapped me."

"He's in Argentina," Margoletti said. "In South America."

Duh. I knew where Argentina was. I didn't know as much about where I was, and it didn't sound like this man, in major denial, was going to help figure it out.

"No, he's here," I shouted, wondering why I had bothered.

"Wait, wait," he said, the first measure of doubt creeping into his voice. "I still don't believe you, but . . . Let me speak to him."

J.P. was back in the doorway. I held out the phone and looked my entreaty.

"No way," he said and stepped out of sight.

"He can't," I told Vince. "But I'm sure he wants to explain—"

"—stay there and I'll come over."

Was he not getting this? "Stay there" as if I had options? "There isn't time. Call the police station. Talk to the chief, but only the chief. There's a crooked cop in this. I think he's headed over here." But Margoletti had hung up.

"Your father's on his way. I told him to call the police. We should stay away from the windows," I said, speaking to the hallway. "Is the door locked? Maybe McManus will think we're not here."

"My car . . ." J.P. began, and stopped to swear viciously. It was past sunset but there was enough light coming in from the streetlights so we weren't in complete darkness. The space was both dangerous and intimate.

"I'm still trying to figure it out," I said, speaking softly into the darkness and silence. "You have a special interest in a handful of expensive paintings, for which there doesn't seem to be as much regular documentation as for the rest of the collection. Those paintings are, I'm guessing, on the accountant's list, the one Larry had that was worrying him, but not on the list your father's lawyers drew up for the gift. I'd assume that only meant your father didn't intend to give them to Lynthorpe, except that people have died because of the discrepancy, and now you're threatening me while someone outside is after both of us."

A loud exhale but nothing else from J.P.

"Something criminal, then. Meanwhile, Vince has demanded Lynthorpe accept the gift without looking further into any discrepancies. He is definitely trying to paper over something, and having all that art come to Lynthorpe is the answer. You, on the other hand, are trying to intimidate me into going away without finishing the job, which could slow things down."

Still nothing from J.P.

"I thought about money laundering, something to do with drug cartels."

A harsh laugh. "He's ethically compromised, but not that much."

"You?"

Another laugh, quieter this time. "Who would ask someone with no money to start moving large sums around? No, not me." Silence, then "All I have to do is get the Lichtenstein."

"The Lichtenstein is missing. I remember that."

"Actually, it's not. Not yet, anyway. I got it from that Loros guy but the deal to move it is still in the works."

"Got it?"

"Told him my father was going to expose how he took someone else's idea and ran with it to the tune of a few hundred million unless he gave him something extra nice for the collection."

"You were blackmailing the CEO on your own?"

"I have a buyer in Austria waiting for it."

"Then someone told him that the inventories didn't match, the accountant, I'll bet, and Vince knew somehow that you were stealing from the collection. That's why he's been so determined to transfer everything to Lynthorpe, to stop you."

"He doesn't know," J.P. insisted. "The accountant was worried and told Saylor. The accountant guessed it was me because I'd been in the San Jose storage facility a few times when the staff was there, but he had no proof. No one wanted to tell my dad."

"I think he does know, J.P. He knows, but he's protecting you."

"No way. Even if he figured it out, he'd only care about the money he was losing or the embarrassment if it came out."

Maybe, but I was sure Vince cared about J.P. and J.P. cared about his father, wanted his approval. Tragically, father and son were talking on different channels. "Were there others? I only saw a few that had incomplete or unusual provenance."

"Don't need many. That O'Keeffe? It's on its way to a private buyer in Mexico right now."

"You're kidding. You can't disappear a major piece like that."

"Dad's mistake was to leave the collection in the hands of bean counters who don't know what they're looking at. They write down what they see, going by the labels."

"So you substitute forgeries?"

"No, just fancy photocopies of the originals in frames."

"Giclees." A lot fancier than photocopies and so good that artists who supervise the printing often sell them openly as prints. "Hey," I said, suddenly remembering. "The Sam Francis?"

"My first. A disappointment. Not enough to set me up and cover old debts. A contact in Argentina found me a buyer in Europe who would pay cash for bigger names, no questions asked. The good news is he's panting for the cartoon painting."

"Roy Lichtenstein," I said absently. *Good going, Dani. As if an art lesson matters right now.* "Let me guess. You knew Sotheby's would be fussy about letting the painting leave their custody. They'd hardly hand it over to you. So, you had it delivered to the facility where the dealers knew Vince kept his art with proper climate control and high security."

"I wish. It wasn't supposed to make it into the warehouse. The Sotheby's sheet and the papers came to me and I planned to have the painting picked up in New York by a friend. But Corliss screwed up, had it sent over to the storage place on his own. So I had to rescue it, and then try to erase it from their list. Corliss paid more than twenty million for it, did you know? Of course, I'll only get half that if I'm lucky."

"Weren't you afraid he'd go directly to Vince?"

"Nah, he hated my dad by that time. My father made such a big deal about what he'd done for Corliss whenever anyone asked, and I bet Corliss was just waiting for the other shoe to drop. I think he was relieved that he could deal with me instead."

"You must feel bad that he's dead," I said into the dark room.

"Dead?" he said, standing up straight suddenly, his voice rising an octave. "He's not dead. What do you mean?"

"You didn't know? He threw himself under a train in Palo Alto a few weeks ago. I think your blackmail convinced him Vince would hold his actions over his head for the rest of his life."

"Not from anything I said. I told him this was it."

"All blackmailers say that."

A string of curses, and then suddenly his fist slammed into the door.

J.P.'s phone rang and we both jumped, jarred out of our dark cocoon. He grabbed it from the bed and frowned. "Why is my father calling me?"

"Why don't you answer and find out?"

"Why don't you?" he said, tossing the phone in my direction. My reflexes kicked in, I caught it, and before he could change his mind, I hit the talk button.

"Mr. Margoletti? Did you call the cops? You're in your car? Great, but did you talk to the police chief?"

J.P. wasn't making a move to terminate this conversation. "You'd like to talk to him? J.P., what about it? The police are on the way. Why don't you explain . . ." J.P. had disappeared again. I lowered my voice. "There are several paintings in the collection you're giving to Lynthorpe that aren't accounted for. Do you know which ones I mean?"

There was silence for so long I wondered if he'd hung up on me, but then Vince said, "Put him on now. I insist. Tell him he has to talk to me right away, while there's still time. I can help him. Tell him I'm on the way."

I repeated the message in a loud voice to J.P. He laughed from somewhere in the apartment, not a good laugh. "A little late, don't you think? Ask him about risk and reward," he shouted. "Ask him how hard it would have been to give me a fresh start when I asked for it. Tell him I have some very nasty people looking for me, thanks to his not giving me some cash to pay them back. Tell him none of this would have happened if he hadn't been so hard-nosed. Let him think about that for a few minutes."

Sharing this with his father wasn't my highest priority right now. "Did you or did you not call the police?" I snapped into the phone.

"Yes, and they're coming, as am I. Why are you even involved in this family dispute?" the senior Margoletti said in a cold voice. "Let me speak to my son."

"I would if I could. He doesn't want to talk to you, but I do." All I can say is I was tired, I was stressed, my head hurt and I don't usually talk to donors this way. "Your son has been pointing a gun at me for two hours and he keeps threatening to kill me, so I guess I am involved. He's talking about goons who want to kill him and plots to extort money to pay off the goons."

"I'm pulling into the parking lot now. The police are close by. Tell J.P. I want to come up there. We can talk about it in person."

I turned around. "He wants to come up here. He says you can talk about it here. Listen." In the silence, we both heard sirens.

"No," the son yelled. "Keep him away from me."

"I heard that," the senior Margoletti said in my ear. "Give him the phone. Please."

I walked out to the living room. "Tell him yourself," I said to J.P. and held the phone out. He lashed out with his free hand and slammed the phone from my palm to the floor, where it skittered into a corner. There went my lifeline. "Are you crazy?" Stupid question. Of course he was crazy.

"If I am, you're the reason," he shouted.

We might have continued bickering like an ill-matched couple but there was a sharp banging on the apartment door. At the same time, we heard sirens getting much closer. Could be a highway crash, or a fire, or a meteor crashing to Earth, but I was hoping it was Detective Kirby and the entire Bridgetown police department, minus one dirty cop.

TWENTY-NINE

*M*y kidnapper cocked his head and listened as he pushed the gun barrel into my side.

"J.P., it's me. Open the door." The bogeyman had arrived.

"Don't do it," I whispered. "He's dangerous, J.P."

Another knock, this one more like a slammed fist. "Let me in, pal. We only have a few minutes before the cops get here. We gotta get you out of there."

J.P., proving once and for all that he was less intelligent than the average fifth grader, left me standing in the center of the living room and undid the chain lock and the bolt. He actually believed Macho Cop was here to rescue him? If I'd had anywhere to run that wouldn't have cornered me, I would have bolted. The door banged open as McManus, in uniform, pushed his way in. He had left his mirrored shades somewhere. His eyes swiveled immediately over to me. He drew his gun from his holster and held it at his side. "You. Of course. I heard an APB on the radio there was a hostage."

"She's not a hostage," J.P. said in a rising pitch. "Not exactly."

"Here's what we have to do," McManus said, riding over J.P.'s protest. "First, put her in the bathroom."

McManus was a lot more decisive than the junior Margoletti. Plus, if J.P. was telling the truth, he had shot two people, which was a bad omen for me right now. The younger Margoletti grabbed my arm and yanked me hard back toward the hallway.

I started babbling. "You can't trust him, J.P. He framed Dermott. He'll frame you too." He had pushed me into the bedroom before McManus appeared in the short hall and said, "I said the bathroom."

"No lock," J.P. said in a voice aimed at appeasing the stronger man.

"Okay, the bedroom then. Doesn't matter. You're going to shoot her, but I guess you'll have to be in the room when you do it. Can't be sure to hit her through the door in a larger room."

"Me? Why me?" J.P. said, in a high-pitched whine.

I pulled my arm free of his weakened grasp and slid down the wall so I wouldn't faint. J.P. didn't try to pick me up. He didn't seem any more willing to go into the bedroom than I was. "You left her there to die," I whispered, looking up at the pale-eyed cop. "An innocent woman, and you shot her for no reason at all. She thought you were one of the good guys."

"Me? Is that what he told you?" McManus grinned. "Why, daddy's little boy is quite the shooter. They already have the gun and, guess what, it has your prints all over it, J.P., so you'll be the one the police arrest."

J.P. started to sputter, but I raised my voice. "Wait. That can't be true. The gun from Dermott's apartment has his prints on it. J.P., he's trying to trick you."

"I didn't do it." J.P. was beginning to babble. "I was there for the papers. He was only supposed to scare her so she wouldn't tell anyone."

"My job was to get you out, buddy. Like it is now," McManus said. "C'mon, J.P. Do her. We don't have any time left."

"I don't think we have to kill her, she won't say anything." J.P. was sweating and waving the gun around like a handkerchief.

The sirens had stopped and I had given up on that rescue, but now, all of a sudden, bright lights stabbed into the hallway, and an amplified voice filled the space. "Mr. Margoletti, we know you have someone in there. Let her come out of the building by herself. You won't be harmed if she comes out safe."

McManus whipped his own gun out and made a grab for me, but I rolled out of reach. "Let me go, J.P." I said. "You didn't kill Gabby—"

There was confused shouting going on outside the apartment door, and the cell phone J.P. had knocked out of my hands moments before began to ring. I scrabbled to it on my hands and knees. Before either man could grab it, I hit the button and started yelling, "In here, we're all in here." I would have said more but Vince Margoletti's voice was roaring in stereo, which took me a minute to figure out. He was outside the apartment, yelling into his phone. I hit the speaker button, and held it toward J.P.

McManus reached down and yanked me to my feet, but he would have had to let go of me or holster his gun to get the phone, and he apparently decided having the gun trumped everything else.

Vince was yelling. "I know about the art, son. I can make this go away. Please, J.P., trust me."

I jammed the phone in my pocket and began kicking and twisting to get out of McManus's grip. With the cop distracted, J.P. rushed into the living room. McManus strode there with me still more or less in his grip, his gun pointed at the ceiling.

A new, mechanically amplified voice chimed in. "Mr. Margoletti, this is Captain Benders of the Bridgetown police department. We need to talk with you. Can you come to the door?"

"Don't open the door," McManus said, still gripping my arm. "They'll kill you."

J.P. stopped in his tracks, but so far he hadn't put the gun down for a moment, and McManus had one too. Two people were dead and another injured, and I wasn't even counting the guy back in San Francisco who went under a train. All I had was a smart mouth.

"Talk to your father," I said. "He's right outside. If you release me, the cops will back down." Or, maybe not, but once I was outside, J.P. wasn't my problem any more.

"Don't, J.P.," McManus said in a low voice. "We have one chance to get you out of here. I say I've captured you and get them to stand down while you go out the back window. I'll pretend to shoot at you but only after you have time to get away."

I had a bad feeling about how this was going to end. The cops probably had a SWAT team surrounding the building by now, and then there was me, who knew too much and would be alone in the room with a crooked cop.

The red lights from the police cars rolled rhythmically across the ceiling and the wall. We'd been stuck in this airless place for hours and J.P. had gone into panic paralysis as far as I could tell. McManus was twitching badly, and I couldn't think of another argument they'd buy to let me out of here. I had the phone, but what use was it if taking it out of my pocket would only make McManus come for it?

Now he said, "Time to roll, pal. They'll be storming this place in about a minute. You," jabbing at me with his gun, "back in the bedroom. And you," looking hard at J.P., "no more second thoughts. Shoot her or give me the gun and I'll do it."

J.P. looked confused and panicky. His eyes jumped to McManus's gun.

"Can't use this one, friend, it would be traced to me."

"See, J.P.? He's going to frame you for this," I said, jerking back as the cop's arm grabbed for me.

THIRTY

$\mathcal{M}$acho Cop held me by the neckline of my Donna Karan jersey top, which made some small part of me mad since it was a favorite. I cursed myself for my inability to stay focused on remaining alive, and concentrated on breathing and trying to salvage something other than clothing from the moment. If I was going to get shot, I'd at least capture some kind of confession on the phone in my pocket, assuming anyone out there was listening. "You killed Gabby, didn't you, McManus? You shot Dermott, then framed him when you were sent to search his apartment. You hit my car, didn't you," I squeaked, "and followed me later. How much did you get paid for all this?"

"The car stuff? No way. That was his job," he said, grunting as he dragged me along. "I do the shooting, he does the easy stuff. That's why I get the big bucks and the babes, Rio style. No more hick town for me. "

"But if he hasn't paid you yet, you can't kill him." I choked and tried to ignore the ripping sound at my neckline.

"You think I'd risk it without getting the money first?"

Divide and conquer, as good an idea as any right now. "J.P., you trust this guy? He kills Gabby, shoots her husband to frame him. You're sure he won't shoot you?"

Score. The preppy polo player, novice blackmailer, and all around amateur crook pivoted, stuck his arm out straight and pointed his gun at McManus. "Not if I do it first. And I'll have better lawyers." His eyes were unnaturally wide open. He licked his lips and pulled the trigger.

McManus froze. I flinched. Nothing happened.

J.P. swore, grasped the gun harder and fired, sending a bullet flying somewhere but not hitting either of us. The sound was enough to unleash everything Bridgetown's police department had, plus one desperate father. Before I could react, McManus spun toward me and hit me on the side of my head with his gun. I fell, breathless with shock, disoriented, as McManus dropped my arm. Dimly, I heard a loud crashing noise. Squinting from my place on the floor, torn between curling up in a ball and trying to find a way out of this hellhole, I scooted away from the killer and leaned against the far wall as the front door begin to splinter. McManus and J.P. both turned their guns in that direction.

"J.P., it's me," a voice shouted. Other voices were shouting other things and time seemed to slow down. I was willing myself not to squeeze my eyes shut and pretend it wasn't happening, if only so I could try to dodge any further attacks.

"Go away," J.P. screamed as his father's face showed through the fractured doorway. Another hit and the door gave way. A uniformed policeman attempted to pull Vince away.

I jumped when there was a sudden shout next to me. McManus hollered loudly, "You can't get out of here, Margoletti. Drop the gun. Don't shoot her."

Dimly, I heard J.P.'s father yelling "Don't shoot, don't shoot," at somebody.

"Mr. Margoletti, you shouldn't be here right now. It's too dangerous." McManus spoke in the same loud voice he had used on Dickie, his official voice, a good cop concerned for a citizen's safety. I wanted to scream that he was lying, but no one would have heard me right then. There were shouts outside the door, and from inside the room, but they were beginning to recede from my consciousness. I was seeing bright spots and had a nasty feeling I was about to throw up.

The cop, who had been struggling with Vince, turned and yelled something over his shoulder. J.P. was screaming, "This is your fault. If you'd just given me the money." His voice was ragged. He raised the gun with two hands and pointed it at his father.

Vince Margoletti started to speak but was stopped by the sound of a gun going off. J.P.'s face registered equal amounts of shock and horror as he threw the gun down. It slid toward me. I dimly registered McManus moving in front of me before another shot was fired. McManus's foot appeared and kicked J.P.'s gun back in his direction. I was reeling from the sounds, but I couldn't take my eyes away from Silicon Valley's most powerful attorney. He looked surprised as a hole on the front of his beautiful suit jacket began to stain red. He fell backward out of the door, replaced by three or four swarming cops.

I looked at J.P., but he had crumpled to the floor. McManus began to yell, "He's down, he's down," and the cops in the room converged on J.P.

What happened next took a nanosecond. McManus squatted down next to me and pressed his gun deep into my side. I thought he meant to kill me, but all he did was murmur, "I can always find you," his breath hot and moist in my ear. I could hardly hear him, but I caught the malice in his voice perfectly. Then, standing and turning away from me, he said in a loud voice, "I had no choice. He was going to kill her next."

THIRTY-ONE

*W*hen I woke up, there was daylight, which stabbed at my eyes and made me groan. I closed my eyes quickly and started to turn my head away from the window. Very bad idea.

"Dani? Are you awake? How are you feeling? Nurse, she's waking up." It was Dickie's voice, loud in a stage whisper, but what was he doing here? For that matter, where was here and what was I doing lying in a bed that wasn't my own? "Dani? It's me. Can you hear me?"

My ex was talking rapidly and squeezing my hand so tightly that I finally said, "Ouch."

"Nurse, she's in pain," Dickie said loudly, still hanging onto my hand as if it might fly off by itself.

"Quit it, Dickie," I whispered, tugging my fingers loose. "I'm fine." Which I wasn't. My skull hurt and my temples throbbed, and there was a stabbing pain in my eyes when I opened them again.

"Oh boy," I said when I squinted and turned my head a millimeter on the pillow. "How many ways can one head hurt?"

"Lots," said a new voice, cheerful and loud and right over me. A young woman with tightly braided hair and dark-rimmed glasses leaned over me and held a coffee-colored finger in front of my nose. "How many?"

When we had agreed it was only one digit, and when she had done a variety of small things to measure how alive I still was, she retreated with the good news that I had a concussion but that I would live. That left me alone with my ex, who was looking worse than I felt.

"How did you get here? I mean," I said, working hard to form coherent thoughts, "how did you know where I am? In fact, where am I?"

He smiled a bit raggedly. "First, you're in the hospital in East Quince, fifteen miles from Bridgetown. Second, I found out because I got two phone calls, one from Charlie Sugerman and the other from Quentin Dalstrop." I must have looked puzzled because he went on, "Quentin Dalstrop, your lawyer? Charles Sugerman, the cop you were calling while you were held captive? Although why you'd call him for help when you thought he was all the way across the country, I'm not sure." The look that wafted over his face before it became determinedly cheerful again told me he had some idea.

The memories of the past few days were descending on me. Amnesia would have been preferable. "Vince Margoletti? Is he. . .?"

"Alive, and he'll recover. His son was a better polo player than shooter."

It took me a minute to get it. "Was? Jean Paul?"

Dickie is sunny by nature, but there was no trace of cheerfulness on his face now. "Your favorite cop shot him when J.P. pulled the trigger on his dad. He died instantly. You don't remember?"

I did remember. What had McManus said?

"Jean Paul told me again and again that he didn't kill Gabby. He was adamant," I said, thinking out loud.

Dickie grabbed my hand again. "Of course he'd say that. Why would he confess to murder?"

"Someone's confessing?" said another voice from the doorway.

"Charlie?" I said and, for some reason, began to cry.

Later, after I slept some more, Charlie replaced Dickie in the single chair in my hospital room, while Detective Kirby leaned against the wall.

"I don't understand," I managed this time.

"Thunderstorms. I was hanging out at Logan waiting for my delayed flight when you started sending me these cryptic messages, so I came back. Good thing I did."

"Agreed," Kirby said. "I'm sorry you had to go through so much scary stuff before we got you out. J.P. was one desperate guy by then."

Holding Charlie's hand, I said, "He admitted he caused Saylor's death by shoving him into the pond on the golf course, even though he could see Saylor was having a heart attack. But he wasn't the one who killed Gabby. McManus shot her."

A muscle worked in Kirby's jaw. "We heard Mr. Margoletti senior's phone."

"It worked? I wasn't sure . . ."

"Well enough. We're putting the pieces together now, but I'm sure we've got enough for a charge. I just need to hear it from you."

"Can I sit up?" I said as a couple more people came into the room.

"Yes," said the doctor, the same woman who had waggled her fingers at me.

"Well," said the nurse.

"No" said my ex, who had tiptoed in to join the crowd.

"If she's well enough to ask, I need ten minutes alone with her," said Kirby, straightening up from the wall.

"Got it," Charlie said. "I need to call Weiler anyway."

It took that long to get me upright and over my gasping at the dizziness. The doctor warned Kirby ten minutes was the limit since it had been less than twenty-four hours since I'd been hit hard, and Dickie let it be known he would be right outside and counting. Briefly, I wondered if Miss Rome was sitting patiently in the hospital's cafeteria, drinking weak American coffee and dimpling at the doctors. If she was, I loved her for it, I decided.

"McManus is a bad cop," I began in a rush. "He shot Gabby and framed Dermott Kennedy and broke into my hotel room. He's threatened to come after me if I talk."

"He threatened you? When?" Kirby looked concerned.

"Yes, right after he shot J.P."

"He's in custody, insisting he was framed. We should have warrants for his bank accounts and emails in a couple hours. I'm guessing we'll find evidence." He smiled.

"Evidence?" This is what happens when you've been hit on the head more than once, I reminded myself, been dragged around with guns pointed at you, and heard bullets fired a couple feet from your head. You get stupid.

"Deposits from Margoletti junior. The father handed his phone to the chief when he realized it was picking up something vital, and he picked up enough information to tell us where to look. We still need details, but I feel good we'll convict him for the murder of Gabriela Flores."

"Wait," I said, holding up a hand and waving it weakly. A thought that had been nagging at me had worked its way to the surface. "Was McManus assigned to help search Dermott's apartment after the shooting?"

"No, he was off that night and the next day, said he went fishing."

"Good, gotcha, you creep. Not you," I said quickly when he looked over at me, startled. "You need to go back to Dermott's apartment. There's evidence there, too, a toothpick."

Kirby's friendly smile disappeared. "And you would know that how?" If I thought Kirby would thank me for my brilliant detective work, I was wrong. I explained I'd been kidnapped outside Dermott's apartment, and admitted that I'd spent some time inside, hoping to clean up but getting scared after J.P. came looking for me. Kirby lectured me about disturbing evidence, but he admitted it might be a useful tool in shaking McManus's alibi. My head was aching and I had already told the detective I had to take a break when Dickie poked his head in. Kirby nodded and promised to get back to me.

"Wait," I said, the queasiness coming back as I imagined myself in the room with Vince, J.P. and McManus. "You need to know this. J.P. had already dropped his gun when McManus shot him. J.P. wasn't armed. McManus shot him to keep him from talking. I saw it."

Kirby looked at the floor and sighed. "I wondered. His fellow officers haven't said anything, but I got the feeling they were bothered by something. The two shots were close in time, however, and McManus says J.P. had turned the gun on him."

"No. J.P. dropped his gun," I said through teeth gritted as much in anger as in pain. "I know what I saw."

"You'll testify? His word against yours?" Kirby looked thoughtfully at me.

"Yes, but," I added as I eased back down to a prone position to combat the dizziness that threatened to overwhelm me, "if Macho Cop—I mean McManus—gets out on bail, I don't feel comfortable. He said he'd come after me."

"Oh, he's not going to bother you," Kirby said grimly. "Joe Ricocetti, his partner, says he caught sight of McManus coming from behind the building where Flores was killed before the 911 call was relayed to them. At the time, he thought McManus was goofing off, but we'll revisit every minute of that time to see if it'll tie to the shooting."

"The elevator," I said. "They took the elevator to the basement. J.P. told me."

"Good. We'll look for DNA in the offices and the elevator," Kirby said, "but I'm betting the best evidence we'll find is a large cash deposit to Officer McManus's bank account and a one-way, first class ticket to Buenos Aires."

"That's in Argentina," I said, beginning to drift. "Will you charge him with Gabby's murder?"

"At least," Kirby said, and we sat in silence for a few seconds.

"That clears Dermott. I'm so glad."

"The only thing that pointed to Kennedy strongly was his fingerprints on the gun. But that was a big one."

"I guess Macho—er, McManus—wasn't such a bright guy," Dickie chimed in.

Kirby didn't seem to notice the nickname. Even in my fuzzy state, I realized this episode was going to rattle the little Bridgetown police department. Most cops are honest, dedicated men and women. The occasional bad one hurts the whole force. It meant no one would cut McManus any slack. He'd be thrown to the legal system with no lifeline, which was precisely what I wanted and what Gabby's and Larry Saylor's memories demanded. Bart Corliss's widow would have to learn the sordid story too.

With a small grimace, Kirby left us. Dickie was subdued as he took the chair Kirby had vacated. "Your Macho Cop is bad news through and through. You're lucky, you know?" he said, patting my hand. "If you hadn't left your phone on, with its tracking capability, who knows what might have happened to you?"

"It was Charlie who called the police?" I murmured, already drifting to sleep.

"Yes, and I heard they were already searching for the exact location of the apartment when Vince called for help. Your Macho Cop must have picked it up on the patrol car's radio."

"Not my cop, ugh."

"Anyway, thank God for Charlie." Dimly, I noted that he sounded completely sincere.

They kept me in the hospital for two days. Kirby came twice, with another police officer who took copious notes. Quentin Dalstrop not only came to see me, but brought a huge bouquet of lilacs, solving the mystery of Lynthorpe's scented campus. "Oh my, yes," he beamed as I inhaled deeply. "I have a half dozen bushes in my backyard and they're all blooming like crazy right now. Lynthorpe's known for them."

Rory Brennan and Coe Anderson were too busy to come, but the college sent a rather grand floral arrangement with a subdued note of condolence for my trauma.

The doctor who visited me every day told me Vincent Margoletti was confined to his bed on another floor in the hospital after surgery. His lung had been punctured by the bullet, but he would recover. J.P. had been his only child and, as parents do, he loved his son, the rakish polo player and reckless gambler, even if he hadn't known how to show him that not all high risks paid high rewards. I had a hunch that when the tough lawyer woke up from his nightmare, McManus and the entire police department of Bridgetown might suffer, but that would have to work itself out, as would a decision about the donation that had started all this insanity. If I knew my boss, he'd argue for making a bid on the Devor's behalf after a decent interval. I already knew I couldn't be part of any cultivation of Vince's gift in that case, since the sight of me would bring back bitter, sorrowful memories.

Dermott Kennedy came to see me, accompanied by a middle-aged woman who looked so much like Gabby that tears filled my eyes. Dermott babbled so often that I'd saved him that I had to command him to stop. Mrs. Flores held my hand in her soft ones and thanked me for being with her daughter at the end. I didn't see how that had changed anything on that dark day, but I kept my thoughts to myself. Anything that helped ease her pain was good.

Oddly, the one person I didn't hear from was Charlie. The last time he had stopped by my bedside, he had kissed me gently and apologized, saying he had to get back to work now that he knew I was okay and that McManus was locked up. I left a handful of phone messages for him, but all I got in return was silence. Could he be that wrapped up in an investigation, or multiple investigations?

On the last day of my hospital stay, when Dickie showed up again with a box lunch better than the hospital food that lay untouched on the plastic tray, I asked him how he could spare the time. "Don't you have to meet your friend, Miss...?" I almost said Miss Roman Holiday, but that was uncalled for. If she was in Massachusetts with Dickie, she was a good sport.

"Isabella?" he said. "She went back to Rome."

"How do you feel about that?" I said, treading lightly.

He thought for a minute. "Sorry, at least a little. She's smart and fun."

"I liked her." I finally got up my nerve to ask, "Did she come to the reunion?"

"To my prep school? Lord, no, why would she do that? A lot of old guys standing around drinking and telling bad jokes? Not her style at all. Yours either, I know," he added quickly. "Listen, I talked to Peter and he wants you to take all the time you need before coming back to work. Teeni says she has everything in hand. How about taking a week to rest on Martha's Vineyard? I could rent a house. It's quiet up there at this time of year and you can sleep and sit in the sun and eat fried clams."

It was the promise of fried clams that did it. Not a whole week, but a long weekend marked by the smell of fresh sea air and the sound of gulls, and waves breaking in the distance. I made it clear the primary condition was separate bedrooms and he agreed without argument. In fact, he never tested my resolve, maybe because he was afraid my head would split open if I were crossed, or maybe because Isabella had left a serious dent in his affections. I took a few long walks by myself, played Scrabble with Dickie in front of the fire, and thanked the universe that I was alive. I promised myself that never again would I let my curiosity and stubbornness tempt me into dangerous situations. Never.

I was in a peaceful frame of mind when I unlocked the door of my apartment. Yvonne or Suzy had obviously been there because there were more flowers, and I saw a bag of freshly ground Peet's French roast on the counter. Fever was happy to see me if I read the upright tail correctly. As I sat on the sofa flipping through the accumulated mail, a handwritten envelope caught my attention and the return address made my heart jump a little against my ribs.

Dani,

I need to talk with you. Call me when you get back, okay?

-C

We met at the North Beach café that was becoming our special place. He hugged me and squeezed my hand when I arrived, and asked me how I was feeling. I sensed something was making him nervous. For a nanosecond, I wondered if he was going to propose, maybe not marriage, but a whole week's vacation together, something to signify a new stage in our relationship.

"I'm so glad you thought to call me when that bastard kidnapped you," he said after toying with a piece of pizza for five minutes. "That was smart, Dani, but it could have been so much worse, and that scares me."

I waited, not sure where this was going.

"I deal with death every day, but I'm having trouble letting it get as close to me as it does when you get drawn into these situations. I work hard to keep the violence I have to investigate impersonal, so I don't get sucked into the pain it causes. That's how I can keep doing my job day after day." His voice had taken on a pleading tone and the green eyes were dark with emotion.

I started to say how sorry I was for worrying him, but he held up a palm to stop me. Then, taking my two hands in his, he said, "I need to back off for now and think about our relationship. I need time."

I looked at his face, so sincere and so unhappy, and had to admit to myself that he was right, in a way. I was a pain in the butt, not that he would ever put it that way to me. I knew when I went to the golf course that it was not the smartest thing to do. Ditto Dermott's apartment after he had been shot. I couldn't expect a cop from all the way across the country to rescue me if I couldn't control my impulses. But, my inner voice said, leaping to my defense, you couldn't let the bad guys get away with this stuff.

Later that evening, after Charlie had dropped me off with a tight hug but no kiss, and promised to call me when he'd had time to think about it all, Fever agreed with my defense, or at least that's what I think he meant by climbing on my lap for a change and beginning to purr.

I plan to call Charlie if he doesn't call me first. I'll give it a few weeks—well, two weeks, anyway—and we'll see. In the meantime, Dickie has been so well-behaved that I agreed to drive out to Stinson Beach with him in the yellow Ferrari, which is due to arrive from Boston on a truck any day now. He says he's going to sell one of the Porsches to make room for it in the garage of his Pacific Heights house, but I wouldn't bet on it.

He told me Isabella is coming back to San Francisco on business in the fall. Maybe Charlie and I can have dinner with them. I owe her something by way of an apology.

Teeni's dream job came through. She'll be at the Devor through the Funk Art exhibition opening and I'm planning a memorable send-off after that. I deliberately bought a slinky wool jersey Donna Karan dress to spur me into jogging the Pacific Heights hills every morning for the next couple of month. I've sworn to eat only dark chocolate for dessert, because I read somewhere it's good for you. Most of all, I'm determined to keep busy with everything but trouble.

Acknowledgements

The third in the Dani O'Rourke series, this book took a circuitous route to publication, and for all her help and support, I must first thank my tenacious agent, Kimberley Cameron, whose faith in it and me is humbling. She has kept Dani company for the journey, and we are grateful. Thanks to Mary Moore, Lisa Abellera, and the Reputation team for their time and attention.

Writing about police business is tricky, and I have tried to get it right as it might play out in a small town with few resources. I thank Corporal Matt Shoup of the Sausalito Police Department, who had recently commanded one of the 7000-person town's rare murder investigations when I asked him for help. He was gracious, forthcoming, and clear. Where the good cops are believable in the book, it's his doing. Where I got procedures wrong, it is completely my error. Similarly, Arlen Hooley, an experienced EMT now in medical school, saved me from a few egregious mistakes, to my (and his) relief.

As always, every one of my characters is an invention, as is Lynthorpe College. Impressive gifts of art are not, thank heavens, and I salute the generosity of collectors who make donations for all the right reasons.

About the Author

Susan C. Shea lives in Marin County, California. She is a member of Sisters in Crime and Mystery Writers of America.

Visit her at SusanCShea.com.

Reputation Books

CPSIA information can be obtained at www.ICGtesting.com
Printed in the USA
LVOW11s2326170316

479695LV00004B/19/P